LOVESICK BRAVES

CROOKED ROCK URBAN INDIAN CENTER BOOK 2

PAMELA SANDERSON

Cover design by Holly Heisey (www.hollyheiseydesign.com)

Editor: Lorelei Logsdon, (www.loreleilogsdon.com)

Visit the author's website at www.pamelasanderson.com.

❀ Created with Vellum

---

*E*ster hurried across campus, head down against the bitter wind. She pulled her flimsy coat more tightly around her shoulders as if that might help. In the brief time since she'd left her desk, the cold drizzle picked up and turned into a driving, slushy rain. Any other day and she would have abandoned this mission. Now that the center had moved to campus, she had plenty of opportunities to sneak into the computer lab.

However, today she was ready to talk to the guy. She would throw out a confident smile and make small talk like regular people. She'd open with a comment about the weather followed by a question asking what classes he took. The words would come out naturally, except that was a joke because every time she stood in the same room with him, she got so nervous there was nothing natural about her.

Ester entered the computer lab from the back door and found an open terminal in the corner. From this spot she would be able to keep an eye on him until she was ready to say something. She typed in the login borrowed from Audra and loaded the clips she was working on. Would he be wearing the gray hoodie, or the gray hoodie? She peeked over the monitor.

A long-limbed blonde with don't-mess-with-me eye makeup sat at the front of the room. She caught Ester's eyes and tilted her head to one side, as if to say, *Not the lab assistant you're looking for?*

Ester sank back into the seat, embarrassment turning into disappointment. Then she grew cross about being disappointed. This turned into annoyance because her feet were ice cubes, her pants were damp and she had to walk back across campus in the crap weather before she could be safe at her desk, deluxe space heater doing its job on her chilly bones. She'd gotten herself into this predicament so she could run into and, seriously this time, say hello to a guy. A guy who probably would have said hi back and never thought of her again.

The man in question was the usual lab assistant at this hour. He was a big guy, both in terms of height—he had to be a least a head taller than Ester—but also brawn. This guy looked like he spent his spare time tearing trees out of the ground and smashing them over his knee. He'd caught her eye because of his warm brown skin and long black ponytail. She liked the way he moved, his giant hands working over the computer keyboard, or his careful sidestep when he worked his way through a row of computer terminals, like Godzilla, only trying to *avoid* knocking over a building. And the way he responded to requests to put paper in the printer with a weary suppressed scowl. She was ninety percent certain he was Native.

She'd planned her entire day around running into him today. Probably wasn't a tragedy that he didn't show up. She would have chickened out or sputtered and forgotten what she'd planned to say. The Ester who existed in her head was much braver than the Ester who put on pants every morning.

She turned her attention to the screen and reviewed her clips and images. The lab's larger screens and faster machines made it more fun than using the computers at the center. The current project was another short film to appeal for help in finding a permanent home for the Crooked Rock Urban Indian Center. After much cajoling, her boss, Linda Bird, the executive director of the UIC, relented and did another interview about the various homes the UIC used or hoped to use.

According to the online tutorial, the challenge of telling a good story was getting all the information in, placing the images in the best order, and timing it right. She rearranged the same bits: the Chief Building they planned to buy, the cramped space in the strip mall they'd vacated months earlier, and their current home, which was a meeting room on campus. She added an early photo of their founder, Margie, typing into a boxy computer on her kitchen table, then shuffled the clips back and forth, unable to sense what worked best.

A quiet tone sounded on her phone. She glanced at the display.

Linda texted: *Conference call?*

Crap. Once her head was in a film project, everything else fell away.

On my way.

She hit save, yanked on her coat, then grabbed her backpack and hurried from the room. Students crowded the hallway, forcing her to push through before she ran out of the building and into the cold rain. Someone touched her shoulder.

"Excuse me."

Ester turned to find herself face-to-face with the guy. Her mouth went dry. His golden-brown eyes gazed into hers, narrow with suspicion. He must have taken over the lab while she was working and figured out she wasn't a student. Instead of her rehearsed small-talk, he was busting her for using the lab. This was not the conversation she'd envisioned having with Mr. Super-Ind'n and she didn't want it to continue.

"You in Kathleen Stone's vis-comm class?" he asked.

The ground grew unsteady under her feet. Instead of a gray hoodie, he wore a gray T-shirt, the filmy kind that clung everywhere. His chest was ridiculous. Out in the cold air, her ears stung, and he stood there without a coat. She slipped a hand into her pocket for her hat, then stopped when her fingers touched the fuzz of the frayed wool. No way would she put on the dingy hat in front of this guy.

Whenever she complained about getting nervous talking to guys, Rayanne would say, *Act natural. Don't over-think it.*

Ester didn't know how to act natural. She shook her head.

"Which class, then?" His voice wasn't what she expected. She'd imagined pure bass but this was more baritone, warm and buttery. She guessed he had a nice singing voice. What was the question again?

"I have a conference call?" she said, not sure why she made it sound like a question. Who knew what the punishment was for using someone else's login? What if they kicked her off campus? That would make going to work a challenge.

"Are you in the digital arts class?"

"Nice talking to you," she said. She turned around and considered how it would look if she sprinted across the greenway.

"Hang on," he called. His hand tapped on her shoulder again. "You forgot this."

Brawny guy held her portable hard drive. The drive was common except for the round sticker with the Crooked Rock Urban Indian Center logo on it.

She stared at it. His hand was huge. She wanted to put hers next to it to compare.

He said, "If you don't take it, I have to plug it in and snoop through all the files to figure out who it belongs to."

"It's mine," she said, trying to remember whether she had any files worth snooping. There were a few he might find interesting. Her fingertips grazed his palm when she took the drive.

"One more question," he said.

This time she looked at him. He wore a gray knit cap with a Pacific-Northwest-style whale on it. She'd seen similar caps at the crafts market in the park. His eyebrows knitted together like an angry cartoon character, equal parts menace and humor.

Brawny guy pointed his chin at her. "You in the Native American student group?"

"Not really," Ester said

"But you're Native."

Ester nodded.

"From where?"

"Eastern Shoshone."

"Wyoming?"

Ester nodded again.

"I'm Theo," he said. "Jicarilla Apache. I lived on the rez when I was a kid."

She knew she was supposed to share something about her background except she didn't want to get into it right then. If she had social skills like a normal person, she might steer the conversation in another direction but instead her brain ground to a halt. She tried to smile but sensed that she was peeling her lips back from her teeth while the corners of her mouth twitched.

She couldn't tell whether the conversation was finished. She asked, "Do you have to go back to work?"

"Work?" Theo smiled as if he'd heard something amusing. "You mean lab assistant? Nah, that job didn't work out."

"Oh, sorry," Ester said.

"The guy in charge of the lab assistants would rather schedule the lady students. I lost out." Theo shrugged.

Ester stared at his mouth and the hard line of his jaw, the way the muscles worked in his neck, the goose bumps that covered his upper arm. He scrubbed his hand over it as if to brush them away. Her eyes flicked from his hand to his face. She'd never stood this close to someone so attractive.

"How about you?" he said. "You said you had a call."

"I do," she said, the importance of her work at the office flooding back to her. "I have to get going. Thanks for bringing my drive..." She patted her backpack and edged away. "Theo," she added because she wanted to say his name.

2

---

*S*he was gone before Theo could catch her name. The Native woman fled into the falling rain. He didn't blame her for running after he'd rushed after her like that. She'd caught his eye when he worked in the lab, always choosing a seat in back and keeping to herself. She would stare at the screen with complete focus, her dark eyes narrowed while she struck the keyboard like a pianist picking out notes. Her intensity was wildly appealing and he would have introduced himself the first time he saw her if he thought he had time to make friends.

But Professor Stone's project gave him a good reason to talk to her. His instructor needed help finding a Native family for a film she was making and she counted on Theo to deliver. The only problem was, Theo never met Natives on campus. His mom was always urging him to look for a Native student group and he might have given it a shot except for the half-dozen jobs he juggled every minute he wasn't at school. All the leftover time was for homework. The only thing left to give was sleep and there wasn't much to give. Even if he showed up at a meeting, clubs did things, and doing things took time.

He headed back into the building to get his backpack and get to class. The chase after the girl made him late again and a closed classroom door greeted him. No way to get around it; he ducked inside and closed the door softly behind him. Professor Stone's eyes flicked to the classroom clock and then to him, her expression radiating disapproval. Theo had two classes with Stone this quarter, lucky him. The vis-comm class, his favorite, and this media writing class, which was kicking his butt.

Only five minutes, he mouthed even though it was closer to ten. He mustered up his most charming smile. A lone empty seat beckoned from front and center. Professor Stone paused long enough to ensure that everyone's attention drifted to him as he worked his way to the empty spot. The woman in the adjacent seat jerked her backpack out of the empty chair without meeting his eye.

"I want you to consider point of view when you tell your story," Professor Stone said. "If you commit to telling the truth, whose truth are you telling? What do you bring? What is your unique point of view for the story?"

When Theo had signed up for digital journalism, he'd prepared for regular reporting, only, on the Internet. He hadn't been prepared for Professor Stone who challenged them to think about the act of reporting itself. They had a responsibility to the subject and the readers, she had told them.

The time passed quickly and Professor Stone wrapped up the lecture. She complained about late and missing assignments as she did at the end of every class. Subtle remarks intended for him. Sure enough, as the class cleared out, Professor Stone called him over.

"Walk me to my office?" she asked.

He followed her out. She put on a wide-brimmed rain hat with a funny cord that she tightened under her chin. The sky was cloudy and the air heavy and damp from the earlier rain. A brisk wind stirred the tree branches, spattering them with cold droplets. Theo wished he hadn't left his sweatshirt in the car.

"What happened with the lab?" she asked.

"I'm surprised you heard about that."

"It's a good job for you. Not so much scrambling. You can stay on campus and focus on school."

7

"Not going to argue with you."

"So, what happened?" She made it sound like he'd lost the job on purpose.

She wouldn't understand the real explanation. "The guy in charge of the staff prefers to schedule a different type of student."

"You mean, one who comes to work on time?"

Theo had been late twice. That was the official reason for letting him go, but the student in charge of scheduling was socially bereft and there were lots of cute young women who wanted the job.

"We can go with that," Theo said.

Professor Stone slowed her step as if in deep contemplation over his future. She was in her late thirties and one of those high energy, outdoorsy types. He imagined her cross-country skiing, or biking across town. As an instructor, she rode that fine line of being approachable but no-nonsense. She encouraged her students but refused to hand-hold. When she'd first taken an interest in him, he hadn't been sure what to make of it, but she understood his financial aid troubles and volunteered to be his advisor.

"I'm doing fine juggling school with my other jobs," Theo assured her. He gave her a rah-rah student smile.

She made a doubtful noise. "You're already behind. You're averaging three journal entries a week. The assignment is five. You're already a good writer but you need to take these assignments seriously."

"Unexpected setbacks," Theo said, which wasn't entirely true. There was nothing unexpected about his situation. "I can keep up. Can I make up the missing work?"

"Can you?" she said. "You're already hanging by a thread. We barely got you through class last quarter. What about vis-comm?"

"I'm bumping along," Theo said. Every minute they spent re-hashing his academic shortcomings was time away from study or making a buck.

"Are you certain there are no untapped resources so you don't have to work so much? You need to pass all your classes to stay in school."

As if this would be his first choice if he had an easier way.

"I'll get an app and organize my time better," he said. "If I can get it done, can I do extra journal entries?"

"I'll read whatever you turn in," Professor Stone said.

"You said I could get credit for helping if I found someone for your film project."

"You said you didn't know anyone."

At this point he would do anything to pass those classes. "I might have someone."

"Sounds vague. Tell me more," Professor Stone said. She didn't sound convinced.

"You said you want several generations in one home? I have someone in mind but we're still getting to know each other."

Professor Stone turned her head away. He imagined her rolling her eyes. They arrived at her office, where she unlocked the door but left it shut. "And your class project, how is that going?"

"I have a friend who does yarn installations."

"I wouldn't have predicted that. The yarn bit, not that you have friends." She smiled.

He smiled, playing along with the joke. "It's a group of women, some of them with rough backgrounds. They knit together for a social thing and they plan these art things only with yarn."

Professor Stone nodded. "I hoped you'd do something with your heritage."

"Why is that?" Theo asked.

"Don't you have a story you're in a unique position to tell?"

This was what she thought? He had an exotic story to tell?

"I thought that's what I was doing." It came out more sharply than he intended. He smiled again. "I'll keep working on it."

---

*a*s soon as she got through the door, Ester sank into her desk chair and snapped on the space heater she kept at her feet. She gave herself a few moments to thaw before she got up to start a fresh pot of coffee. In their current office, the kitchen was a narrow table with a coffee maker, a box of sugar packets and a box of creamer packets. They used heavy cardboard cups since there was no place to wash dishes. Ester tried to use the same cup one more than once because otherwise it seemed wasteful.

A few months earlier they'd been operating out of a temporary location shoehorned into a strip mall. They had planned to move into a permanent home, a place known as the Chief Building, to be purchased from the city. At the last minute, the city had killed the deal and wouldn't disclose why.

Meanwhile, the lease at the strip mall expired and they'd moved into this even less useful space at the community college. Ester and her three co-workers worked together in one room. The only thing worse would have been to close the center and have no job at all.

Rayanne, her friend and co-worker, came in the door with her boyfriend, Henry, close behind. Ester was still too unnerved by her close encounter with Theo to tease them about the obvious nooner.

She could tell by the giddy lunatic glow in their eyes. Henry had his hands on her waist and she was smoothing the front of his shirt.

"How was lunch?" was the best she could come up with.

"Lunch was great," Henry said. He hadn't taken his eyes off Rayanne since they'd entered the room. What was that feeling when you were happy your friend had found someone but witnessing her endless bliss made your own life feel hopeless?

Rayanne kissed Henry goodbye and then unwound a long flannel scarf from her neck. "Give me some heat," she said, coming to stand by the heater. "How about you? What did you do?"

"Nothing," Ester said. She adjusted the heat to blow on Rayanne. She rubbed her hands together and opened the spreadsheets she needed to go over with Linda by the end of the day.

"What happened to getting a new coat?" Rayanne said. "Yours is so worn you can see through it."

"Haven't gotten around to it yet." Ester didn't want to explain that she'd misplaced the gift card from the Big Stop Outdoor Store that her parents had given her specifically to buy a new coat. She thought she had put it in her dresser drawer but it wasn't there last time she checked. She hadn't had time for a thorough search yet.

"Let's go after work. I can drive you over there and then take you home."

"Not today," Ester said in a tone intended to end the conversation.

"Sure," Rayanne said as the coffee finished brewing. She poured two fresh cups and handed Ester one, then she slid her chair over to Ester's desk and took a sip. "What a nice hot drink after that cold air outside."

"You're not kidding. My hands froze into claws out there." Ester wrapped her hands around the cup. Rayanne gave her a look—a look that Ester herself had perfected. A suggestive, questioning look.

Uh oh.

Ester took a big sip of coffee. "I'm feeling warmer already." She returned her attention to her desk, rearranging her documents and files. "Does anyone else use this room?"

Rayanne stayed where she was. "Who were you talking to?" she asked in a casual tone.

"Seriously," Ester said, waving her hands over her things, "someone comes in here and disturbs my files and leaves empty cups behind. They could be stealing our supplies or—"

"—or our grant research?" Rayanne asked.

"Yes," Ester agreed. "People could be after our valuable paperwork."

Rayanne shook her head.

"I'm setting up a spy cam so I can find out," Ester said. She opened a desk drawer as if searching for the camera that she already knew was in a box at home.

"The guy?"

"What guy?" Ester said, her voice going up a half octave. She shifted her attention to her computer screen and the spreadsheet she'd made to map out how much coffee they drank.

"Outside the computer lab? I recognized your crummy coat."

"No one."

Rayanne leaned forward and in a knowing voice said, "No one?"

"Correct. I have no idea who you are talking about," Ester said. She busied herself formatting cells in fancy patterns.

"Big guy. The kind of big that could inspire fear, except cheekbones for miles. His hair was hidden under a hat but he's built like a Maori rugby player. Super-hero muscles, big hands—"

"Okay, okay. I was talking to that guy. I left my drive in the lab and he gave it to me. It's no big deal."

"Are you sure? Your face is bright pink." Rayanne sat back again, a sly smile on her face.

"It's working. I'm embarrassed. Are you happy now?"

"Embarrassing you isn't what makes me happy. Who is he?"

"Theo. Jicarilla Apache. That's all the intel I have. He worked in the computer lab and I've been crushing on him. That's the first time we spoke. He asked me a bunch of questions and I froze up and then ran away. I like his chest muscles, too, if you must know. That's it, you know it all. Will you leave me alone now?"

"Look at you, all grown up. When are you seeing him again?"

"Did that count as seeing him once?"

"It does," Rayanne said.

"I don't know. He doesn't work in the lab anymore."

"What did you guys talk about?"

"I'm not sure. I was staring at his face, and my ears stopped working."

"We can track him down. Theo, the studly Jicarilla Apache from the computer lab."

Ester chilled all over. "I don't know his last name. Do we have to keep talking about this?"

"Come on, girl, you talk a big life. You whine about never meeting dudes. You talk about going home alone. Make a plan about this guy."

"We're not all born confident like you are," Ester said.

"It's not confidence. I just don't let doubt control me."

"People with confidence are always saying they aren't confident and then ordering the rest of us to get over it. It's not easy for me."

"It's not easy for anyone. What's the alternative? Either you take the risk or you wait until some imaginary perfect person finds you and does all the work to turn you into a couple. So you get nervous when you talk to him. Think of three things to say next time you see him. If he doesn't want to talk, he'll duck out of the conversation and you move on."

"Do you think he would let me touch his abs?" Ester said.

Rayanne laughed. "That can be one of your three things."

"I never imagined myself with someone built like a linebacker. I would need a stepladder to hop on him."

Rayanne leaned forward. "That would be the fun part. Think of three things. You can practice on me later."

Their coworker Tommy came in. He shook his coat off and hung it over his chair.

"Fresh coffee, hooray," he said.

"If you like fresh coffee, I can show you how to make it," Ester said, "for next time."

"I don't need to make any, a fresh pot is right here," Tommy said with a smile. He dragged his chair over to join the conversation.

"Did Henry recruit you?" Ester asked.

"He did," Tommy said. "The bus is booked and I am your trusty driver."

"For the birthday celebration?" Rayanne asked. "Where did you guys decide on?"

"Frenzy's." Ester mimicked the radio ad and sang, "Everyone is going to Frenzy's." She jumped to her feet and circled her hips while tilting her head side-to-side like a pop star.

Rayanne sang with her, "All your dreams come true at Frenzy's. Make new friends at Frenzy's."

Tommy made an unhappy grunting sound. "Henry did not make that part clear."

"I love Frenzy's," Ester said. "Not the drunky, meat-market part. But the two levels of loud pounding music and flashing lights so I can dance my feet off part I like a lot. The first time I heard the ad I thought it was Friendsies, like a cute plural of friends."

"It isn't a place you want to be stone sober," Tommy said. He'd given up drinking before they knew him but this was the first time they'd recruited him for designated driver duties.

"Are you changing your mind?" Rayanne asked.

"Nope," Tommy said. "I'll get through it."

"What are you wearing?" Rayanne asked.

Tommy glanced down at his outfit. "Pants, shirt, shoes. That okay?"

"Not you." Rayanne shot Ester a pointed look.

"Pants, shirt, shoes. That okay?"

"No. It is not okay. Wear the cute little black dress you wore for the festival. You were radiant that night."

Ester was mostly shaped like a boy except for her breasts. Her body was all limbs and no shape except for the two that poked out in front. Nothing looked good on her. "It's winter. I'll freeze to death getting from the bus to the club. Plus I spent that entire night pulling it down. While I was in the midst of my best dance moves, that skirt rode up like it was trying to escape. I don't want my butt dangling out for all to see."

"That's the whole point," Rayanne said. "Show a little skin."

"My entire butt skin?"

"Let's shop for something new. It would be fun."

"Did I tell you the one about how I'm dead broke?" Ester said. She normally didn't complain about it because she didn't want anyone to guess how tight things were for her.

"Cody and Sam are attending," Rayanne said.

"Cody and Sam? Cody of the huge biceps has never set an eyeball on me and paused to think about it. Sam is an awkward tech nerd who is too sweaty and nervous. Our combined poor social skills would create a black hole to end the world. Besides, I thought you were trying to set me up with the computer center guy." She pointed at Tommy. "Why don't you pick on him?"

"Whose side are you on?" Tommy said, with humor in his voice. "What computer center guy?"

"Whose side are YOU on?" Ester said, but she was laughing, too.

Tommy pulled his chair back to his own desk.

Rayanne put her hands up in surrender. "I'll drop it. But it would be fun to dress up. Especially since we hardly ever go out like this anymore."

"I'll think about it," Ester said. She already knew she was wearing the little black dress; she had no other going-out clothes to choose from.

4

———————

*A*fter his last class, Theo headed to the parking lot to warm up his car. With the lab job gone, the pressure was on to drive more. He signed into the ridesharing app and then cracked open a book to study while he waited. If he could travel back in time and tell the younger Theo—the version who skipped school and drove around getting high—that he would voluntarily return to school, what would that kid say to him? He didn't skip class now, and the time after school was for study and for work. He'd traded in his pickup for this dumb car so he had a more appealing ride.

As expected, within a few minutes of logging in he had a ride request from on campus. A short ride, too. He drove around to the Student Services building to pick her up. This was his favorite type of job. He could fit in more than one before going home to get ready for his night job.

A light rain had started up, the kind Theo referred to as a driving mist. He drove as close to the entrance as he could and waved. Two women in fancy white coats hurried to the car, their heads down. The first one hesitated when she saw Theo through the window. He offered a reassuring smile and motioned her into the car but by that time the other one had the door open, tossed in her book bag, and crawled in after it. The first followed and, once settled, they pushed back their fur-trimmed hoods and dipped their heads down to their phones.

"Hey," Theo said, glancing back via the rear-view mirror. Neither woman looked up. "Warm enough for you back there?"

"Sure," one of them said. Her eyes never left her phone, one finger sweeping across the screen. "Can you pick up one of our friends?"

"Where is she?" Theo asked. He waited for a full minute but neither one answered. He put the car in drive and headed for their destination.

"Never mind," one of them said. They tilted their heads together and kept their voices low. A lot of rides didn't start a conversation and, strange as it was to sit in his car with another person in silence, he rarely made the effort himself. The car hadn't even come to a full stop in front of their apartment building before they had the doors open to get out. They both wore high-heeled white boots, an extravagance he tried to find humor in. If he compared other students' situations with his own, he would never get out of bed in the morning.

They left one of the car doors ajar and he had to get out to shut it. "You're welcome," he muttered.

He drove to the local mini-mart to pick up an energy drink. The driving mist had ramped up into a steady cold drizzle. He checked the time. He could squeeze in one more ride.

Instead of reading, he worked on a journal entry for Professor Stone. She had told her students they needed to practice writing well and completing pieces quickly. The assignment was five short articles every week; the topic wasn't important. She didn't ask for a bunch of research or interview sources, but she wanted to see a variety of stories about real issues, not lazy work like interviewing friends about student loans or covering sports.

All of his ideas circled back to finances: students finding jobs that worked with an academic schedule, on-campus jobs run by nerds who want to meet cute girls, students with no family resources trying to support themselves, the foolishness of taking on a car loan to get a better car for ride sharing.

His phone rang and he checked the display.

Jess from the moving company. Finally, good news. Jess paid better than the muscle-for-hire app and he paid cash. Any time Jess had work, it took some pressure off.

"What's going on?" Theo said.

"I got two jobs tomorrow. Four hours total. One hundred bucks."

When Jess said four hours, it meant more like six.

"That's my whole day," Theo said. "I have the chance for a bigger job but don't have the details yet. Yours sound better if you can come up with more money." This wasn't true but if Jess was calling at the last minute, it gave him some leverage.

Jess sighed. "One fifty."

"Hm," Theo said, pretending to mull it over.

"I know other people if you don't want the work."

"Okay, okay," Theo said. Jess was playing him right back, but that was okay. They needed each other and Jess knew Theo was reliable. "Text me a time and address. See you in the morning."

Thanks, Theo."

The ride-sharing app chimed again and he headed back to campus.

This time a friendly stoner guy hopped in the front seat. "What's up? You're Theo? I'm Theo, too." He shook Theo's hand and gave him a wide smile.

"Theodore?" Theo asked. He liked stoners. They always seemed so content with whatever the world offered. He wished he could get into that headspace.

"That's me. When I was a kid, I was Teddy. You don't seem like a Teddy."

"I'm not," Theo agreed.

"I get you," Teddy said. Theo had already pulled away but his ride announced, "We're going to Big Barn to pick up booze for the weekend."

"Sounds good," Theo said. "You have your own ID?"

"No worries," Teddy said. He laughed. "All legal and on the up-and-up. People ask you to buy for them?"

"Not often," Theo said. "I say no."

"I hear you," Teddy said. "There are so many ways that can go wrong."

Theo thought the guy seemed familiar. "You in Professor Stone's class?"

"Vis-comm. You too?" Teddy gave Theo the once-over. "I didn't think you were a student. That's a good class. How are you doing in it?"

"She's busting my ass over the final project," Theo said.

"Yeah, she is an ass-buster, but a good teacher."

Theo pulled into the Big Barn parking lot.

"You come in, help me out and take me back, I'll give you another twenty bucks," Teddy said. Even the hippie kids had money to throw around.

Theo checked the time. "Why not," he said.

Throughout the store Teddy kept up a steady stream of conversation. He mentioned another digital reporting class that Theo hadn't gotten into yet, the latest snow report, and the two dogs he had brought back to his folks because it was a pain to take care of them while in school. Theo watched in fascination as the guy loaded the cart with boxes of beer and big jugs of hard alcohol, trying to fathom having the money to pay for all this.

At one point Teddy smiled. "Typical college weekend."

Theo nodded like he understood even though he'd yet to experience such a typical college weekend.

They checked out and Theo drove Teddy to a rundown older house. The neighborhood was filled with similar homes that had been remodeled with student housing in mind. He helped carry in the booze. The house smelled like stale beer and wet dog. They stacked the drinks on a scuffed table in what would have been the dining room.

"Thanks, dude," Teddy said, using his phone to transfer the promised twenty. "You should come back later. Good crowd, not the usual types. Hang out."

"Thanks," Theo said. "Night job."

"Doesn't matter," Teddy said. "We'll be up late."

"I'll keep it in mind," Theo said, wishing it were true. He couldn't imagine having anything in common with Teddy and his friends.

He headed home for a power nap and quick shower before he had to get to work.

His mind drifted back to his new favorite Shoshone. Something about those brown eyes and the way her brows knit together before she said something. Her closed-mouth smile, as if she knew something she wasn't going to share. She had shown zero sign of interest and he was in no position to start something even if she had. But his thoughts kept going back her anyway. Maybe the attraction came from a deeper place. She reminded him of home. Plus she was smart. He always had a thing for the smart ones. But the smart ones knew well enough to stay away from him.

---

5

*E*ster boarded the bus last. She strutted down the aisle, slapping everyone's hands. "This bus smells like elders, basketballs, and hope."

"That's a song title," Jack, the guest of honor, said. She gave him a birthday hug before she sat down. Jack was like a Labrador, loyal and even-tempered. He was Henry's childhood friend and the lead singer of a band called the Beat Braves.

Sam, the band's bass player, gave her a nervous wave before typing into his phone. "I'm making a note of it." He was more techie than she, and great at television trivia. He was always wanting to tell her about some computer problem he'd solved.

She sat down next to Cody. He was their guitar player and a mechanic. He was the one who helped Tommy get the center's bus running when they first purchased it. Cody looked like a rock star yet acted surprised when women surrounded him.

Ester had met the band when they played a show for the UIC. Everyone on the bus was Native except Jack's girlfriend, Nicole, a talkative blonde who had been intimidating at first. She turned out to be sweet and genuine and Ester looked forward to seeing her.

Ester waved until she won Rayanne's attention and then pointed at her outfit. She'd worn the little black dress and put on eyeliner, too. Rayanne winked at her. "You're gorgeous."

"So are you," Ester said. Rayanne looked amazing. She could spend the night sleeping in dumpster and crawl out looking cute. Ester pulled the skirt down. Cold air seeped up from the floor. "This bus is freezing," she said.

From his rear-view mirror, Tommy spotted her rubbing her hands together. "The seat behind mine is the warmest," he called.

Ester moved to sit behind him. "Crank it up all the way."

"If I blast it, you'll overheat in ten minutes," Tommy said.

"I wouldn't mind."

"We're almost there, Ester."

He must have cranked it up a notch anyway because after a moment warm air blasted around her feet. She put her hands out like it was a camp fire.

"Thanks, Tommy."

He drove the bus with steady hands at ten and two. They crossed over the river and headed into downtown. By the time she was comfortable, they arrived. She had no sooner jumped off the bus than her warm feet were cold again. She shook her hips and shoulders and danced from foot to the other, trying to keep warm.

"Save something for inside," Tommy said. He collected parking money from each of them, with Ester tapping her phone to transfer her contribution. She had scraped together enough money for a drink and to throw in for drinks for Jack. If anything unexpected happened, she'd have to mooch and pay someone back later. She managed day-to-day expenses okay but anything extra took planning. A night of flashing lights and a bass beat was a welcome treat.

They headed for the entrance, early enough to beat the cover and the long line that would wrap around the block later.

"I'm ready to get inside," Rayanne said, her arm linked with Henry's. She rested her forehead on his shoulder and he tilted his head against her. Ester stood behind, admiring for the millionth time how easy they were together.

Rayanne spun around. "Your dude is here," she hissed.

"I have a dude?" Ester said.

"From the computer lab."

Ester's stomach lurched. She searched the line until she got to the front and saw him sitting on a stool by the door of the club, checking IDs. He was wearing brown slacks and a long-sleeve maroon Henley, a combination that most folks would agree didn't quite match. He had his sleeves pushed up over his manly forearms. She exhaled. In the computer lab he seemed plausibly attainable, but now the idea was absurd.

"He's the bouncer?" she said, her mouth gone dry. He met a hundred women a night. She wanted to go home.

The women in the group ahead crowded around him. They had obedient hair, clever makeup, and accessories, ladies the opposite of her. They laughed and one of them leaned against him while he examined their IDs. His expression remained neutral, but she imagined he was taking his time.

He glanced up and spotted her. He twitched an eyebrow before returning his attention to the lady in front of him.

"Did you think of three things?" Rayanne said.

"No. I thought I had more time. I planned a brainstorming session this weekend to find different topics and opening sentences—"

Rayanne elbowed her with a playful smile.

"I don't know," Ester said, her panic genuine. "What would you say?"

"Something about class?"

"But I'm not a student."

By this time their group reached the front. Rayanne gave her an encouraging smile before she took Henry's arm again.

Theo checked out their group, curiosity in his face. He made a point of catching Ester's eye and she smiled in a way intended to convey more like *what a surprise, campus acquaintance* and less *I am crushing on you bad.*

Theo took Tommy's ID. He used his chin to gesture over their heads. "You skins ride on that bus?"

"We did," Tommy said. "It's a fifteen-passenger Drivemaster 1600 loaded with extra options. Some of them work, too"

Theo cracked a smile. "Is that so?" He returned Tommy's ID. "Never seen this many Ind'ns together in the city. You all know something I should know?"

"It's Jack's birthday," Nicole said, nudging the birthday boy forward. Jack handed over his ID.

Theo checked it and handed it back to him. "So it is. And you came here?"

"We like to dance," Rayanne said.

"I suppose I can see the appeal," Theo said. He continued working through the group, looking at each ID.

The closer she got to him, the more Ester's heart pounded. Three things. She needed three things. Her eyes drifted to his big brown hands, his wrists, the edge of his sleeves. He wore a bracelet with silver beads on the hand that rested on his thigh while the other held up the ID. His hands were probably nice and warm. She couldn't think of one thing.

At this point Theo had seen all their IDs but Ester's. To her great alarm, everyone entered the club, leaving her alone with him.

"We meet again, Shoshone," he said with a smile. His shirt was one of those waffle weaves and clung to him. No coat. What was up with this guy never wearing a coat? He hid her ID in his hand and studied her face.

Three things, three things were the only panicked thoughts in her head. Weather? Too stupid. Traffic? Not relevant at that hour. Favorite sandwich? Obviously grasping.

He saved her by saying: "I was going to guess but I don't know any family names for Eastern Shoshone."

He flipped up her ID and squinted at it. "Ester Belle Parker?"

"My birth mom is Eastern Shoshone," Ester said.

"Ah," Theo said, conveying a lot of understanding in that single syllable. "Welcome to Frenzy's, Ester Belle Parker."

"This your new job?" Ester asked.

"I have many jobs," Theo said. "Starving student, you know?"

"Ah," Ester agreed.

He still had her ID. "Twenty-five," he said, as if impressed. "Older than I am."

Before she could ask, three women arrived at the door. Theo gave Ester her ID but motioned for her to stand next to him. He checked their IDs and sent them on their way. He turned his attention back to her.

"You don't strike me as the Frenzy's dance-club type," he said.

"I'm not," Ester said. "But I like dancing, and it's okay with a group."

"Not here on the prowl?" Theo said. One side of his mouth curved up.

Ester made a face. Three things. Three things. She wanted to keep talking to him. She bounced from foot to foot, trying to ignore the cold.

Another group approached the door. Theo put one of his big hands, which was indeed pleasantly warm, on her back and nudged her toward the door. "Have fun, Shoshone."

THE IMPRESSION of Theo's warm hand stayed with her as she made her way into the club. His voice was like she remembered. His manner was looser, verging on playful here at the club, unlike in the lab with his stony face.

The group waited for her at the bar. Henry handed her a draft beer, the cheapest beverage choice on the menu, which she took with a grateful smile. They raised their glasses.

"Happy birthday, Jack."

There wasn't much action on the dance floor so they moved upstairs and crowded around a couple of empty tables.

"Aren't you glad you wore the little black dress now?" Rayanne said.

The entire group had its attention on her. Ester said, "You guys all happy with your clothing choices?"

"How do you know that guy?" Nicole asked.

"He goes to the college. I've seen him in the computer lab," Ester said. "Moving on. Have you guys picked out your porn star name?"

Rayanne raised her voice above Ester's. "He talked to her on campus today. I think he's into her."

"You called it," Ester said. "He handed me the external drive I left in the lab. Minutes ago he checked my ID. Any day we'll get hitched and poop out Ind'n babies."

"He's cute but intense," Nicole said. "I wouldn't want him to catch me with a fake ID."

"No one?" Ester said. "No one wants a porn star name? Isn't it your first pet and the street you grew up on?"

Sam said, "My porn star name would be Pup Smokehouse."

"I thought it was your grandpa's middle name and your favorite food," Henry said. "Mine would be Norbert Steak, or Norbert Red Meat."

Tommy said, "I think it should be the place you lost your virginity and your favorite superhero. Mine would be Rodeo Batman."

"You lost your virginity at a rodeo?" Rayanne asked.

"Pendleton Round-Up," Tommy said. He leaned back with a satisfied smile.

Ester exhaled, relieved that she'd deflected the attention elsewhere. She wiped her still-sweating palms on her skirt.

"What about you, Cody?" she asked.

"My porn name is a secret. You started this," he said. "What about you?"

"Grandma's first name and famous nature thing near your reservation. Ramona Jackson Hole."

They all burst out laughing. Rayanne had just gulped her beer and had to slap her hand over her mouth until she got control of herself.

Nicole shook her head. "You people are too funny."

"You people?" Henry said, feigning indignity. "Did you hear that? She called us you people."

Jack stood up and grabbed her hand. "I'll rescue you. Let's go shake your thing."

They made their way to the dance floor. Cody trotted downstairs, too, and stood near the bar. Seconds later, ladies surrounded him. He knew how to work the exotic-dude thing. Henry and Sam talked about the band's next big show.

Tommy moved to sit next to Ester. "When they get into reverb and looping, I can't follow." He'd finished his soda and rattled the ice cubes in the tiny glass. "Who was that guy?"

"We're never going to stop talking about him, are we?" Ester said.

"He's the guy from the computer lab," Rayanne said.

"I never pictured you with a meathead," Tommy said.

Ester reached over and thumped him on the shoulder.

"Sorry. I was expressing a thought. You're so brainy. I always figured you'd merge with some fellow brain."

Ester considered suggesting Theo might be a fellow brain but that would only encourage them to keep talking about him. "Talk about something else," she said.

"Sure. What's the latest with crazy McKayla?" Rayanne asked.

Ester shook her head. "I don't know where to start."

Tommy shook his glass again. "Who's crazy McKayla?"

"MacKenzie," Ester said. "My roommate, Dennis, the guy who owns the house, has a new girlfriend. She was okay at first but she's developed a busybody vibe. Like tonight, about three minutes after I got home, she asked me what my plan was for paying the rent. Dennis wasn't around when she asked."

"You mean for the month that doesn't start for two weeks?" Rayanne said.

"That's what I said, and she tried to make it sound like I wasn't getting her point."

"What would her point be? Besides, do you pay her the rent?" Rayanne asked.

"I pointed that out, too. Then I closed myself up in my room. I hate feeling uptight in my own living space."

"Have you talked to Dennis?" Rayanne asked.

"To say what? You used to mope around here and worry about being alone forever, but this girl you like treats me weird."

Henry stood up and held out his hand. "It's time," he said.

"You can hope the conversation will come up by itself," Rayanne said. She gestured for Ester's hand.

"Sure." Ester finished her beer.

"I'll keep the table," Tommy said.

"Me too," Sam said.

"I'm doing my dance thing." Ester made her way to the dance floor with the others.

~

THE CLUB MANAGER radioed Theo to ask how many people were waiting outside. As the hour had grown later, the line stretched halfway down the block. Theo slowed things down at the door as Pete had instructed. A group consisting of several couples waited at the front of the line. They'd started their night elsewhere and had decided it was their turn to get in the club.

"How much longer?" one of guys asked.

Theo gave him a bland smile.

"It's cold out here," one woman said, as if he were unaware of the air temperature. Another guy growled into his phone about the jerk who wouldn't let them in. Theo tuned them out.

He got up from the stool and scanned the line for brewing trouble but all was clear. The closer they got to closing the more likely it was that things would change.

"Buddy, you gonna let us in there?" The guy put his hand on Theo's arm. He shook it off with a fierce glare. "This is ridiculous," the guy said.

They were arguing over whether to offer him cash when Pete came from inside.

"Everything like we want it?" Pete asked. That meant, did the line stretch to the end of the block? After a certain hour, the club owner liked it that way.

Theo nodded.

"Great. Time to trade," he said. He took the radio.

Theo let Pete sit down. "Inside?" Theo asked.

"The usual. Lots of people who want to do sex with each other. Wow, it's colder out here than I thought." Pete made a shivering motion at the group waiting at the door.

They smiled back, relieved that this door guy understood their situation.

"Let me see the ladies' IDs," Pete said.

"About time," one of the guys said with a huff.

Theo suppressed a smile as he headed back in. Pete would make them wait, too, but where Theo played indifferent, Pete acted like their buddy. He chatted them up and made them feel like they were friends, so they put up with a longer, more drawn out admittance. They didn't like being ignored.

The stuffy throb of the club contrasted with the refreshing air outside. He waited at the bar until his favorite bartender spotted him.

"Hello, dear," Fran said with a bright smile. She was a tall blonde, with the demeanor of a concerned big sister, which worked equally well with belligerent customers and the ones in the midst of a night out disaster. Theo had unexpectedly unloaded on her one night when he could hardly stand up straight he was so exhausted and over-whelmed with school. She was one of the few people he trusted. She had a cocktail shaker in her hands. "Coffee?"

"Water's fine."

"Give me a sec." Fran turned around and poured drinks, ran a card, set up a row of glasses, and then came back to hand him a glass of water. He admired her brisk efficiency.

"Thanks, Fran," Theo said. He used his elbow to show her where he'd be standing if they needed him.

She nodded and returned to mixing drinks and opening beer bottles, always with a smile.

Theo crossed the club and stood in the corner and scanned the room. Once he had a handle on that, he searched for Ester. She said she liked to dance so he checked the dance floor first.

The club was busy but not at capacity. The dance beat thundered over the sound system while the bodies on the dance floor surged together and apart, arms pumping overhead. People jammed the benches and tables around the perimeter, the guests shouting above the music. He liked being in the mix without being a part of it.

He couldn't find her and the disappointment surprised him. How hard could it be to spot a group of Ind'ns in a place like this? He thought about leaving his post to take a lap around the upper level and then chided himself for acting like a school boy.

Then he spotted her. Her group clustered together on one side of the dance floor. They all laughed, somehow exchanging words over the music. They took turns with a dance move that the others would copy. Ester moved with more energy than he would have guessed. She had both arms above her head and swiveled her hips with the beat. One hand dipped down to tug her dress where it was riding up high on her thighs. Her shoulders shimmied as she bounced around, her eyes bright and her mass of curly hair swinging around her face. Her arms were shiny with sweat. He wouldn't mind getting to know the texture of that skin and the taste of it. She yanked down her skirt again.

He forced himself to tear his eyes away and scan the club again. This wasn't the time for getting his personal business stirred up.

A curvy brunette came over and touched his arm. "Can I talk to you for a sec?"

Theo had learned to be cautious about making assumptions about women approaching him. For every come on, there was a lady with a legit problem. Some guys didn't like the word no.

He leaned down so he could hear her better.

"I'm S----la," she said.

Shayla? Sheila? He couldn't be sure over the music.

"Is there a problem?"

She swayed a little, and he touched her back to steady her. Encouraged, she leaned into him. Theo glanced over her shoulder. A group of women watching turned away. Everyone who worked at the club got hit on and, depending on the night, it might be flattering but tonight he had eyes for one.

Theo walked her back to her friends and peeled her off of him. He stood at the table long enough to learn their names and confirm they weren't having a problem before excusing himself.

Then he found a different corner to stand in. This time he spotted Ester upstairs, sitting at a table with the group. Whatever they were talking about involved elaborate hand motions and much laughter. It took a minute to sort out that the feeling tugging at him was envy. He couldn't remember the last time he'd been that loose and relaxed with a group of friends, much less Natives. Ester's outgoing friend spotted him and tugged Ester's arm. Her head swung around. The friend gave an expressive lecture, which he hoped would end with Ester coming to talk to him. He tried not to smile when Ester stood up and came downstairs to stand next to him.

Theo slouched down and tilted his head to hear her.

"Are you allowed to talk to people?" she asked.

"As required by the job," he said. "Anyone giving you a hard time?"

"Rayanne," she said, flashing a dark glare upstairs.

"You want me to throw her out?"

"Kinda," Ester said. "Have you ever thrown someone out, as in picked them up and booted them into the street?"

"No," Theo said. "If they bust their heads, I would be in big trouble."

Ester nodded, her expression serious. Her eyes drifted back out to the dance floor.

"Do I want to know why you have your own bus?" he asked.

Those gorgeous dark eyes met his again. "We know each other from the Crooked Rock Urban Indian Center. The bus belongs to the center."

"Urban Indian center?"

"We provide services for Indians who live in the city. Healthcare referrals, elder assistance, some cultural activities. Our office is on campus until we get a permanent location."

"On campus? I've never heard of it," Theo said.

"Clearly our outreach program is a total failure," Ester said.

Theo couldn't help smiling. "Well, I don't get around much."

"Yeah, well, there have been complications with the center. Funding. Location. Long story."

"Sounds like it," he said. He imagined Ester coming on to him. A coy smile, a roundabout invitation with clear meaning. He would follow her to her place, a small apartment like his with solid color, practical sheets on the bed. She'd push him down and climb on top of him, that sexy smile never leaving her face.

Ester didn't come across as the one-night stand type.

"Urban Indian center is your day job?" he asked.

"Manager of health programs, slash, class clown," Ester said.

He glanced up to see Fran frantically waving him over.

"Sorry, Shoshone. Gotta run."

He spotted the problem right away. A couple of guys in standoff mode in front of the bar. They weren't throwing punches yet, but they wanted the other to think that could happen. Theo said nothing. He sidled into view and stood there. They made a point of eyeing him and then each other again, before backing down and ducking their heads to their group of friends. One left the club with his group, so he didn't bother following the other one.

"No one breaks up a fight like you," Fran said. She gestured for him to come closer. "We're picking up burgers and having a beer at Pete's after closing. You coming?"

"Not tonight," he said. There was a group that often got together to unwind after a Friday shift. He had joined them a few times, but he wasn't up for it tonight. "I got school projects in the morning and I have a couple moving jobs."

"You can always change your mind," Fran said.

"You still doing my interview?" he asked.

She made a face but nodded, then side-stepped to her spot to take a drink order.

The rest of the evening passed with the usual amount of drunken incidents and lovers' spats. Shortly before last call, Pete swapped with him again and he returned to sit at the door. They turned people away unless they were tracking down a friend or lost something in the club. The latest part of the night had the potential to be the strangest but on the nights when things stayed calm, he liked the way things wound down.

Ester's group burst out, rowdy and loud like people who had a fun night out. Ester raised her eyebrows and gave him a wave as she walked by.

She was a few steps down the street when he called out, "Ester, I want to ask you something."

The entire group stopped. Ester looked back at him, but he wasn't sure what her expression meant.

"There's a frybread feed on campus next week. You have lunch with me?"

Ester froze.

Her friend Rayanne called out, "She'd love to."

Theo gave her a tight smile. "I'll wait for Ester to answer."

Rayanne made an *ooh* face at Ester and urged the group to keep walking.

Ester stepped closer. "Okay." She could hardly look at him. "Where should I meet you?"

"Campus longhouse. If it's cold, I'll meet you inside."

"Okay," she repeated.

"Goodnight, Ester."

"Goodnight." She hurried to catch up with her friends.

A couple of regulars came out to say goodnight. One of them leaned on him and put her chin on his shoulder. The other wrapped her hand around his arm.

"You going to Pete's?" the one huddled against him asked.

"Not tonight," he said, trying to sound regretful. He leaned back and gently shrugged her off.

"You have other plans?" the arm holder asked.

"Sleep. I have a lot to do tomorrow. Goodnight, ladies," he said, urging them back inside.

He watched the bus pull out and drive off into the night.

6

*L*inda Bird read the email for the third time.

The Native American Tribal Government meeting is at the convention center and coming up soon. We need something to tell our story. Not just the usual talk. Something.

What did Arnie mean by *something?*

Something crazy like burlesque? she wrote and just as quickly deleted.

Something like, reenact the Dances with Wolves *tatanka scene?* Backspace. Backspace.

I'm good at the usual talk, she wrote. But she deleted that, too.

Arnie Jackson had joined the urban Indian center's board of director's only months earlier but he managed to be a consistent pain in the ass. At first she thought they worked well together but since she'd successfully pleaded for one more year to get this vision of hers off the ground, their relationship had grown strained.

Linda believed the problem came from too many people giving her input and no one trusting her judgment. The board asked her to do everything at once rather than solve one problem at a time.

Their biggest problem was location. They'd busted their tails putting together a deal to buy a building. They had contracts and funding in place, but the city backed off. She needed a clear answer so she could decide how to move forward. Instead, the board had her applying for grants, talking to potential employees, giving speeches at meetings, and visiting every entity that might be a fundraising opportunity. She couldn't accomplish anything when she was running around.

I'll work on it with the staff, she typed and hit send.

She crossed her arms and put her head on her desk.

"Knock, knock," someone called from the door.

She sat up. "Why, it's Audra, the attorney with a heart of gold."

"It's impossible for an attorney to have a heart of gold," Audra said.

"Thanks for the warning. This is a public facility, you don't have to knock."

Audra came in and sat down next to her. She gave a mock-admiring look around the room. "Love what you've done with the place. Open work space. None of this cubicle business."

Linda tried to laugh. She was the executive director of a non-profit organization that months earlier had been on the verge of moving into its own permanent home. Now her group was crammed into a single room at City College, a cluster of desks pushed together in the center of the room.

"They offered to let us borrow some of those dinky student work stations. They were so depressing we said no. If we need privacy, we take our cellphones and go outside. If it's cold, we talk fast."

"You're lucky your staff is loyal," Audra said, admiring the stacks of boxes.

"For now. Welcome to the Crooked Rock Urban Indian Center. What took you so long to visit?"

"The usual—working, teaching, living it up in the high glamour world of Indian law. I stopped by on a whim. I thought you would have gone home by now."

Linda and Audra had met years earlier when Audra was fresh out of law school and wanting to volunteer some time to tribal organizations in town. Linda had always admired Audra, who worked tough hours and pulled off an effortlessly casual look like the magazines talked about. She had her dark curly hair pulled back off her face and wore a business suit that made her look like an attorney on a TV program.

Linda wore a droopy skirt with a salsa stain from lunch. "I operate under the delusion if I put in enough time, I can fix it all. It never works out that way."

"Not an uncommon delusion. How is our former mentor? She still keeping her fingers in the mix?" Audra referred to Linda's predecessor, Margie, an elder who had retired months earlier with health issues.

"She's a lean mean fighting machine. My dream is to be that together when I'm her age. She has live-in care so she can stay at home. She lends me an ear when I need to vent but she's letting me sink this ship on my own. Which is why I have to ask if you're here with bad news for me?" Audra had saved her ass by talking the college into letting them use this room, but from day one the college made it clear it was temporary. "Is our time here at good old Harney Hall ending?"

"Not that I know of," Audra said. "I'm not in charge of facilities but I think you're in the clear until the end of the quarter—maybe even the school year. If worse comes to worst, we can set up a tent in the parking lot."

"A tent or a teepee?"

Audra laughed. "No word from the city?"

"They could avoid us easily during the holidays but I'm back on it with gently escalating persistence. Margie helped me track down Paul Douglas. He was the guy who set up the Chief Building deal the city canceled. After he retired, he and his wife wintered in Spain. I wonder if I'll ever winter anywhere. He's back in town and coming to meet with us. We'll get the story and get the deal back on track."

Linda shut down her computer and piled everything on her desk into a single stack. "Would you like a mission?"

"I am plenty busy. What kind of mission?"

"I need clothing advice. I was thinking about walking through the mall to check out the sales."

"Special occasion?"

"I need something new. All I wear are dumpy long skirts, often flecked with lunch."

Audra smiled. "I'll tag along if it means saving you from dumpy skirts."

∿

THEY TOOK an escalator to the upper level. The bright lights and shiny fixtures of the department store promised more than clothing could deliver. Linda caught sight of herself in one mirror after the other; the entire place was made of reflective surfaces. Her underlying framework was still strong, but she'd grown lax on minding the details.

"He tosses out projects with no concept of how things work," Linda said, meaning Arnie. "An open house. A mass mailing. More, bigger social media. A detailed reference of every funding source under the sun for him to review and mark-up so we can direct our efforts."

"That's not an uncommon management style," Audra said.

"Now he's directed me to do something for NATG. Like he's had this great idea: we need something. My job is to come up with something. What does he think I do? Every minute of my life I'm thinking of something."

They arrived in the professional women's-wear section. Linda said, "You can never mention this to Rayanne. She's the one who suggested my wardrobe needed help."

"Why not bring her with you?"

"She'd have me in a skintight minidress and towering high heels and those tights that hold your gut in."

"For the office?"

"She's in love. She thinks everyone needs to be in love. She suggested I'm too dowdy. Or frumpy. I can't remember the word she used."

"You aren't even close to dowdy or frumpy but a, uh, more streamlined look never hurt anyone," Audra said.

"How diplomatic. Fine, take her side," Linda said, ignoring the display of neutral-colored work skirts and heading straight for a rack of flowy long skirts. "I'm allowed to look." She held up a skirt of the same color and material as the one she had on. "What would you do? We had a deal to buy a building. All the reports and environmental tests. Numerous packets of paperwork. The city pulled out and they're dragging their feet about even talking to us. What are our options? Stand at the front of city hall and throw rocks?"

Audra put the skirt back and led Linda over to a rack of dresses.

"Throwing rocks wouldn't get you far. Why not threaten to sue?"

"Arnie says no lawsuits. Too expensive. Only the lawyers win. Don't want to create the impression we're a litigious organization."

"Do you have to run everything by Arnie?"

"We've known each other a long time and have a lot of respect for each other," Linda said, wondering if it were still true. It felt like Arnie was pushing her into a corner and then blaming her for the problems it caused.

"You'd be surprised what a sternly worded letter can shake loose," Audra said.

"We can ask him again." She held up a long-sleeved gray sweater-dress. "Rayanne would force me to try this."

Audra smiled and took it from her. "Good idea. Who is Rayanne in love with?"

"Arnie's nephew, Henry. Another one of Arnie's forced orders. We had to hire him. I guess it worked out okay." She moved to another rack and searched for her size.

"Didn't you have a thing for him in college?"

"Arnie?" A pang of something—embarrassment?—stung in her belly.

"Schoolgirl crush, perhaps," she admitted. "We were friends. We're still friends, but now he's the boss."

Audra held up a navy-blue sheath dress. Linda made a face.

"You could wear it with a cardigan. This screams sexy professional. Try it on."

Linda took the dress. "We work well together."

"You're still talking about Arnie?" Audra said, a touch of a smile on her lips.

"If you let me finish, the problem is me. I always envisioned myself as a leader and here I am, everything I touch turns to crap. I'm always reacting. I can't seem to make anything happen."

"You inherited a mess," Audra said. "The board can't expect you to turn it around overnight."

"I've been working on this longer than overnight. Maybe this won't happen, I'm not the one who can do it."

Linda turned to the closest mirror and held up another sheath dress, this one with a sunny yellow pattern. "I'd get toner on it the first time I wore it."

Audra put the dress with the others. "Perhaps you need more time. Let's talk about something else. Are you seeing anybody?"

"Nice segue," Linda said. She took the dresses and found the changing room. Audra sat on a stool outside.

"When? I never meet anyone. I see the same people and no one is date material," Linda said.

"Is Arnie seeing anyone?"

Linda strained to understand what she meant with the question. "Are you asking for you or for me?"

"Just wondering."

"I think he sees lots of people." She waited but Audra didn't say more. She stepped out of her skirt and studied her reflection. "Why do changing rooms have such terrible lighting? I look sallow and lumpy."

"Try on the blue one I picked out. There's no way it isn't flattering. I have someone for you to meet. He's an attorney I work with sometimes. He's Native, one of those California rancherias. I forget which one."

"Go on," Linda said.

"He's super nice."

"You mean he wears patterned sweaters?"

"He's sharp and great at his job."

"You mean he knows lots of big words and never fails to return his shopping cart to the store, even in the rain. Your omission of a remark about his appearance doesn't bode well. What's wrong with him?"

Linda zipped up the blue dress. Audra was right. She didn't usually pick outfits so formfitting, but the cut was flattering. The material had give and wouldn't be uncomfortable at the office. She stepped out of the dressing room.

"It's perfect. Rayanne will approve," Audra said.

"I like it, too. I'm trying the sweater-dress." She returned to the changing room.

"He's attractive. Not leading man, but his face has character."

"Cartoon character?"

"No. He's a regular guy. Easy to talk to."

"If he's so great, why is he available?" Linda wiggled into the gray dress.

"You're great, why are you available?" Audra said.

"Because I work too much and I'm flawed," Linda said.

"You're not flawed. You're complex. He's kind of quiet," Audra said.

"You see me with someone quiet?"

"Not really. But ten minutes ago you complained you never meet anyone. How about a coffee date? Assuming I can convince him to go on one."

"What do you mean convince?" Linda said.

"Ambitious Ind'n woman, often late and over-extended, runs a non-profit and thinks grant-writing is fun. You're not an easy sell either."

Linda came out to model the sweater-dress.

"That one's cute, too. But the skirt is sort of baggy."

"I like the other one better," Linda agreed. "What's his name?"

"Virgil Harris."

"I'd always envisioned falling for a Virgil. I'll meet him," Linda said.

7

_E_ster inhaled a scent like a heated bucket of sour cheese. "Did something die in here?" she asked.

Linda came away from the microwave with a folded bundle wrapped in a napkin. She dropped a steaming knot of orange-tinged bread that was leaking an acidy orange sauce onto a paper plate.

"You mean this hot Italian roll?"

"You're spoiling my appetite," Ester said.

"Don't like it, don't eat it," Linda said. She took a big bite and then fanned her mouth.

"No frybread?" Rayanne asked.

Linda pointed at her computer.

"You don't want to see Ester's date?"

"I'd love to. Bring him by," Linda said.

"Not happening," Ester said, her eyes glued to the screen. For the first time, someone had shown up on her spy-cam footage and that someone was Tommy. According to the timestamp, he'd arrived after nine. He'd gone to his desk and sat in front of his computer with his feet up for a couple of hours, then left. No clue what he was up to. She shut the program and saved it to a password-protected folder until she figured out what to do.

Her eyes drifted to the time. Her date with Theo was at 11:45. She'd never been so mindful of the clock.

"It's pouring again," Rayanne said, coming away from the window.

"It does that," Ester said.

Rayanne came to stand behind her. She combed Ester's hair between her fingers as if that would do any good. "Did you buy the products I recommended?"

"I did," Ester said. "It's weird, I can't find them. I must have spaced out and put them in a weird place like in a box of old books or a coat pocket."

Linda said, "I've done that. Once I was so tired, I left the TV remote in the refrigerator."

Ester caught another whiff from Linda's monstrosity and her stomach flipped. The drawback of waiting days to see Theo again was she'd accumulated a lot of nerves.

"Are you prepared with three things?" Rayanne asked. "Conversations starters, not yes-or-no questions. Ask him about the highlight of his weekend."

"You're making me more nervous," Ester said. She put on her coat.

"Sorry," Rayanne said. "Just remember, you're a great person. Let that shine through."

"Would a great person be nervous about a get together involving frybread?" Ester said, wishing she were a normal person who didn't work herself into a lather over a lunch date.

She put up her hood and hurried across campus toward the longhouse. The whole way over, the vision of those two women at the club hanging onto him crept into her memory. A guy working at a club must meet tons of girls. He could take home a different one every night. On a good night, he could go home with both of them. That sour thought canceled out much of her elation after he'd asked her to lunch. Lunch wasn't much of a date, anyway. It was one point bigger than a coffee date—brief and easy to escape.

The building they called the longhouse wasn't even a replica longhouse like other schools had. Whereas a traditional Pacific Northwest longhouse was built from wood, City College had a rectangular building with high ceilings and a lot of Native art and cultural objects on display. There was a commercial kitchen and a space for events. Since the UIC had moved to campus, she'd attended numerous gatherings in that building.

Inside, the room was packed. She threaded her way through a group jammed in front of the door. She pushed her hood back and scanned the room, when she heard "Hey, Shoshone!" Theo waved her over.

He wore a rain jacket—so he did own one, and carried his backpack slung over his shoulder. He had his hair pulled back, and he wore small silver hoop earrings. After seeing him at the club, it was funny seeing him like a regular student. A regular student so gorgeous he should have his own holiday. The muscles around her mouth went slack and she couldn't force out more than a whispered, "Hi, Theo."

"It's nuts in here," he said. "They moved everyone inside because of the rain." The line stretched around the perimeter of the longhouse. Next to the kitchen, three students frantically filled plates while a fourth collected payment.

"You want to wait or would you rather go someplace else?"

Ester didn't mind waiting anywhere if Theo was involved. "This is fine," she said, dreading going back into the rain. "Some of the folks at the center don't approve of frybread."

"What's wrong with frybread?" Theo asked.

"Not healthy. Not traditional. Part of our mission is fighting cultural stereotypes."

"You want to protest the Native students' fundraiser?"

Ester shook her head. "I like fried food."

"*Phew*. I was nervous we were off to a bad start." Theo didn't look even a tiny bit nervous. She tried to remember her three things. Or anything.

"What was the highlight of your weekend?" she said. Would he tell her if the answer was "going home with two girls"?

"Besides talking to you, my weekend didn't have a highlight."

He said it with an easy confidence that made her blush to her toes. She played with her hands in her pockets.

"How about you? What was your highlight?"

He looked at her like she was the only person in the room. She tried to remember what she did over the weekend.

"Going out to the club. We had a lot of fun. Do you like working there?"

"The money is decent. The hours aren't ideal but I've become a strategic napper."

"I guess it's good you look like that," Ester said, then—realizing how it sounded—wished to take the words back. She was incapable of carrying on a normal conversation.

"Like what?" Theo said.

"Tall. Intimidating. It's good for a bouncer." The words came out in a stammer.

"Maybe," he said. "Sometimes scares people off in regular life. If I want to ask someone a question, like about class work, and they run in the opposite direction."

Heat crept into her face. The notion of intimidating people with your looks was so far outside her experience. They'd barely traveled halfway around the room; she needed another conversation starter.

"Do you have roommates?" she asked.

"I live alone," Theo said. Which was perfect if you wanted to go home with two girls.

"Lucky. My roommate has a new girlfriend. She's sort of...I don't know what the word is, abrasive?"

"Abrasive? That's a strong word," Theo said.

"She makes me uncomfortable."

"What does abrasive girlfriend do?"

"I can't relax when she's around. Like, I get up Saturday morning and I'm minding my own business. I have a cup of coffee and I'm reading a book in bed. She knocks on the door and asks if I left a glass in the sink. That kind of thing."

"Wow. Abrasive isn't a strong enough word," Theo said. "You tell her off?"

"I rode my bike to the library."

"That's one way to deal with it," Theo said.

The conversation quieted again. She should have let Rayanne give her more conversation starters.

"You never told me what class you're taking," Theo asked.

"I'm not. I goof around with social media for work," Ester said. "The UIC is in the middle of a situation and I've been collecting footage of things we've done. I put short clips online."

"Like a documentary?"

"That sounds much more professional than what I'm doing," Ester said. She was embarrassed to talk about it with him.

"Is that what you do? Make movies about the center?"

"I wish. That would be fun. Right now the center is a barebones operations so I do anything related to computers, data, spreadsheets and assist with whatever anyone needs. The films are for social media."

They reached the front of the line and the student asked for payment. Ester had her card out but Theo pushed it away.

"I invited you, Shoshone," he said.

"I don't mind. We're supporting Native students. It's practically my job." She'd begun talking faster.

"You fighting me on this?" he asked with a half-smile.

Ester shook her head, fretting that she'd offended him. All the progress she'd made on being not-awkward erased again. Her face was hot as she took her plate and picked up a can of soda. The long-house had set up rows of cafeteria-style tables. Theo pointed to an open spot and Ester sat down onto the bench first. Theo squeezed in next to her, his warm thigh pressed tight against hers. All thought disappeared except the awareness of that spot, with Theo's hip against hers, his elbow brushing at her side. A jolt of heat turned her insides to liquid. The distracting sensations destroyed her ability to eat.

"This okay?" Theo said. He could have been asking about anything, and here she was looking into his eyes, desire interfering with her ability to think straight.

She nodded, her attention divided between worrying about her poor communication skills and trying to get the food down now that her appetite disappeared. She sipped her soda, then asked, "What classes do you have?"

"Two with Professor Stone. Visual communications and an online journalism class, too."

"You want to do journalism?"

"I'm not sure what I want to do," Theo said. "Financial aid wants you to pick something, so that's what I picked. I like writing."

Ester tried to align the image of Theo writing with the tall slab of muscle sitting next to her.

"I also took cultural anthropology. If you want to read ten thousand pages a week, that's the class for you."

Ester smiled. "I've taken classes like that. If you get behind, you're toast." She relaxed enough to take a bite of food.

"As I am learning," Theo said. "I'm way behind in Professor Stone's classes, so we talked about me helping her with a film she's making."

"She's making something?" Ester asked.

"She makes documentaries. I wanted to ask you about that. I might have told a fib."

Ester raised an eyebrow. "A fib?"

"Professor Stone wants to talk to some Ind'ns. She asked me since, obviously, I'm acquainted with all Indians."

Ester smiled. "We joke about that, but truth is, once you get to know the Indians in town, the circle is pretty small."

"Do you think someone at your urban Indian center could talk to her?"

"Talk about the center in a movie? That would be great," Ester said, calculating how she might get involved. "A real filmmaker making a real movie would be great for us."

"I could use the points, too," Theo said.

"If you get the center involved, they're going to get you involved with the center. It's like its own Ind'n tractor beam, reeling in our people to support the cause."

Theo laughed. "I'm not getting involved in anything. I'm helping out the professor in order to stay on her good side."

His casual tone made Ester's heart sink. This lunch wasn't personal interest, it was about finding someone for his instructor's project. She looked down at her half-eaten food.

"How's your nontraditional lunch?" Theo asked, nodding at her plate.

She shook her head and slid it toward him. He surprised her by grabbing the plate and finishing it.

Off her surprised look, he said, "Did you want it?"

"I was done," she confirmed.

"I'm always hungry," he said.

They got up and threw away their paper plates. Theo got out his phone and waved it at her. "Trade numbers? You can let me know when you talk to someone."

8

_L_inda grabbed a copy of the meeting agenda from Rayanne.

"What's the occasion, boss?" Rayanne asked.

Linda had on the new blue dress and her prized, least-pilled sweater. "You told me I was frumpy."

"I think my words were, 'You could use more style.' You look terrific," Rayanne said. She passed the agenda around the room. They'd spent the morning moving computers and pulling desks around until they formed a square. The board had arrived, and they waited for Arnie.

Ester and Tommy came through the door loaded with carryout trays of coffee and a paper bag with what Linda hoped were the chocolate chocolate chip cookies she loved. They passed out the takeout cups to the board members.

"Our coffee pot now fails to do the only thing it's good for," Ester explained. "We didn't want you to endure a meeting without this magical elixir so this is from the campus coffee outpost. I think they brew up a vat in the morning, burn it, and then let it simmer all day. These cookies are other-worldly, though." Ester passed around napkins and cookies. She winked and left the bag with Linda. Two cookies were left inside.

Ester sat next to Audra.

"Can I get in trouble for using the computer lab?" Ester said to Audra.

"Did someone say something to you?" Linda asked, taking one cookie and hiding the other one for later.

"No, just wondering what would happen," Ester said.

"Technically, you're not supposed to use it," Audra said, "but you're not doing anything illegal, right?"

Ester lifted an eyebrow as if to say, *you never know.*

"You're working on material for the center. The center is affiliated with the college at the moment," Audra said.

"You're a lawyer, do you know for certain?" Ester asked.

"If you're uncomfortable, don't do it," Linda said. "It's the same old social media projects. You can do it on our machines."

Ester shrugged. "I like the school's equipment and I'm learning more tricks."

"Then stick with it. We'll visit you in jail if you get busted," Linda said. Rayanne was the one who could talk her way out of anything. Ester did better with non-speaking roles but she was sharp and a fast learner. Linda could use another Ester.

When they sat side by side, it was hard not to notice Ester and Audra shared non-traditional wavy hair. Linda said, "You two have the same wild hair. When I was a kid, my aunt practiced giving perms on all the kids. It was like you got your hair cut in the dark and then went to sleep with it wet."

Ester smoothed her unruly locks. "Don't mock the hair the ancestors gave me."

"You're adorable, Ester. Excuse my poorly worded affection," Linda added.

Audra ran her fingers through her puffy tangle and compared it to Ester's hair. "Maybe we have the same grandfather?"

"Origin stories are complex," Ester agreed.

Arnie burst through the door. "Sorry I'm late. I've been circling the parking lots trying to find a spot. I ended up on the other side of campus."

"A legitimate drawback of this location," Linda said. "We're not complaining, Audra, we appreciate you getting us in here."

"I'm more upset about the bad perm remark than your disparaging the college's parking."

Ester handed Arnie the last coffee. Linda realized the extra cookie was for him. She was tempted to keep it for herself but with the news she had to share, shoring him up with a treat might help. She put the cookie in a napkin and handed it to him.

He gave her a grateful smile, the same beaming Arnie smile that dropped panties all over campus back when they were in college together. Probably still did. She gave him a chance to get settled before addressing the room. The usual subjects were assembled with the executive board, the people who trusted her to produce something out of nothing.

"Bad news first," she said. "We didn't get the big grant we went for."

Arnie covered his face with his hands. She should have told him ahead of time but he was late to the meeting and she'd put off making the call because she couldn't bear to hear the doubt in his voice.

Pauline was a gray-haired Tlingit and one of the calmer board members. She threw up her hands. "You were certain about this one. You begged us for one more year. And here we are, *again*."

That stung. If Pauline was this wound up, what were the rest of them thinking?

Linda took a deep breath. "It's only been a couple months since you gave us an extension. It's one grant. We have other options."

"That's all you've produced is other options," Pauline said. "When are you going to give us something? This isn't an urban Indian center. This is the idea of an urban Indian center. You need to secure local support." She tapped a finger on the table to emphasize each word. "Your little festival was a good start but you need local partners so you can build something."

They couldn't make big plans without a suitable location. The board had agreed to prop up their funding to keep the UIC going for one more year. In return she had to deliver two things: additional funding that would let her deliver the services she wanted to deliver, and a stable home for the center. Linda kept her mouth shut.

Arnie made a general calming motion. "Funding is always an issue. Linda's right, this is one grant. You've got others?"

Linda nodded at Ester.

"I've been researching like a maniac," she told them. "I'm checking private sources, too. I realize those require a different approach but why not try everything?"

"Let me see before you try anything crazy," Arnie said.

And there he went, wanting to oversee before they did anything. Discussion about the budget gave way to the Native American Tribal Government meeting.

"That's a good place to chase down tribal leaders," Pauline said. "Some of them gaming tribes set aside money for this kind of thing."

"We're working on building relationships," Linda said. Approaching tribal leaders at a multi-day government issues conference wouldn't be her top idea but she could figure out an approach.

"Let's talk about specific things you can do," Arnie said.

Or, let Arnie dictate her approach.

He looked around the room expectantly, as if he were the only one trying and forcefully dragging the rest of them along after him.

"What is more specific than talking to people?" Linda asked.

Arnie waved the comment off.

Fine. She could act more serious. "Is there an open announcement period? Can we advertise our social media in the conference bulletin?"

"How about a brochure in their welcome packets?" Rayanne said.

"Stickers," Tommy said. "Kids love stickers."

"Could we set up a monitor somewhere? We could do a repeating slide show with information," Ester said.

Arnie nodded. "I like that one. Sounds like you're on the right track. Keep working on it."

Linda scrawled *argh!* across her agenda. "Thanks. Next agenda item is the building. If you remember, a friend of Margie's who worked for the city brought the Chief Building to our attention. When the deal fell through, we tried to contact him for help but he had retired and spent time out of the country. He's back and he should be here any minute." She glanced at the clock. "Meanwhile, any thoughts about how to proceed with the city? What should we do to get the city talking to us again? I'm feeling like I'm ready to get extreme. I think it's time to talk about a lawsuit."

"No one is suing anyone," Arnie said.

"Then...what, picket city hall? Is there a civil rights or outside group we can file a complaint with? We can get involved in local elections."

"I appreciate where you're coming from," Arnie said, "but I think it's too early for extreme measures."

"They've been jerking us around for months," Rayanne said. "Last fall they said they'd schedule a meeting, which was pushed back until it was the holidays. Then they pretended to want to see us, urgently, right before Christmas like their heads are in it at that time of year. They met with us and said there was nothing they could do until after the holidays. Now it's January and everyone is too busy again."

Linda's phone chimed. A text from Paul Douglas.

Can't find you.

"Paul is on campus but he's lost. I'll get him."

ARNIE COULD HARDLY TEAR his eyes away from Linda. She wore a snug fitting dress in a dazzling color blue. She pulled on her coat and ran out the door. Rayanne caught him staring and smiled in an unsettling way. Arnie turned away.

"Ester," he said, "weren't you making a movie about the center?"

"I make short little clips for social media," Ester said.

"You'll have to show me one sometime," Arnie said.

"They're online," Ester said. "You can look at one anytime you want."

Arnie still hadn't figured out his relationship to Linda's staff. Sometimes he got the impression they were being hostile but they were also protective of her. Her group had stuck together through a lot of uncertainty, so it wasn't a surprise they weren't chummy with him. Everyone knew what was at stake here. The center needed to come up with something big soon or the board would shut them down.

Linda returned with Margie's friend, Paul Douglas. He was tan and fit with a pleasant face and the calm demeanor of a man who had spent an extended vacation in a sunny climate. Linda introduced him around.

"He's the former facilities manager for the city. He was the one who suggested the Chief building for us." The building was named the Chief after one of the city founders.

"Been looking forward to talking with you," Arnie said, getting up to shake his hand.

"I grew up around Tahlequah," Paul said. "Lots of friends in the Cherokee Nation. I know a little bit about Native Americans, which was why I wanted to help out your organization. The city wasn't utilizing that building productively and there was talk of handing it off."

Arnie waited for him to sit down. "You understand the delays?"

"I need an update," Paul said.

"The city gave us a checklist," Linda said. "We did all the inspections and walk-throughs. We had all the financing in place except one piece and that's when the deal fell apart."

"But they told you there was no problem," Paul said.

"Correct," Linda said. "But when we had our final piece in place, they told us there was a delay on their end. At first I assumed, we have delays, they have delays. I understand how governments work. You need to get a group of people on the same page. But then they delayed us again and then communication vanished. Then some of our staff went to the Chief Building and were told there was no deal."

Paul rubbed his chin. "Get a name?"

"Cranky old guy," Rayanne said. "Taller than you. He wore a suit."

"That narrows it down," Paul said with a smile. "I asked around when I first heard you were having a problem. No one could give me a specific answer, only vague theories. Said someone wanted to shoot it down."

Already Arnie didn't like where the conversation was headed. If no wanted to talk about it, the problem was bigger than he thought.

"It was suggested that this project would only benefit one group," Paul said.

"One group?" Arnie said. "You mean, Indians."

"I'm trying to read between the lines," Paul said, his face apologetic. "They weren't against Native Americans specifically."

Arnie fumed. Linda met his eye. *Don't make it personal.* As long as they'd known each other, whenever he got worked up she talked him down. But there was no question this was personal. He knew Linda was suppressing her own rage but she wouldn't show that face to Margie's friend.

Linda cleared her throat. "This is all rumor. You don't know who is behind it. What do you suggest? Can you connect us with a person who can be straight with us so we can work through what went wrong or is this completely hopeless?"

By all rational measures, it had been hopeless for months. They needed a new plan. Linda should have had a backup plan all along. He began a mental list for where to go from here. Linda was persistent for good reason, since the building was a perfect fit for the center. They could have classes, events, child care, elder meals. There was plenty of room for the organization to grow with Linda's plans. They'd worked so long on this deal, no one wanted to let it go.

Paul took his time considering what he'd heard. "I don't think it's hopeless at all. Yeah, it's a government but it would be unusual for them to cut you off with no formal communication. I will track down someone who can give a straight answer. Sorry this has caused you such struggles."

Arnie couldn't join the optimism. They needed more than another promise. The longer they waited, the more opportunities they would miss.

The other board members had questions for Paul before they

wrapped up the meeting. Paul proposed to get them a meeting and they would make their next move from there.

"How's Margie doing these days?" Paul asked. "I was sorry to hear she retired. She always told me she would stick around until they had to carry her out."

"That's not far from what happened," Linda said. "Pneumonia. Gave us a scare, but she's hanging in there. She's still in her house with in-home care. And she tells me what to do whenever she can."

"Glad to hear it."

Once Paul had gone, they wrapped up the meeting. Arnie caught up with some of the board members while Linda's staff shoved chairs and desks around to get their work stations set up again.

Arnie had a few last things to go over with Linda before he went to his sister's for dinner. He heard Rayanne ask, "When is your date?"

He turned to see who she was talking to. Ester was at her computer, typing as if chased by wild dogs. Tommy squatted on the floor, going through a box of books.

Rayanne sat at her desk with Linda at her side.

"After work," Linda said.

Without thinking, he said, "You have a date?"

"Don't sound so surprised," Linda said, laughing the question off. "I know, what am I doing trying to date, on top of everything else? Audra wanted me to meet someone. I said I would. I get tired of being alone sometimes. You know the feeling?"

Arnie didn't know what to say.

Linda laughed. "I'm kidding. Of course you don't know the feeling. The original Indian player."

"I don't know what you've heard," Arnie said, adjusting his tie. He went along with the joke, even if it weren't true. When he was younger, sure, but these days it was all work.

"It's barely a date," Linda said. "It's coffee."

"You like coffee," Arnie said, surprised at the uncomfortable twinge of something that felt suspiciously like jealousy. So Linda had a coffee date. That had nothing to do with him.

"You have something for me?" Linda asked.

"We can do it later. I'll send you an email."

"I've got time now," Linda said.

Arnie hesitated. "No, I got a few errands to do and then dinner at my sister's."

"Henry and I will be there too," Rayanne said.

"See you there," Arnie said, eager to get away.

9

*E*ster met Theo at the arts building. Today he wore jeans, a black hoodie and giant puffy bags under his eyes. He moved like a man who'd slept on a bag of rocks.

"Tough night?" she asked him.

"All nighter for a paper," Theo said.

"For Professor Stone?"

"Other class," Theo said.

"How do you think you did?"

"Good enough," he said.

Ester had been up late, too, researching Professor Stone. Several of her films were available online plus several syllabi and a talk she had done at a film festival. Ester fell in love with her work. She wanted to know how Professor Stone approached her interviews and figured out what images to use. Ester watched one film three times. She didn't know what to anticipate from this meeting but she imagined the instructor taking an interest in her and wanting to see her succeed. If she was lucky, she could sit in on a class or get advice. Rayanne's advice about three things echoed in the back of her mind.

"This is it," Theo said, opening the door for her. She caught a zing of his body heat as she moved past him, and her thoughts jumbled again.

"Professor Stone?" he called. "It's Theo Dunne."

"I'm here," she said. Theo urged Ester down a hallway until they reached a tiny office crammed with paper and books. The disorganized jumble was the same disaster Linda's desk would be if Rayanne didn't keep after her.

"You told us to stop by," Theo said. "This is Ester."

Ester expected a soft, friendly teacher. This woman did not give out a welcoming vibe. Professor Stone didn't smile when she looked up. "Nice to meet you, Ester." She dropped a handful of memory sticks into a small paper bag with a handle. The bag came from one of those upscale makeup stores. Ester had visited the one downtown to get makeup advice but couldn't afford to buy any of the fancy cosmetics they were selling.

"Nice to meet you." It came out in a whisper. Everything else she wanted to say vanished from her mind.

"This is insane. I find them everywhere," Professor Stone said. She shook the bag for emphasis. "I'm glad you're here. I need muscle."

Ester bent her arm and patted her bicep.

"I meant him, but even better, I have two helpers," Professor Stone said, less frosty now. Maybe she wasn't so scary.

The professor handed her a heavy messenger bag and a potted plant. She pointed to a shiny hard case and said to Theo, "Can you carry that?"

Theo lifted it and swung it back and forth. "I can carry another if you've got it."

Professor Stone used her foot to slide another case toward him. "Great. This equipment goes to the car."

Theo picked up the other case and winked at Ester, making her warm all over.

"Follow me," Professor Stone said. She picked up a box, and they headed out. They went back the way they came and into the winter air, the point of this meeting lost in this new task.

"At least it's not raining. On the news they said there's a big storm coming next week." Professor Stone pointed to the path to the campus adjacent parking. "Ester, are you part of the Native student group?"

"I'm not a student at the moment," Ester said.

"What's your background? Where's your family?"

"I was born on the east side and grew up here. My mom is a social worker. My dad works in HVAC."

"Which reservation?"

Ester flashed Theo a questioning look. She didn't understand the sheepish shrug he gave her.

"I'm not sure what you mean. My family lives here. My birth mother is Eastern Shoshone but I don't have a connection to the rez."

Professor Stone stopped next to a beat-up SUV parked in a faculty spot. She opened the back and checked her phone while they loaded the equipment. The back already had another box and something wrapped up in a padded blanket. Theo leaned forward to shift something aside and his top rode up and exposed a narrow band of brown skin above his waistband that she stared at as long as the view was available. Ester glanced at Professor Stone, but she remained glued to her phone. Theo took the messenger bag from her and stuck the plant where it would be secure.

"Why are you taking the plant?" Ester said.

Professor Stone put the phone away. "It's going home, I'm tidying up my office." The professor's office needed more than that to be considered tidy.

Professor Stone shut the SUV's back door. She crossed her arms and leaned against the truck, the humorless expression back on her face.

Ester took this as her opening. "We'd love to have you over to the center. There's not much to see now but if you knew about our history and purpose, I think you'd find there's a story there."

Professor Stone looked bewildered. "What center are you talking about?"

"The Crooked Rock Urban Indian Center," Ester said. "I thought you were making a documentary about Ind'ns."

"I've never heard of it. What does the urban Indian center do for the campus?" Professor Stone asked.

"Nothing. This is a temporary location. The center provides services to urban Ind'ns, like healthcare referrals, after-school programs for kids, cultural activities. One of our upcoming events is an elder lunch in the longhouse."

"Because they can't afford to feed themselves?" Professor Stone asked.

"Because it's part of our culture to take care of our elders," Ester said, not able to prevent a tart tone from creeping into her voice.

"Interesting. Let's head back up," Professor Stone said.

When they reached her office, Ester said, "My idea is a film that will tell our story. We have so many plans like an elder hot-meal program and outreach in the community. That's a major goal. We want Indians in town who might feel disconnected from home...we want them to have a place where they can be around other Ind'ns. Some of us need that."

"I'm not sure what's going on here," Professor Stone said, giving Theo an irritated glance. "My film is almost done. What I need is an interview. I want a Native American family with multi-generations living under one roof. Preferably a family living on a reservation."

Ester's mind raced through the Natives she knew for anyone who might fit this description. "What kind of film?"

"It focuses on the way different generations intersect and are viewed in terms of culture and socio-economic factors."

"Oh," Ester said, not sure she understood. "My family isn't connected to the rez and we don't have multi-generations living under one roof."

"How about at your center? Do you know anyone on the reservation?"

"I could ask Arnie. He's from Warm Springs," Ester said.

"Who's Arnie?"

"He's on the executive board. He lives on Warm Springs rez. They've got a huge family out there."

"He's Warm Springs tribe?"

"Wasco. I'll ask him for you." Ester wasn't sure how excited Arnie would be to have a filmmaker come out and interview his family.

"Terrific," Professor Stone said, her mood brighter. "How soon can you get in touch with him? Can I contact him directly?"

If Arnie agreed to the film, perhaps Ester could work with Professor Stone. But how to get Arnie to agree?

"Let Ester talk to him," Theo said. "Not everyone wants to be in a film. It's a cultural thing."

Ester laughed inside. At the center they used that expression when they had trouble explaining something to a non-Indian. *It's a cultural thing.*

"Of course," Professor Stone agreed. "Tell him I would love to talk to him and tell him more about the project. It would be short interviews with various family members. We can do it in one afternoon. It would really round out the diversity for my project."

"I'll tell him," Ester said, too shy now to talk about her personal filmmaking goals. She'd arrived thinking she was doing something for the center, but the momentum had shifted. There was still a chance she could get something out of it personally.

"So we're good?" Theo said to his instructor.

Professor Stone looked amused. "If we get something set up, you should plan to come out and help with the interviews. I'm a filmmaker but you have a cultural advantage."

"An afternoon at Warm Springs?" Theo repeated. A flash of emotion she couldn't identify crossed his face. "I've told you about my jobs."

"It's one day. You'll learn a lot," Professor Stone said.

"Can't wait," Theo said, sounding less than thrilled.

If Ester wanted to get involved, now was the time to ask. But she still had to talk to Arnie.

"Glad to meet you," she said.

Professor Stone handed Ester a card. "Here's my email. Contact me as soon as you can. I'm looking forward to it."

~

THEO HAD STARTED out with the mission of meeting Ester and connecting her to Professor Stone to win points for class. What began as a mild attraction was growing into something more. He'd enrolled in school with the single-minded mission of completing a two-year degree like he promised his mom and his grandma. He'd never had time for relationships so it never came up.

Now, every time he saw Ester, he wanted more, a more that he didn't have to give. This thing was bound to end in disappointment. Thrilling now and eventually breaking down and then disappointment. He couldn't bear to do that to her.

Theo put a hand on her elbow and guided her out of Professor Stone's office, calculating how much money he would lose by taking a day to go to Warm Springs for the extra credit he needed. One more stress on top of everything else.

"Can you convince Arnie to do it?" he asked.

Ester yanked her arm back and slipped ahead of him. She picked up her step so he had to hurry to keep after her. They exited the building, Ester keeping a brisk pace.

"Hang on a minute," he called to her.

Ester stopped and waited for him, irritation flashing in her eyes. She'd cooled during the visit with Professor Stone and was getting cooler now. "Was there something else you needed from me?"

Screw cold turkey. He needed more time with her, especially if she was unhappy about the meeting they'd just had.

"She's like that," he said. "I should have warned you."

Her face twisted into an irresistible look of confusion. Whatever was going on for her, she wasn't pleased with him, but all he could think about was kissing her.

"I thought she needed a subject, like an urban Indian center," Ester said. "I'm such an idiot."

"Not you. Me. I should have explained it better. This is her personal project she's finishing."

"I wish I'd understood that before," Ester said.

Theo needed to do homework, get out and make money, or take a nap. And there was a preference to those activities but only one where he might convince Ester to join him. Theo tried to smile. "I'm going to the computer lab to work on my short interview project. Come with me?"

"So you do need my help." The normal spark of humor in her eyes had disappeared.

Whatever feeble connection he thought he'd forged, he'd screwed it up. He could use the help but wanted her company. He didn't know how to respond.

"Why do you want me to talk Arnie into it?" she asked.

He wanted to put his hand on her again and take her someplace. A nice coffee shop with snacks so they could talk properly instead of standing between buildings with a steady stream of students coming and going around them. "Can we talk about this somewhere else?"

Ester shook her head.

He faltered for words. "I'm not sure what you're thinking. There isn't a dark plan behind this. I'm on academic probation. I didn't get enough credits last quarter. Professor Stone agreed to help me out but I'm falling behind this quarter, too."

"Aren't there student services or something to help you study or figure out your course load or whatever is going on?"

"My problem isn't studying," Theo said, the words coming out more hotly than he intended. "The problem is I'm juggling too many jobs. The solution is to work less."

"But you need the money," Ester said, her expression changing.

"Exactly," Theo said.

"You helping her with her personal thing will save your grade?"

"Extra credit for time put in. I'm trying to make a good impression," Theo said. "She asked me if I knew someone. I found you and you suggested Arnie."

"Do you learn a lot from watching her?"

"She's a good teacher."

Ester nodded, the thoughtful look back on her face.

Theo couldn't find the words he was searching for. The all-nighter had turned his brain into a hazy mush. He went for the dull truth. "If I can't finish the class, I lose my financial aid. If I lose that, I go home and learn cable installation. I want to finish. Could you ask him? I can go with you to talk to him."

Ester wrapped her arms around herself. "I'll ask him."

"Thanks," Theo said. A coil of Ester's hair had fallen over her face and he was so out of it he caught himself reaching to push it back and had to stop himself. Common sense was slipping away. "I'm off to the lab. See you later?"

She took her time responding, like the question was way more complex than it was. "I can go for a little while," she said. "I found an old drive with some footage I wanted to upload and play around with."

"For your non-project?"

"It's a real project. I have a bunch of footage from the center. Historical clips. I was hoping to learn something from Professor Stone."

"Sign up for her class," Theo said.

"No classes right now," Ester said. "No money. No time."

"You should ask her about going to Warm Springs." An afternoon working for Professor Stone wouldn't be bad if Ester were there.

"If Arnie wants to do it."

At the computer lab, they found side-by-side open computers and logged in. The guy who'd fired him was the lab assistant on duty. He offered Theo a nervous smile of recognition and looked relieved when someone came over to ask him a question.

Ester plugged in her drive and her earbuds and got to work. He couldn't follow what she did as she easily swapped between clips and views, eyes glued to the screen.

Theo dug his drive out of his backpack and plugged it in and brought up his project. He fiddled with it a while before reaching over to touch Ester's arm. She took out an earbud and gazed at him with those sweet dark eyes.

"Are you good at the editing software?" he asked.

Ester raised an eyebrow. "So that is what you brought me up here for," she said, her tone playful. This woman had no idea how sexy she was. Purely the inflection of her voice stirred him up with surprising potency.

Theo swallowed. "Perhaps."

Ester scooted closer to him, her arm alongside his. She smelled like cookies. He closed his eyes and briefly considered ditching caution and asking her if she wanted to take a nap with him. She nudged him and he returned his attention to the screen.

Fran's face was on the clip. She had invited him to a knitting club meeting and showed him some of her projects.

"What's this?" Ester asked.

"That's Fran. She's a bartender at Frenzy's." A glimmer of recognition crossed Ester's face. He continued, "She does this knitting thing with a group. It's called yarnbombing."

"I don't know what that means," Ester said.

Theo changed the view to a clip showing Fran seated on a park bench, the backrest covered with colorful yarn.

Ester studied the image. For a small person, she radiated a lot of heat, or maybe it was his imagination. He was having a tough time keeping it together.

"What is the point of the yarn art?" she asked.

Theo cleared his throat. "Fun. Build community. Street art. Modern urban cultural activity."

Ester sat back up. "That's a good idea for an interview."

"Tell Professor Stone," Theo said. "She never likes my ideas. She thinks I should be more interested in my 'heritage' and using my 'unique perspective.'"

"Does she ask the other students to choose a topic by their heritage?" Ester asked.

Theo laughed. "I hadn't thought of it that way."

"You guys need to keep it down or go out in the hall," the lab assistant said. He stood over their computer stations and did a poor job of conveying his authority.

Theo offered an insincere smile.

Ester turned her attention back to her monitor and worked quickly, switching between the different screens. Theo tried to follow what she was doing. He leaned over and whispered, "Can you give me a two-minute refresher?"

"We're not supposed to talk," she said through the side of her mouth.

"He told us to keep it down," Theo whispered back.

"Review your outline and your list of clips. Let me finish what I'm doing." Ester put the earbud back in and focused on her monitor.

Outline? List? Between his non-existent free time and Fran's reluctance, he had four clips. Fran wouldn't have done it at all except he had swayed her with his woeful *I'm on the verge of failing* story. Then he had to promise all kinds of cleaning and stocking favors at work.

Ester finished and turned off her monitor. She put her drive away and then scooted her chair next to Theo's.

He opened the web browser and pulled up the syllabus. The assignment was to ask three questions and edit together with different angles. Nothing fancy, just get a feel for talking to a subject and putting together something from the results.

She pointed to the screen. "You can see your clips here and you can drag them to where you want. Or you can insert things. That's what you have? Four? Put them in the order you want. For the different angles, I go by instinct. I don't know what Professor Stone taught you to do." She nudged the mouse at him.

"Me either," Theo said. "I've already learned more from you than I did from class." He enjoyed the pleased smile that crept into her face. He dragged the clips into the order he thought was best.

"I would be curious to see how she works in Warm Springs. Like, how she does the interviews and sets them up." She picked up her bag. "You can figure out how to finish. I gotta get back to the office before they send out a search party."

Theo put a hand on her arm. "You should go to Warm Springs."

She blushed. "I don't think Professor Stone wants someone like me tagging along. Besides, I don't have a car so I'd have to borrow one, and it's a big pain to be watching the clock the whole time."

"You could come with me," he said, momentarily forgetting that earlier he'd planned to unhitch from this steam engine. Once he started talking, he couldn't stop. "I'd take my own car rather than drive with her. It's no problem."

Ester stared at the floor. "We don't even know if Arnie will do it."

"If he does?"

"I'll ask him. I need to go."

Ester slid her arm out and squeezed his hand before she left.

---

10

*L*inda tried to ignore the florescent tube popping and flashing in the corner. The lights emitted a high-pitched whine she could ignore, but this was something louder and more distracting.

"Isn't that what happens right before the monster comes and tears everyone apart?" Ester asked.

"You guessed my concern," Linda said. "Getting torn apart. Who do we call? I'll jump out the window if I have to listen to that all day."

"We're on the first floor, jumping out the window won't save you," Rayanne said. "Can we assign that problem to Tommy?"

"Do we want to get it done sooner or later?" Linda asked.

"I'll figure it out," Ester said. She made a quick note and taped it to her monitor before joining them at Linda's computer.

Linda carved out time to do a massive status update. She'd been running around meeting with other tribal people in town, trying to gather support, and collect more contacts and make friends wherever she could. They were finding new supporters, not as fast as she'd like, but it was progress.

Ester handed over the list of grant opportunities they'd promised to do for Arnie. Linda marked off the ones that wouldn't work.

Knowing Arnie, he would direct them to target opportunities they were unlikely to get and then balk at their failure.

"Delete those before you hand off to Arnie," she told Ester.

"But Arnie said he wanted to see everything," Ester said, feigning shock.

"Then he can research himself," Linda said, the words coming out crankier than intended. "We have lots of ideas that are better suited to the way we work. The real work is finding something Arnie will go for." She tried to pinpoint the moment this job had turned into making Arnie happy.

"What happened with your coffee date with Nerdgil?" Rayanne asked.

"Virgil," Linda said, "and thanks for asking. I enjoyed it." She meant it. The conversation was easy, they had a lot in common. He had a charming smile and quick wit. He was the kind of quiet guy she would have overlooked in college but now realized was worth her attention. She liked him immediately but wasn't sure about a physical attraction. "We hit it off. He's Native and works with tribal organizations. He talked me into going to one of those Native professionals get-togethers they have downtown. We all should go."

"Are we professionals?" Ester asked.

Linda threw a paper clip at her. "As I was saying, he's a good guy. We'll get together again."

"I'm not hearing enthusiasm," Rayanne said.

"Like what?" Linda said. "Did I want to rip his clothes off as soon as our eyes met? No, but I'm not twenty-two anymore."

"Did you ever rip anyone's clothes off as soon as you met?"

Linda didn't answer. She wasn't about to explain her history of social weakness to her staff.

"But you wanted to with someone, I get it," Rayanne said. "How about you, Ester? You and the bronzed warrior seeing each other again?"

Ester blushed and studied her spreadsheets. She showed a page to Linda. "Do you want me to do anything with these sources?"

"Keep in a separate list," Linda said. "Who is the bronzed warrior?"

"Theo is the guy from the computer lab. I guess we'll see each other again."

"'I guess' is weak but we can work with that," Rayanne said. "What are you wearing next time you see him? Do you have any matching bra-and-panty sets?"

"We're not even close to the panty viewing stage. I'm not sure he's even thinking about my panties," Ester said. "Are they really supposed to match?"

Rayanne's eyes grew wide in mock disbelief. "Did you hear that, Linda? No matching bra-and-panty sets."

Linda offered an embarrassed smile. Ester wasn't the only one with a sorry underwear drawer.

"You neither?"

"We had coffee. Next we'll go to dinner. My underwear is my own business."

"See?" Ester said. "We ate frybread and hung out in the computer lab."

"You're missing the point," Rayanne said. "Matching bra-and-panty sets have power."

Linda and Ester cracked up. Ester stood up and shook her tail. "How much more power can this take?"

Rayanne laughed with them. "I'm taking you ladies underwear shopping. You need me."

"Do they have powerful panties at the bargain store?" Ester asked.

"I have tips for low cost options," Rayanne agreed.

The door opened and Arnie walked in. Linda blushed for no reason. Rayanne had better quit with the panty talk in front of him.

"Am I interrupting something?" he asked. He wore a dark gray suit she'd never seen before, and a tie with a subtle Native design.

"Not at all," Linda said. "Nice tie."

Arnie smoothed his hand over it. "Thanks. Gift from a friend."

Another girlfriend, no doubt. "You must be here for your coat," she said. He'd run off from their last meeting without it. With the winter weather, she'd expected him sooner. She'd resisted the urge to try it on but she couldn't help checking the pockets, obviously in case he'd left his phone. She learned Arnie carried breath mints in three different pockets. Who was all that minty good breath for? She was about to joke about it but she didn't want him to know she'd been nosy.

The jacket hung on the back of her chair. Before she could move, he came up behind her and his hands brushed her back when he slipped it off. The brief contact gave her a surprising shiver.

"Did you guys need to talk alone?" Rayanne asked with exaggerated innocence. That woman missed nothing.

"Nope," Arnie said. "I had a message from Ester so I made a point of getting here when she would be here. What's up?"

Arnie pulled up a chair and folded his coat over his lap.

"I met a documentary filmmaker," Ester said. "She wants to interview a family on a reservation."

"Does she want to do something about the center?" Arnie asked.

"It's her own project. I said I'd ask you."

"I don't understand. What kind of film is it, exactly?"

"You can find out about her online. I think she's good. If I could, I would take her class. She had an award in her office from the film center downtown. Her film has to do with culture and family generations. It's not about Ind'ns. I thought of you."

Arnie dipped his hand into the pockets until he found a tin of mints. Linda suppressed a smile when he popped it open. When he offered her one, she shook her head. He put the mint in his mouth and put the tin in his shirt pocket.

"Why don't we be strategic about this?" Arnie said.

"Meaning what?" Linda said, wary now. For every bad idea Arnie had, he had an equally good one. *Please let this be a good one.*

"We will find her an Ind'n family if she can help us with a movie about the center."

"If you want a movie, let Ester do it," Rayanne said. "She's great at that."

"No, I'm not," Ester said. "I'm learning."

A film about the center. The *something* he wanted them to do had turned into a film. He was going to make her figure out how to do this. "You think we need a movie?"

"It would be perfect for NATG."

Linda disagreed. She had a plan, to hand-deliver their message to carefully identified individuals. Creating entertainment wasn't what she had in mind. "What if she's not interested?"

"I can be very convincing." Arnie exaggerated a winning smile.

Linda ignored the warmth creeping into an unexpected place. He'd always had this power over her, to stir her up, especially in the most inappropriate moments. She made a point of avoiding Rayanne's eyes.

Arnie took out his phone. "What's the timeframe?"

"She's amped up, so…soon?" Ester said. She pushed a business card across the table.

Arnie picked it up and studied it. "We can do this. I'll talk to my brother Mike. I can bring Grandma over to his place and they've got kids. They don't live under one roof but close enough."

"Do you think I could help?" Ester asked.

"If you want to," Arnie said.

Linda didn't want Ester to encourage him but her staff took on so much grunt work without complaint. Ester deserved an opportunity to do something she liked. Ester graced them with a pleased smile.

Arnie stood up and pulled on his coat. "Any word from Paul Douglas?"

"He's not getting far either," Linda said. "I was giving it a week before following up with him."

"Good idea. One more thing," Arnie said. "I realize things are already cramped in here but I'm on the planning committee for the National Association of Tribal Governments so I'm going to be around a lot until then. I'm bringing in a bunch of cousins and kids from the rez to be interns and get them some experience around tribal leaders. Could you set me up with keys and a work station here?"

"You're the boss. Who is going to coordinate your interns? Henry?" Linda wasn't sure if she was happy or annoyed about having him around more often.

Arnie laughed. "He's one candidate. Thanks, Lulu. See you, ladies."

"Lulu?" Rayanne and Ester said after he'd left.

"Old nickname. Don't start or I will give him your work stations and make you work on the floor."

"What's your favorite tree?" Ester asked.

"I don't know. Giant redwood."

"Your porn star name is Lulu Giant Redwood."

"Thanks, I needed a porn star name. Something to go with my matching bra and panties."

"Now you're getting it," Rayanne said.

---

11

*E*ster kept everything except kitchen items in her room. That included her hair dryer, her spare linens, and her laundry soap. She even brought her winter coat and boots into her room. If they were wet, she'd let them drip onto a piece of newspaper. It was just easier if her things weren't mixed up around the house.

The problem was, between all the different stacks of storage containers, she couldn't always find the item she was looking for. Her brand new winter hat, a great find in the post-Christmas sales, was missing. The wool watch cap, described on the label as Old Rust, still had the tags on it. She'd gotten it specifically so she wouldn't have to wear her ratty old hat in front of Theo.

Arnie had talked to Professor Stone, and they were on their way to spend the day at Warm Springs Reservation.

She pulled out her under-bed boxes and checked those again, and then she rechecked the floor of her closet.

Dennis called from the front room, "Ester, your friend's here."

"Be right there," she said.

She opened the bottom dresser drawer and tossed through all the folded T-shirts and sweatpants before checking around her backpack again. The wisdom of searching the same places over and over again for something that clearly wasn't there wasn't lost on her but she was certain she'd brought it home.

She went out to the living room. Theo leaned against the door. He had on jeans and a fleece pullover that looked new. He didn't say anything, just lifted an eyebrow in a way that made her heart quiver.

Dennis and MacKenzie sat side by side on the couch in front of the TV.

"Have you guys seen a brownish-red winter hat?" Ester asked. "I bought it a couple days ago and now I can't find it."

"Haven't seen it," Dennis said. "Was it in your room?"

"I thought so," Ester said.

Dennis nudged MacKenzie. "Did you see it?"

MacKenzie shook her head, her eyes glued to the television.

"I still have my old one," Ester said, preemptively embarrassed by its shabby state. She slung her backpack over her shoulder and headed for the door.

MacKenzie came to life at the motion. "Are you guys planning to spend a lot of time here?"

"We're not spending any time here," Ester said. "We're going to Warm Springs Reservation. We'll be gone all day."

"Is that where you're from?" MacKenzie said, shifting her gaze between Ester and Theo.

"No," Ester said. "We're from here."

"Have you seen the weather?" Dennis asked. "There might be a storm or something."

"I haven't paid any attention." Ester looked at Theo.

Dennis switched the channels until he found the weather.

MacKenzie reached for the remote. "I was watching that."

"For a second, so they can see," Dennis said, holding it out of her reach.

"We'll be okay," Theo said.

"I'd check to be certain," Dennis said.

"They said they were going," MacKenzie said. "Do you guys know what time you'll be back?"

Ester gave her a cold stare. "No, we don't."

75

Dennis burst out laughing. "Come on, Mac. Who died and made you the house mother?"

MacKenzie shrugged and snuggled against Dennis. He put his arm around her. "Safe travels guys," he said.

Ester yanked the door open and let Theo go before stomping out after him.

"She does have a whiff of crazy about her," Theo said.

"You hang out around a lot of crazy women?" Ester asked without humor.

"I'm a bouncer at a dance club," Theo said.

"Yeah, I bet you've seen crazy," Ester said. Leaving MacKenzie improved her mood. "What do you think about the weather?"

"Professor Stone is on her way. She wanted to get some B-roll. I have to show up. Would you rather stay?"

"With them? No way." Ester stopped and gaped at the car in the driveway. "You drive a silver Jetta? Isn't that a shiny sorority-girl car?"

"Silver is the color of my people," Theo said, his hand on his heart, as if offended.

"Too bad you don't have turquoise interior," Ester said. She got in the passenger seat and marveled at the perfectly clean interior, an artificial pine scent in the air. "I predicted you would have a truck with a dented bumper and beef jerky wrappers on the floor."

Theo climbed into the driver's seat and started the car. "I used to. It was old, beat-up and paid for and I loved it. Unfortunately, it wasn't great for ridesharing, which I need to help with my income. I made a critical error and bought this thing so now it takes two weekends of ridesharing per month to make the car payment."

"It's nice," Ester said. "Clean. I can give you money for gas today."

"Professor Stone gave me money for gas," Theo said. "I negotiated that at least, but thanks for offering." He drove out to the highway that would take them east to Warm Springs. "What do you drive?"

"Ugh, I don't," Ester said. "I had an ancient Mazda that, gasping and wheezing, got me through college. At one point I lived in that stupid car. The kind of car that breaks down any time you need to go somewhere important, and you need to keep a jug of water, a jug of oil, and jumper cables in the trunk at all times. I put her down and use the bus. I want to get another car but I'm paying off my student loans first." Remembering that car brought up dozens of humiliating memories. When Theo didn't say anything, she asked, "Were you at the club last night?"

"I was. Tonight, too," Theo said. "Friday and Saturday nights until close. That's how I pay the rent. Didn't see you there."

"No," Ester said with a small smile. "Rayanne and I used to go dancing but now she's with Henry, so we don't go out anymore."

"Not the type to go by yourself?"

"To meat market central? No thanks. I stay home and hide in my room while Dennis and MacKenzie watch superhero movies."

"You don't like superhero movies?"

"I'm not invited," Ester said. "I mean, Dennis wouldn't care if I joined them, but being the third wheel isn't so fun. Plus dealing with MacKenzie's scrutiny."

"What do you think he sees in her?" Theo asked.

"Besides the giant boobs?"

Theo smiled a little but didn't comment.

"She's good to him. He doesn't have the best luck meeting women, so he's motivated for it to work. I think she's territorial and Dennis having roommates interferes with her desired possessory interests."

"There are more roommates?"

"Used to be. Lorenzo just moved."

"You lived with two guys?"

"You sound like my mom," Ester said. "We lived in the same house. It's a good location. I've known Dennis for years. He's a good friend. It's his girlfriend that's not great."

Theo had his phone in a cradle on the dashboard with a map of their progress. Traffic was light but Theo drove with purpose as if on a tight timeline. Probably used to it from ridesharing.

"How did you end up with so many loans?" he asked.

Ester sighed, going for the easiest version of the story. "I picked an expensive school because I had scholarships. But after two years the money was reduced, so I borrowed to get through. I'm voluntarily living like this to get the things paid off. Eighteen more months."

"Then what?"

"Then I have choices," Ester said. "I can get a car. I'm not super adventurous, but maybe travel or do a film workshop. I was going to ask Professor Stone for ideas on that."

"She has a lot of resources. I bet she could help you out."

Theo was quiet after that. She pulled out her phone and found a suggestive text from Rayanne that she hurried to clear from the screen.

The sun broke through the clouds but disappeared again. Ester calculated how much time they would be on the road. "We probably won't get home until after dark tonight," Ester said. "Will you have time to get to work?"

"Hope so. Turned down other work for this thing. I can't afford to miss my night job, too."

"How many jobs do you have?"

Theo smiled. "I sometimes do one of those muscle-for-hire apps. I help move things. There's also a mover in town who hires me. I like working for him because it's cash and easy."

"Do you like the bouncer job?"

"The money's not bad. My co-workers are great. The guests are crazy sometimes. You like your job?"

"Most of the time," Ester said. "It's a good group and I'm accomplishing something. But other times it's like pushing keys on the computer. It's hard to plan for programs when we don't know where we'll be next year."

She'd hoped it would come up naturally but she had to know. "How old are you?"

"Twenty-five, why?"

"You said I was older."

Theo grinned. "Three months. You worried you were robbing the cradle?"

Ester shook her head and smiled back.

Theo had a lunch cooler with a couple bottles of water. He asked her to get him one for him. She pulled one out and he twisted the top off and took a long swallow. Her eyes went from his lips to his throat, then to his forearm as he handed the bottle back to her, every movement a highlight.

Get a grip, Ester.

"Is there anything about being a bouncer that would surprise me?"

"There are a lot of things about the club that would surprise you," Theo said.

Ester pictured women lined up to throw themselves at him. The whole point of a club was hooking up, dancing, dressing up in pretty clothes and finding people to grind up against. The bouncer got to talk to everyone.

"Often the women are harder to deal with than the guys. You know, when things get out of hand."

"What do they do?"

"Guys will back down as soon as a bouncer shows up. Like he's a badass, but he's forced to back down because the bouncer is there. They stop to save face. Women..." He shook his head. "Sometimes they're going at it and they get serious when you try to break them up. And with a guy I'm not concerned about being rough, but with a lady, I don't want to manhandle them, no matter what they're doing."

"Do you meet a lot of women at the club?"

"I do," Theo said.

Ester's face grew hot. She didn't know why she'd asked.

"Sometimes they offer a favor to get in. What kind of person wants to get into Frenzy's that badly? Sometimes they're too socially inept to talk to club guests so they come talk to me."

Ester didn't know how to respond. A burst of rain spattered on the windshield. The heavy drops had some slush in them. "The weather is going to hell," she said.

"As long as it's not freezing rain or a blizzard, we'll be fine," Theo said.

"How did you do on your interview project with the knitting?"

"She hasn't reviewed it yet," Theo said. "I edited by instinct like you said. I think it's okay. It's her other class that's killing me. I'm behind on my daily writing assignments. That's why I need extra credit for this."

"How behind?"

"We're supposed to do five stories per week. About five hundred words, not polished. She wants us to practice writing as if on a deadline. I've been turning in two or three."

"That sounds hard. What kind of stories?"

"She wants clever topics. I want to interview Arnie. You, too, about being adopted away from your tribe. Do you mind talking about that?"

"Not at all. My birth mother was Eastern Shoshone but living in Oregon. My real mom is a social worker. She knew the adoption would have to go through ICWA—"

"ICWA?"

"Indian Child Welfare Act. It's a law where if a baby is eligible for tribal membership, then that tribe gets a say in the placement."

"I never heard of that," Theo said.

"A lot of times they'll try to place the baby with the family but Mom said it wasn't an issue. Since my parents are both Native and they wanted me, the adoption went through. I wasn't raised as a traditional Ind'n, but culturally I never felt left out like some adopted Ind'ns."

"What do you mean?"

"Have you ever met anyone adopted away from their tribe? A lot of times they feel...wrong. People describe it differently but it's like,"—Ester tapped her heart—"something is missing and they don't fit."

Theo didn't answer. He was silent for so long Ester thought the conversation was finished. She was wrestling over whether to come up with another thing from her list when Theo said, "But you don't feel that?"

"No. But I'm not a great example since my parents are Native and I've lived around cultural stuff. Have you been out to Warm Springs? We used to come out and stay at the resort. We would camp in a teepee and go hiking."

"I've driven through a few times," Theo said. The rain changed back into a light drizzle. The day was turning into a regular late winter gray Saturday.

"Will we make it by noon?" Ester asked.

Theo nodded. "For once I'm on time. Professor Stone won't recognize me."

AN ENTIRE MORNING sitting in the car with Ester was more intoxicating than Theo would have guessed. The space was too small when she was in there with him. She had a sweet floral scent and a funny way of waving her hands as she talked. After a long pause in the conversation, she would puff out a sigh before making a new comment to fill the silence.

"Reminds me of where I grew up," he said when he turned off the main road. "It's either mud or dust." A single lane dirt road headed up a gentle slope and curved past several houses. The first house had portions of plastic sheeting visible; one corner flapped in the wind.

"Must be tribal housing," Theo said. "You can tell because it's not finished."

Ester laughed. "I forget you grew up on your rez."

"Moved when I was little," Theo said.

"Do you visit?"

"Not often," Theo said, remembering his last visit. He'd driven down with his mom before moving to go to school. They'd arrived during late summer into days of blistering hot sunshine. The air smelled like warm grass and something else he couldn't name.

She pointed to the next house. Theo spotted Professor Stone's rig and pulled in next to it.

As soon as he stepped out of the car, a cold rush of air knocked the clarity back into him. If that woman had any notion of the kind of spell she put on him, he would be in serious trouble. An Indian man about a half head shorter than him answered the door.

"Hey, Ester, come on in. Everyone's here." He gave her a friendly squeeze on the shoulder. "Any trouble on the road?"

Ester shook her head. "Theo, this is my boss, Arnie Jackson."

"Boss sounds so serious and official," Arnie said.

"This is a coffee-swilling paper-pusher who holds the purse strings at the non-profit that employs me," Ester said. "Better?"

"I like to think somewhere in between," Arnie said. He shook Theo's hand. "Who are your people?"

"Jicarilla Apache on my mom's side."

"Thanks for bringing this together. Always glad to see new folks getting involved with the center."

Theo held up his hands and shook his head. "Don't give me credit. I'm along for the ride."

The house wasn't much from the outside, but the inside was cozy and pleasantly cluttered. There were at least a dozen people inside. An oversized couch and two recliners draped with Pendleton blankets took up most of the main room. Several boys were running around and chasing a pair of brown dogs. There was a wood stove in the corner and the room was toasty. A pair of windows looked out to a yard patched with dirty snow and some scrubby trees. There were snow-topped mountains in the distance. His heart creaked wistfully, looking out into the open space.

Theo had never been around so many Indians outside of his own family. The din was familiar in a comforting way. A man who looked like a less fit version of Arnie came over.

"The film crew at last," he said.

"You must be Uncle Mike," Ester said. "I'm Ester. I'm a friend of Henry's."

"So, you're Ester," Mike said with a wink. "The woman working the magic in the kitchen is my wife, Jody. Our kids are teenagers—I don't know where they are, and the short people belong to a cousin. Jody's got coffee and fresh huckleberry muffins, if you are in need."

"We need." Ester grabbed Theo's arm. "Henry made those muffins once. They are too delicious to refuse."

"I'd like something," he said. Every time she touched him, he fell in deeper.

"They're better when I make them," an older lady said. She had short dark hair and a serious face behind the smile. "I'm Diane, Arnie's mom. Nice to have you. You're the young filmmakers?"

"We're crew," Theo said.

"Your boyfriend is cute," Diane said to Ester.

Ester's face flushed in an appealing way. He didn't see any reason to clarify the situation.

Before they could grab a snack, Arnie called them. "Come meet Auntie. Katie is talking to her now."

Ester nudged him with her elbow. When he looked down, she had a smile curling at the corner of her mouth. *Katie?*

Theo covered his mouth and turned his laugh into a cough. Professor Stone crouched down next to an elder in an overstuffed chair. She had a sweet round face surrounded by a head of white hair. Her voice was surprisingly commanding coming from such a tiny lady.

"I want to meet the young filmmakers." Auntie reached out her puffy elder hands until Ester and Theo each grabbed one. Somewhere along the way they'd been designated as the filmmakers. Must be one of Stone's tactics to put her subjects at ease.

The elder pulled Ester down and inspected her hair curiously. "Where did those curls come from?" she asked.

"The ancestors?" Ester suggested.

Auntie laughed. She patted Theo's leg. "This one is tall."

Theo squatted down next to her chair. She checked him out with sharp eyes, peering over her funny eyeglasses with a wary gaze. "Who's your people?"

"Jicarilla Apache," he told her. "Lived there until I was eight. I didn't realize how much I miss it until I saw the view from your driveway."

She smiled. "I don't live here," she stage-whispered.

"If you two want a snack, grab it now," Professor Stone said. "I want to get outside for more B-roll out front here. We'll come back indoors for the interviews."

They were ushered back to the kitchen. Someone set down a plate of muffins and a couple mugs of coffee. Ester poured milk into her mug and offered to pour some for him. He shook his head. Theo hadn't realized how hungry he was until the food was in front of him. Ester probably was too. He hadn't even thought to bring food.

Ester closed her eyes and moaned when she bit into the muffin. Her eyes snapped open to see him watching her. When she finished chewing, she said, "Food of the gods. You'll see."

Theo could have moaned himself, watching her. He took a bite and nodded in agreement.

The boisterous activity in the room reminded him of being at his grandma's house with his brother. Two little boys and one black dog chasing in and out of the house all day. Another wave of homesickness snuck up on him.

He returned his attention to Ester. Her eyes traveled around the room, studying something he couldn't see. She caught him watching.

"I'm trying to guess what sort of angles and shots Professor Stone will want. I know what I would do."

"You should tell her," Theo said. "She'd probably like to hear your ideas."

"Ha!" Ester said. "She's in charge. Pay attention to the hierarchy."

Theo thought Ester was the one missing out on the hierarchy but he didn't argue.

He shoveled the last bite into his mouth while Professor Stone stood at the door and waved them over.

They put their coats back on. Ester yanked her flimsy hat over her head. Professor Stone pointed at the gear and they carried it out after her. Outside, they walked along the unpaved road they'd come in on.

"Let's walk up that rise and get the view," Professor Stone said.

A bone-chilling wind whipped up. Ester pulled her coat tighter and crossed her arms. Theo had fleece and a hat but he longed for some gloves. The clouds hung heavy overhead and there was a chilly dampness that promised snow. Arnie wore a heavy leather jacket and Stone had on a puffy winter coat. They walked ahead, most of their conversation muffled. Arnie named the mountains and said something about the reservation's history.

Ester tried to hide it, but Theo could see her shivering.

"You okay, Shoshone?" he asked.

Ester made a face he interpreted to mean, *don't baby me.* At least they both had decent boots. They stopped a couple of times to get a shot Stone wanted but showed no sign of returning to the house. Even Theo grew miserable. They reached the first house on the road, the one with the exposed plastic sheeting. The house lacked a front step, and an overturned milk crate sat in front of the door.

"Tribal housing," Arnie said, repeating their joke from earlier.

Professor Stone pointed the camera at the house. "Will it ever be finished?"

"It is finished," Arnie said in a tone to convey, *isn't it obvious?* Everyone except Professor Stone laughed.

Two little boys played out front, both wearing jeans and boots. They were chasing each other through the mud and jumping around on various detritus in the front yard. There were a couple of wood pallets, an ATV, and several tires. One of the boys made the mistake of jumping on a cardboard box, which promptly collapsed. The other boy ran into the house. Professor Stone caught it all on camera.

The boy on the ground stayed there, crying with his mouth wide open, the tears falling fast.

"Hey, Junior," Arnie called.

He cried louder.

"Should we do something?" Professor Stone asked.

"His grandma is inside," Arnie said. "She'll be out in a minute."

Arnie continued down the road. "If we go a little farther, there's a great view of the mountain all majestic with snow."

"This light is incredible," Professor Stone said. She got her last shot, and they finally headed back to the house to start the interviews.

Ester pulled her hat down, trying to keep her ears covered.

"You got one of them big Indian heads, too?" Theo asked.

"It's like the hat is trying to escape," Ester said.

"I had someone make this for me," Theo said. "I had her make it extra big."

Ester stumbled in the gravel and Theo grabbed her arm to make sure she didn't fall. He held on longer than he had to, and she smiled while she kept her eyes on the ground.

12

They kicked off their muddy shoes at the door. Arnie held the door open for Katie and couldn't help eyeing her butt as she went inside. He'd anticipated someone bookish and self-important with fixed ideas about the rez. From the moment she'd arrived, she'd charmed them all. She learned everyone's name, even the dogs', asked intelligent questions and listened carefully to each response with genuine interest. He'd been half-dreading this event and now he wanted it to continue.

After the brisk air outside, the heavy heat in Mike's front room was oppressive. he ignored Jody's frown when he cracked the front windows to let in fresh air.

Across the room, Katie directed Theo, pointing to where she wanted the camera. He admired her confident manner. This was what the UIC needed, someone with a fresh point of view, who could articulate their message to the community.

He'd worried Grandma would gripe about the camera and he'd had to coax her to agree to the interview. Earlier, when he picked her up, she told him she'd had enough of these people. In Grandma terms, *these people* referred to anyone who caused her grief. This included but was not limited to family, doctors, the neighbors, and the tribal council who she blamed for everything from the wait at the health clinic to the channel selection on her television. They were all fair game.

But Katie had her charmed from the minute they met, complimenting her great-grandchildren and raving about the beauty of the reservation. Grandma approved.

Katie sat off-camera while she asked questions. With her snug jeans and long-sleeved T-shirt, she could pass for one of her students.

Mom sidled over to where he stood. "Something going on?" She flicked her eyes at Katie.

"I'm not sure I'd tell you if there were," Arnie said. Mom's favorite pastime was commenting on his dating life. She used to tease him by referring to his girlfriends as Cindy Lou and Sandy Sue. She would recognize that Katie, with her soft curves and warm yet competent manner, was the kind of woman he would find attractive. He liked her leadership, too. Since she'd arrived, she'd been like a scout leader, upbeat and patient, always keeping things moving forward.

"You haven't had a friend in a long time," Mom said. She used the word *friend* like he was a kid. Arnie resisted the urge to point out she knew nothing about his friends.

"I want the center to succeed, Mom. This is what we need. Someone who can make something we can use." He lowered his voice. "It's frustrating to see them tossing around ideas without accomplishing anything."

"Not everyone solves problems the same way," Mom said.

"So, you're lecturing me personally and professionally?"

Mom laughed. "No lecture. She's nice. You work hard. You should have fun, too."

As if on cue, Katie glanced up at him, something extra behind that smile. Fun sounded nice, but only if he could avoid complications.

After Grandma's interview, Katie had Theo move the camera. She brought together Mom, Mike, and Jody on the couch.

Ester stayed glued to Katie's side, her eyes wide as she scribbled notes. If she wanted to do filmmaking, this was the way to learn. The little boys tumbled into the middle of the interview, oblivious to the camera. Katie convinced them to say a few words before they ran off again.

A short time later, she wrapped up the interview and directed Theo to pack up the gear. Katie waved him over.

"You get what you needed?" he asked.

"This was great." She nodded at the room. "It always like this?"

Arnie studied his brother's place, trying to see what she would see: never-ending commotion. A half-dozen rigs had been up and down the road that afternoon. A cousin came to take Grandma home, but she wanted to stay for dinner. The cousin left and returned with his family and a foil-wrapped baking dish. Jody's cousin had a place not far away, and she had come up to see what the film crew was all about. Grandma had been one of eight kids and then had five of her own. She had twelve grandkids and four great-grandkids. Mom had twenty-two first cousins. The family was close whether they lived on rez or not. Even the smallest family gathering would turn into a mob scene, with kids running around and someone navigating an elder to a comfortable spot.

"Seems normal when you're used to it," he said. "Too crazy for you?"

"Not at all. This couldn't have gone better. Thanks for having me." One of the kids ran over and hid behind her before squealing and dashing for the couch. She broke into a delighted smile. He was surprised by the tug of loneliness in his chest. Mom was right, he hadn't had a friend in a long time. This might be a place where he could land. The moment stretched out between them but he couldn't decide what to say.

"Looks like my team has wrapped up," she said. Ester and Theo carried Katie's equipment outside.

"That's funny, I was thinking it was my team," Arnie said. He laughed.

She laughed, too. "I want to hit the road before it gets dark, but can you tell me what Crooked Rock plans to do? I need a strategy for your film."

When he'd first talked to her, he was unsure about the film idea himself, but she asked the right questions and was anxious to hear his vision for what the center needed. She insisted she could help make something to help them.

"We're in a standoff with the city over a piece of property. No word from city officials and we want an answer before we make plans."

She took out her phone and tapped in a note. "You're in a tussle with the city? How did that come about?"

Arnie explained the plans to purchase the building, and how—at least for now—the deal was off.

"Great conflict," Katie said.

Theo and Ester returned from outside and joined them.

"Ester might have insights. We have a friend on the inside making inquiries for us. We've talked about everything from a protest to a lawsuit. Anything to get them to talk to us."

"A protest?" Ester said, the look in her eyes saying no.

"Yeah. You know, storm city hall with signs and chants."

"That would be great on film," Katie said. "How soon could you put something together?"

Ester gulped and stared at him. "Linda would hate that."

"We need to do something," he said, even though Ester was right. He and Linda had a history with protests. Not some of their best memories. "I'll call Linda on Monday and see about getting something going."

"Great," Katie said. To her helpers, she said, "Am I packed up?"

"Yes, ma'am," Theo said. He waved his notebook at Arnie. "If you don't mind, I'd like to talk to you for one of my writing assignments."

Arnie had made it through the day without getting interviewed for Katie's movie; he wanted to continue the trend. "What would that involve?"

"I want to write one of my daily topic pieces about tribal leadership, on versus off the reservation."

"That's a great idea," Katie said. "For both of you. Theo is a great writer."

Theo reacted with surprise. "Huh, how come you never tell me that?"

"I said you were a great writer. You're terrible at turning in assignments."

"She tells the truth," Theo said. "But I'm working on it."

Arnie tried to reconcile Theo, the smooth talker, with the reserved Ester whom Linda referred to as her favorite brain.

"Turns out that's my favorite subject," Arnie said. "If you're interested in tribal leadership, I have all kinds of information you could check out."

Theo held up his hands. "One thing at a time."

"I hear you," Arnie said. "But we need more leaders. I'm always recruiting."

Theo laughed. "I'm not your man."

Katie rubbed her hand on Arnie's back, a gesture that became more thrilling the longer her hand lingered. "I'm charging out of here while the sun still shines. You two shouldn't linger. Weather forecast predicts nasty weather ahead."

"Thanks, Prof," Theo said.

Arnie walked her to her car to say goodbye. "Feel free to call me if you need any follow-up. I want you to have all the information you need." It sounded a little more come-on-y than he'd intended.

"I will," she said.

ESTER STOOD at one of the front windows and watched Arnie walk out with Professor Stone.

"Those two are acting all chummy," she whispered to Theo.

"That's how she is," Theo said.

Activity at the house notched up again. As Professor Stone's car headed down the narrow dirt driveway, two more trucks turned up their way. The red of Professor Stone's brake lights flashed several times, but both drivers pulled into the mud until she passed by. Arnie waited outside for them to arrive. This time it was a couple Arnie's age with a toddler and a baby. The other truck contained two teenagers and an indeterminate number of dogs.

"I've never seen him like this," Ester said.

"Like what?" Theo said.

"All warm and fuzzy. It's weird."

Arnie picked up the toddler and swung him around. The kid squealed. The woman pulled a giant bowl covered with plastic wrap out of the back and Arnie urged them all toward the house.

When he was back inside, Arnie said, "You're not in a hurry, are you?" He handed the toddler to another relative. Ester had long lost track of how they were all related.

Arnie said, "Everyone will insist you stay for dinner. Theo can get the information for his school piece."

Ester waited for Theo. Even though it wasn't her job, she worried about him getting back on time, but the laughter and warm connection of kin was hard to resist.

"Nothing fancy," Jody called from the kitchen. "Elk burgers with the family's secret barbecue sauce. You've got to be hungry, and it's a long drive back."

Even Grandma weighed in, waggling her fingers at them. "You kids need to eat."

"I don't think we can say no to an elder," Theo said.

"Your mama taught you well," Arnie said.

"We'll stay, thank you," Ester said, pleased by the invitation. "Can I help?"

Grandma said, "Get the big one out chopping firewood."

Theo laughed. "I have plenty of experience. Show me where to go."

Ester thought it would be nice to watch Theo chop firewood. The work would heat him up so he'd be forced to strip to his T-shirt. His big arms would arc overhead, axe in hand, then swing through the air. Her imagination ditched the shirt entirely, and she pictured him shirtless, rolling giant circles of wood around the yard. A pleasant warmth came to her face.

"She's kidding," Uncle Mike said. "We've got plenty of firewood."

"Not plenty," Grandma said, but Uncle Mike guided her away and someone stuck a baby in her arms.

The sky had faded to dark blue. The far-off mountains disappeared in the darkness. Inside, the house was warm and bright. In short order, Jody and the cousins had the counter lined with food and a stack of plates ready to be filled. They fixed plates for the elders first and then the kids. Ester and Theo made their own plates and squeezed in with the adults at the big table.

Ester was afraid the meal might be awkward, but they eased in with the family, trading stories about hunting and talking about the center and Arnie's career. Theo quizzed Arnie about his work on Council compared to his trips to the city and time with the center. Ester was impressed with his thoughtful questions and follow-up responses. Arnie must have been, too, because he asked, "What are your plans when you're done? Where do you want to end up?"

Theo had cleaned his plate and Arnie's mom pointed at it, her face aghast, like he had violated a family rule.

"Mom wants you to get more," Arnie translated.

Theo laughed. "I got that. I have a mom, too. To answer your question, the plan is to get the AA degree. That's all I can deal with right now."

"Think about a four-year and keep in touch, I'm serious. We need our people working for our people. I can find scholarships or make introductions. If I can help, I will," Arnie said.

"Your energy is inspiring," Theo said, getting up for another serving. "I'll keep it in mind."

The talk turned to the filmmaking and interviews. Arnie asked, "What did you think, Ester?"

This wasn't the best time but she couldn't hide her concerns. "I'm learning a lot. Professor Stone is great at what she does. It helps me re-think how I approach my subjects. But I'm, uh...uneasy with a manufactured set piece like a protest. I don't think that sells what we're about."

Arnie didn't hesitate before he said, "I think an outsider perspective is what the center needs. She sees things we can't see ourselves." He wasn't seeking her input; he had already decided.

Ester returned to her meal. Theo was already halfway through his second helping. A starving student knew how to capitalize on a home-cooked meal. When they finished, they cleared their plates.

Theo and Arnie exchanged one of those guy combination handshake-shoulder hugs. "This reminds me of how I grew up," Theo said.

"You're always welcome," Arnie said. "I'm serious about helping. Don't disappear."

Arnie gave Ester a surprisingly familial hug, too, but she didn't mind. It was a good day.

The sky was dark when they pulled out. Ester was full of food and sank back in a contented swoon. The forecast said the storm wouldn't arrive until long after they were home. The drive was smooth. A light rain fell but there were few cars and the road stayed clear. Ester didn't mind the lack of conversation. Theo put the radio on a classic country-western station and the strumming guitars and crooning voices made a perfect soundtrack for the day. Ester wished it didn't have to end. She closed her eyes and dozed off.

She awoke when the car came to a stop. Her heart twisted at the thought of saying good bye, but when she opened her eyes, they were in the bright lights of a gas station.

"I need coffee," Theo said. "You want something?"

"No thanks. How far are we?"

"Over halfway. Sorry, I know we're close but I'm feeling sleepy, too. I have a long night."

Ester sat up and rubbed her eyes. "I should have stayed awake with you."

"You're fine. I'm going to get the tank topped off while we're here."

Ester waited in the car while Theo got out and talked to the attendant. She couldn't hear the conversation but their tones changed.

Theo opened the car door and got out his phone and headed into the mini-mart. She thought about following him but the car was warm and outside the wind gusted. A banner at the gas station had come loose and flapped back and forth.

Theo returned to the car. "There's a problem before we get back into town. There's ice on the road. A semi jackknifed, and the road is blocked. No info about how long it will take to clear."

"Is there a back road?"

"I asked. The guy said he wouldn't advise it. He said it's not a great road in ideal driving circumstances. He's lived here for years and he wouldn't do it at night in this weather if he didn't have to."

"What about Frenzy's?"

"I called. They can deal without me if I can't get there. I've worked there long enough, they know I'll show up if I can. I have many short-comings but flaking out about work is not one of them."

"What should we do?" Ester said. She tried to picture them showing up at Mike's again. They could sleep on the couch or even curl up on the floor. At least they'd be warm. A electric thrill shot through her at the thought of sleeping under the same roof as Theo.

"He said there's a little motel about fifteen minutes down the road. I was thinking we drive that far and see if we can get more news. The other option is going back to your friends. We could be back there in a little over an hour."

"I don't know them that well," Ester said, even though she'd been thinking the same thing.

"Yeah," Theo agreed. "Plus we could get back there and then find out people are getting through and have to come all the way back, or depending on how the storm goes we could get stuck there."

"Let's keep going," Ester said.

Theo got back on the highway. The rain had turned to snow, but nothing stuck. They headed for the motel. Ester tried not to think about what it meant if they had to stay there. Would they get separate rooms? They were both broke. She did a mental check of her finances. She had an emergency stash, it wasn't like she was on the verge of crisis but she hated to throw away money on a motel room. She stared into the dark highway in front of them and willed the road to be fine. Meanwhile, her heart beat a little faster, not certain whether it was about getting home or not getting home. By the time they found the motel, Ester's stomach was a hard knot.

"You okay with it, if we have to stay here?" Theo said. She waited for him to waggle an eyebrow or try to turn it into a joke but his face was completely serious.

"If we don't have a choice—" She shrugged as if were no big deal.

While Theo went inside, she checked the traffic using her phone. Like he said, the only thing she could find was that the road was closed ahead and with the storm coming people were being advised to stay home. She wasn't surprised when Theo came out with a room key.

Tension flared in her belly. This could be a moment although she already knew it wouldn't be. Launching into a physical fling wasn't in her nature. What would Rayanne say about this? She wouldn't tell her. She liked having secrets like that.

When he got in the car, she said, "Let me guess, only one room left."

"You got it," Theo said with a smile. "And only one bed."

Ester cleared her throat. "I can pay for half."

"Since I made zero money today, I'll let you, but give it to me later, I don't want the desk clerk to get any ideas."

Ester laughed.

Theo parked the car and they took their backpacks to the room. He opened the door and flicked on the light to reveal a typical road-side motel room. One bed covered with a dingy bedspread dotted with blue flowers and... That was all Ester noticed. The bed took up most of the room. Of course, that's what people did at motels. They slept. In a bed. There was no other reason to be there.

"Your fine accommodation awaits," he said, letting Ester go in first.

She dropped her backpack on the bed. The room was chilly. "It's not that bad," Ester said, rubbing her arms.

The first thing Theo did was open the controls of the heating unit.

"Fifty-five degrees," he muttered. He hit the buttons until the machine buzzed to life. The room had one chair that he moved in front of the heater. "For you."

"I'm not an invalid. I can handle a little cold," Ester said.

"Good," Theo said with humor. "You'll need to."

There was a framed picture above the bed and he went closer to study it. It was a stylized painting of a bright sandy beach lined with neon-colored buildings. A pair of pink-tinted rabbits were perched at the foamy edge of a bright blue ocean.

"How does something like this even exist, much less end up here?" he asked.

"Probably a giant motel stocking warehouse. Their slogan is, *If it isn't weird, we won't carry it.*"

Theo opened his backpack and got out his laptop. He sat on the bed. "There's nothing else to do. Do you mind if I work on my homework?"

There was something else to do, but Ester wasn't going to suggest it. "Why would I mind?"

"Last I checked I only needed nine more articles for Professor Stone to be caught up."

"That sounds like a lot," Ester said.

"It is." Theo flicked on the TV and flipped through the channels until he found the news. He handed the control to Ester and then went into the bathroom. She'd never seen him so fidgety, like he couldn't stop moving. She tried not to listen but in that tiny room all she could think about was Theo taking care of his personal business on the other side of one slim wall.

The toilet flushed. The water went on and off. Theo came out. "What's the news?"

Ester muted the TV. "Road still closed. Storm still coming. We made the best choice."

"At least the company's good," Theo said. He sat on the bed and picked up his laptop. "I'm writing the adoption one and then the Arnie one. He seems like a decent guy."

"He is. What did he say about leadership?"

"He says you need a plan. He's very ambitious. But I guess if you're a politician, you have to have a strategy." He winked at her before he bent over his computer and got to work. Ester liked how serious his face was when he typed.

She got her laptop and wrote notes from what she learned from Professor Stone. She outlined ideas she had about organizing the center's documentary and footage she thought she had versus what they needed. Professor Stone's syllabus had interview tips, so she brainstormed interview questions. After a couple of hours, the room warmed up and she could take off her coat.

Theo slapped his laptop closed. "Two articles written and several chapters read. That's enough. I'm going to grab something from the car."

While Theo was gone, Ester hurried to use to the bathroom. She was in for a long night if she was too embarrassed to use the bathroom with him in the room.

When she came out, Theo was spreading an extra blanket on the bed. "It's getting icy out there. I almost fell in the parking lot. I forgot Fran gave me some cookies for the trip. At least we won't starve." He set a plastic bag in the middle of the bed. "How about a movie?"

He sat down on the bed and flicked through the channels. Ester wasn't sure if she was supposed to sit next to him or not. She decided not. Instead, she pulled the chair around so she could see the TV better.

"The selection is awful," Theo said.

"Back Country Sleepy Inn doesn't have the latest and greatest movie channels. One star."

Theo laughed. "*Die Hard?*"

"I like that one," Ester said, as if she could pay attention to a movie while in the same room with Theo and a giant bed and a whole night ahead of them. The only thing she was aware of was Theo's warm body and the blood rushing in her ears. She couldn't wait for the movie to end so she would find out what would happen next.

At last the bad guys were defeated and John McClane and his wife went off together.

"You want to watch another one?" Theo asked.

Ester shrugged. "I'm kind of tired."

Theo turned off the TV and went into the bathroom again. She pulled off her shoes and sat on the other side of the bed and waited to see what he would do.

Theo came out of the bathroom and said, "I'm not sleeping on the floor."

Ester looked down at the floor, not clear what they were talking about.

"You're not sleeping on the floor either. Don't worry, I'm not putting the moves on you," he continued. The way he said it with such certainty, she was tempted to be insulted.

"You can get under the sheet, I'll stay on top of the sheet. We'll put a pillow between us. Two people can sleep in the same bed without meeting in the middle. You've shared a bed with someone you weren't doing it with, haven't you?"

"Lots of times," Ester said, even though technically she hadn't shared a bed with someone she *had* done it with. The few times that had happened it had been in the back of a car, or on a sofa in a basement, or once, in a tent.

She wondered how many girls he'd shared a bed with.

"You comfortable with this?"

"Yes," Ester said, the tone in her voice intended to convey, *I don't even know why you're making a big deal about it.*

Ester crawled in between the cold sheets, careful to stay on her side. Theo stayed on top of the sheet, like he said. She pulled the comforter and extra blanket up around her ears.

"Good night, Ester," Theo said. He shut off the light.

"Good night, Theo." She could hardly breathe as if it would bother him if she moved too much. At the same time, she was aware of every move he made, shifting to get comfortable on the bed.

"Do your feet go off the edge?" she asked.

Theo gave a low chuckle. "Not if I bend my knees."

She didn't think she could sleep but the events of the day and the accumulated tension from being around Theo for so long caught up to her.

She awoke with a start. The room was completely dark and cold. An anxious twinge shot through her until she remembered where she was. She put a hand to her face and touched her cold nose. The sound of dripping water came from the bathroom and someone moved across the room and then returned to the bed.

She inhaled sharply.

"Lost power," Theo said, his voice immediately soothing. "Ice must have taken down a power line. They may have a generator, we'll find out soon."

Ester didn't say anything. She was tired of being cold. Pushing aside any doubts, she scooted across the bed and curled up alongside him, the sheet still between them. "Is this okay?"

"Hang on a sec," Theo said. He got up, and the mattress lurched up and then he was back on the bed, bundling her up in the sheet. Then he pulled the blankets and comforter over them and pulled her against his chest.

"Too much?"

"No," Ester said, hesitant about how much to lean into him. With all the wrappings, there was less body heat than she needed, but she wasn't about to complain.

Theo adjusted the blankets again. "You think you can fall back to sleep?"

All Ester could think about was every place where her body touched Theo's. Not only was she no longer cold, she was no longer sure what was happening. It wasn't a feeling of lust as much as a feeling of being pulled into something terrifying and exhilarating and a little bit over her head. He was being a perfect gentleman but she thought about his hands wandering over her while he took his time unwrapping her from the sheets. The feelings of longing were over-whelming.

She swallowed. "My mind is full of thoughts."

"I know the feeling," Theo said. "Before, did you say you lived in your car?"

"You heard that?" Her secret had slipped out and she hoped he'd forgotten it.

"I did," he said.

She'd never told anyone about this. "While I was in college my dad got hurt on the job and he, uh, got addicted to pain pills. That was during the time when my scholarship changed and I didn't want to trouble them. Money became a problem and I had to live in my car."

"That's terrible, Ester," Theo said. The sincerity in his voice made her want to cry.

"It wasn't that bad," she lied. She'd been cold, scared for her safety, and humiliated. The amount of energy it took to keep anyone from finding out made it a miracle she passed her classes.

Theo gave her a comforting squeeze that involved his entire body.

"The bummer is it made me paranoid about things not working out. I don't like to do things unless I'm certain, but then I overthink so I can't make a decision."

"What else?" Theo's warm breath brushed her ear and she shifted into whatever was the opposite of almost in tears.

"My housing. It's been weird for a while. Dennis and I have been friends forever. I thought about talking to him but he could tell me to move if I don't like it. So I tell myself it's not that bad, at least I can pay down my loans. But then I'm stressed because I can't relax at home, but then, it's more relaxing than sleeping in a car. I think about looking for a place but I don't have a car so I have fewer options. But then it's a big city, you never know what's out there if you don't look. But what if I end up with a roommate who's even worse? And so on like that."

Theo made an agreeing sound in his chest.

"Earlier you said you had a lot of shortcomings," Ester said.

"Did I say a lot?"

"You don't have to answer. You can pretend you're asleep."

Theo didn't say anything for a long time so she was surprised when he answered.

"How about one: I'm the opposite. I make decisions without thinking them through. Like coming to school without considering how I would pay the bills and be a successful student at the same time. Is that short enough for you?"

"I think it's a different version of the same problem," Ester said.

His body relaxed around hers.

"You falling asleep?" she whispered.

"Yeah, you're a comfortable place to be."

Ester wasn't sure how to answer. "Me too," she finally said.

Theo pulled her closer. "Thanks for keeping me warm, Shoshone."

14

_____

When Ester woke up, the power was back on and the heating unit wheezed from across the room. Theo was in the shower. So, basically completely naked on the other side of a wall she could kick her foot through. She had to pee. It might be fun to duck in and take care of it while he was in there.

No way would she do that. She hoped he wouldn't be long. It was always weird to sleep in your clothes. She put her sweater back on and considered herself dressed. She rubbed her growling stomach while she checked her phone. There was a text from Rayanne asking if they'd gotten back from Warm Springs okay. Ester ignored it and checked the road report. Still icy in spots but the road was clear and traffic was getting through again.

The bathroom door opened and Theo came out, completely dressed, along with a puff of steam.

"Isn't it weird to take a shower and put on your dirty clothes from yesterday?" Ester asked. His hair was wet, a look that she approved of.

He offered a sheepish smile. "Sometimes you need a shower. You taking one?"

She thought about her being the one completely naked with Theo in the next room. "I'll wait until I get home, but I need to get in there," she said, and pushed into the bathroom. She took care of her business and splashed water on her face. Her hair was a frizzy mess, so she wet her fingers and ran them through the curls until she looked respectable. She wished, desperately, for a toothbrush.

When she came out, Theo was gone. She checked out the window, worried for a half-second that he'd left without her.

Her phone beeped with a text. Probably Rayanne again. Instead it was Theo. *How do you take your coffee?*

Milk. Not the powder.

He returned with two cups of coffee, two tiny Red Delicious apples and two smashed pastries wrapped in cellophane wrappers.

"Oh, you shouldn't have," Ester said. She took a big sip of coffee and unwrapped the pastry.

"Free breakfast bar," Theo said. He handed her a flimsy napkin.

"Good thing we let them feed us before we left," Ester said. She took a bite of the pastry, which was so sweet it made her teeth hurt. "I was about to say I might feel human again but I don't think I'll feel human until I brush my teeth."

Theo took a sip of his coffee and nodded. "The guy in the office said the road is still icy. He thought we should wait an hour or two if we could."

"What about you and work?" Ester asked.

Theo shrugged. "It's so messed up at this point, I don't know what difference a couple more hours makes. You mind?"

"I have nowhere to be." Inside, she was thrilled to spend more time with Theo.

"Show me your film," Theo said.

"It's just for fun," she said, embarrassed to show him the collection of clips.

"I want to see."

Theo reclined on the bed with his computer in his lap, looking ridiculously sexy. If she sat on the bed next to him, she would melt into a puddle. She grabbed her computer and moved her chair to the bed and set up the movie so he could watch.

"It needs voice-over," she said.

Theo put his finger to his lips and turned the screen so he could see it better. He didn't say a word until it was finished.

"I thought you said you were messing around. That's incredible. Why don't you show it to your boss?"

She shook her head. "Your turn."

"I'm serious. Those images tell a great story. You should do something with that. Professor Stone has been encouraging us to apply to a workshop that her mentor runs. I'll get you the information."

Ester shrugged, pleased with the compliment. "I can't do a workshop. Now yours."

Theo explained the ideas he had to expand Fran's interview into a final project. She'd had a terrible home life and left when she was a teenager. This was a common element of her yarnbombing crew. Ester gave him some suggestions and he roughed out an outline.

By eleven a pale sun broke through the clouds and it was warm enough to get back on the road. There were a few spots of slow-going and there was more than one car stuck in a ditch. They made good progress and soon saw signs that they were close to the city. Then Theo would drive off and she'd be stuck at the house by herself with no firm plans to see him again.

Ester's stomach growled. The tiny pastry hadn't been enough to make a dent in her hunger. Theo pulled up to her house. Dennis's car was gone. No Dennis meant no MacKenzie.

Ester blurted out, "Do you want to come in for something to eat? I can't cook, but I can heat things up. We could have soup and toast." Ester couldn't read the look on his face and it wasn't a big deal but somehow she was pinning a lot on hearing him say yes.

"Dennis's car is gone," she added.

Theo laughed. "In that case, I can't refuse."

He followed her into the house. She went to her bedroom and threw her backpack on the bed. Theo stood behind her and pushed the door open a little wider. "This is where the magic happens?"

"That's one way of looking at it," Ester said. She imagined what he would think of her stacks of storage boxes filling every corner of the room. "I don't like my stuff scattered around the house so I keep everything in these boxes."

Theo didn't go in but he took a careful look around. "How long have you lived here?"

"Three years. Since I graduated," Ester said. She realized she was nervous, so she kept talking. "Dennis was a friend from school and this was a friend of his aunt's house. He could get a killer deal but he couldn't afford the mortgage on his own. It works out okay. He never told me to keep my belongings piled up in my room but as he's settled into the house, it made more sense. When the center had a bigger office, I kept things there, and when I had a car, I threw clothes and shoes in the trunk. Now I pile it in here. I don't mind. At least I know where everything is and it keeps me from buying too much. You know, voluntary simplicity." She walked over to her bathroom caddy. "I have to brush my teeth or I will die."

She backed out of her room and pointed to the living room. Theo went to look at the bookshelf while she went to the bathroom. "Those are Dennis's books," she said before she left the room.

"You don't have any books?" Theo asked when she came back.

"I limit myself to one box," Ester said. "Do you have a lot of books?"

"Similar situation," he said.

She took him to the kitchen. "It sounds weird but I have this great soup I eat a lot because it's cheap. Sorry I'm bragging about cheap soup for the food I've offered, but it's not terrible as far as cheap foods go. It's called Aunt Barbara's. Doesn't that sound friendly? Like something homemade. I add frozen vegetables to it. Am I talking a lot?"

He grinned at her. "I like it."

"But the soup on the label looks like dog nuggets floating in golden grease, so I guess it didn't sell well and they sent it to the closeout store." Ester flung open her cupboard and there was nothing there but two cans of refried beans and a box of pasta. She stared at the empty spot where she was positive four cans of soup had sat the other day. She could see missing one, but four cans?

"That's weird," she said.

"You don't have to feed me, Ester," Theo said.

"I know, I thought it would be nice to eat something before you had to work."

"Maybe your roommates ate it," Theo said.

"Dennis doesn't eat my food. If he did, he would leave a note." But now that he said it, she was uncertain. Hadn't this happened before, things weren't where she remembered she put them?

"Maybe whatshername took it," Theo said.

"Why would MacKenzie take my food?"

"Does she have a key to the house?" Theo asked.

"Dennis would have mentioned it," Ester said, uncertain again. He could have mentioned it when she wasn't paying attention. Come to think of it, MacKenzie had been in the house when he wasn't around.

"Why don't you let me buy you lunch?" Theo said. "We'll stop at the hardware store and get a lock. You can lock everything up in your room."

"I don't need a lock." She hated looking like a fool in front of Theo.

"You could ask her," Theo said.

"Ask MacKenzie if she's seen my stuff? I don't want to get into it with her. It's me, I'm sure. Sorry to woo you with food and then have nothing. I might have Saltines." This had turned into a humiliating mistake.

"Another time," Theo said.

"I'll walk out with you," Ester said.

Outside, Theo leaned against the driver's door. The sky was still gray, but the air was warm enough that the threat of ice was gone. "I offered you food and then failed," Ester said, anxious about him going. The last twenty-four hours had been amazing. He held her gaze like he was feeling the same way.

"I won't starve," Theo said. "I know you don't want to rock the boat around here but I think you should talk to your roommate. If he's the landlord, he should know something might be going on."

"Making an accusation won't help," she said. She moved closer to the car as if studying something on the hood.

"You could be diplomatic."

"I'll figure out how to deal with it," Ester said. They'd spent the night together. The adventure should end with a gesture. She might never have another chance to kiss someone so beautiful. Two steps and she could do it. She would count to five and if he wasn't in the car, she would do it. She stared at his lips.

"What are you doing for the rest of the day?" he asked.

Ester met his eyes and smiled. "Buy soup."

He still hadn't moved. She counted to five again while she moved a half-step closer. She hoped he might take the initiative but so far he was hanging back, looking carelessly sexy. But he wasn't hurrying to get back in the car either. If she was going to do it, she had to do it right now.

She chickened out. "I guess I'll see you later," she said.

"I guess so," Theo said, before he climbed into the car.

DRIVING AWAY from Ester was one of the hardest things Theo had ever done. The last twenty-four hours had been like finding a place he didn't know he was looking for. He wanted to pick her up and take her back to that quasi-dorm room she was stuck living in and spend the afternoon pleasing her from head to toe. He wondered how thick those walls were. Poor MacKenzie would have one more roommate issue to complain about.

The entire scenario was impossible. He wasn't in any place to have a girlfriend. He was losing ground taking care of himself and keeping up with school. There was no time for them to do things together. He couldn't afford to take her out even if he had the time. Plus she had her shit together; she wasn't going to stick around for someone like him.

He circled the streets around his apartment until he found a parking spot. He lived in an older building with tiny studios he could afford without having to deal with roommates. Whenever money got tight, he wondered if he should reconsider but seeing what Ester went through, he would continue to live solo.

He didn't mind the small space because he had no possessions to fill it with. He had a queen mattress on the floor with an overturned box next to it with a lamp. There was an old dresser he'd found on the curb with a "FREE" sign. It would be left in the same place when he moved. He found a used table online and he had a single folding chair. The walls were bare except for a tribal flag. He could pack everything he owned into his car and be out of here in a few hours. The bed was the only item he'd be sorry to leave. Everything else that couldn't fit could go out on the curb.

Ester's roommate situation might not have been ideal but even being at her place a short time created unexpected longing for a sense of home. He didn't plan to stay in town long so he saw no point in fixing his place up but he envied her having a place to be settled.

When he got inside, he turned up the heat and perused the pitiful contents of his own cupboards. He filled a pan with water to boil for oatmeal and then pulled out the slow cooker. There was a chunk of beef in the fridge that he cut into cubes. He added a chopped onion and the last of the baby carrots and poured stock over it. That and a bag of noodles would get him through most of the week.

He left a message for Jess but it was already so late he was unlikely to get a moving job. It never hurt to ask. Then he signed into the muscle-for-hire app and hoped for some luck there.

He spread his homework out on the table and set up his laptop. There was an email from Professor Stone thanking him for his help on her project. Nothing about how much the extra time bought him. She liked his two essay submissions, too. She suggested he rethink his ideas for a final project. The day on the rez should have given him fresh ideas.

Fresher than what? She liked to push her students but it was tough to imagine her being this hard on everyone's project.

Ester had given him good feedback on what he had. He wanted to build on Fran's story. As he worked, his mind drifted back to Ester. He couldn't get her out of his head. The way she moved, with her long legs and adorable tiny butt. The way she was so easy around Arnie's family, with her humor and bright eyes.

His phone rang and his hopes rose. He would make money today after all. Only, the display said it was his mom.

"What's going on?" he said.

"Checking in. Wasn't sure if you were working today." She sounded tired.

"Trying," he said. "I got caught in the icy weather so I'm behind on everything. Are you okay?"

"I'm fine. I wanted to see how you were doing," she said.

He wished he could be honest and unload. To let her know how he was so tired of struggling. Tired of being by himself. She would like Ester. He could hear her telling him not to screw it up, he wouldn't get many chances like that. Instead he said, "Swamped with school work. I went out to a local rez yesterday for a school project."

"How was it?"

"Different and the same. Made me miss you guys."

"Grandma asked about you. You should call her."

"I will." Theo blew out a short breath. If he failed school, he would be on his way home shortly. He didn't want to worry her but he didn't want it to surprise her either.

"You doing well in your classes?"

"I'm doing my best," Theo said. "Being a good student doesn't come naturally to me."

"True," she said. "You were always smart, but you never liked to follow directions."

"I haven't changed," Theo said.

"I'll let you get back to your studies. Call me soon."

He disconnected the call. The need not to disappoint her was feeling like desperation. Another unwelcome wave of homesickness tugged at his heart. He wished for some Ester-induced calm. That woman created a peace inside like nothing else. The part of him that endured the solitude didn't realize how thirsty it was until Ester came and filled it up.

He twisted the phone in his hands. He wanted to talk to her. To hear her voice. To make her laugh. No time. He'd get caught up first and then have time for Ester.

He ate his oatmeal with a handful of raisins and read a chunk for his class, working his way through the chapters, typing notes into a computer file.

The muscle-for-hire app sent him a notice for a clean-up and moving job. He gratefully pulled on a sweatshirt and went to the job. It turned out to be a man and woman cleaning out their recently deceased hoarder mother's home. The rest of the day was spent packing garbage into plastic bags and hauling it to a dumpster, then moving around furniture the siblings couldn't handle on their own. By the time he got home he had enough energy to shower, eat a bowl of stew, and fall into bed dreaming of Ester curled up next to him.

15

The minute Ester walked through the door she was hit with the smell of poster paint. Rayanne and Tommy had cleared a corner of the room and spread poster boards across the floor.

Ester groaned. "We're really doing a protest?"

"With signs and everything." Rayanne didn't look up, her face scrunched into a furious scowl. She thrust her brush into a tub of red paint and then dragged it across the board. Ester walked around to see what slogan she'd come up with.

"Raisins out?" Ester said.

"I hate raisins," Rayanne said. "Squishy gross bits ruining delicious cookies and muffins. More people should protest raisins."

Tommy had a streak of black paint down one forearm. His said, *Tired of Making Signs.* He looked like his normal self: shaggy hair, a pair of black athletic pants with a red stripe down each leg, bemused smile as if remembering something funny that happened earlier. She couldn't shake the image of him in the office late at night, by himself, staring at a computer screen, his chin bouncing off his chest while he struggled to stay awake. She wanted to bring it up, but every occasion felt intrusive. She'd spied on him without meaning to.

Ester got down on the floor to join them. "She couldn't talk him out of it?"

"She tried," Tommy said. He went back over the letters again. The paint built up thick and shiny on the sign.

Rayanne said, "The board asked us to do things to attract support for the center. Arnie has decided the center needs a film and that that filmmaker lady is the one to do it. You were out there with her doing her thing. What did you think of her?"

Ester's mind leapt back, the time spent with Professor Stone muddled by the memory of what happened later...Theo pressed against her and the rise and fall of his breath in the dark. Not snoring, exactly, but an audible hum when he exhaled. A warm flush crept into her face. She shuffled the blank poster boards in front of her. "She's a good filmmaker, but I don't think we should protest city hall for the purpose of film drama."

"He's the boss." Rayanne stood up and held up her sign and waited for a response.

"You honor the unheard voices of raisin-haters everywhere. What did Linda say?"

Rayanne flung the sign to the floor. "She clings to the hope she will convince him to drop it, but for now our job is to make signs and recruit suckers to go down there with us tomorrow."

Tomorrow.

As much as she dreaded the idea of marching on city hall and waving a stupid sign, if Professor Stone was involved, there was a good chance Theo would be there too. Something equally happy and sad stabbed at her heart. In the week since they'd gone to Warm Springs, he'd disappeared. She shouldn't have been disappointed since he was up front about having zero time, but he could text or stop by when he was on campus.

She'd wandered by the computer lab once a day, hoping to run into him. The radio silence hurt her heart every time she thought about it.

"Nice glum face. Once you get past the disbelief and dread, you'll settle into resignation like the rest of us." Rayanne tried to pull Tommy's sign away and waved a fresh poster board at him.

"Linda's going to get mad if there aren't serious signs," Ester said.

"Like what?" Tommy said. "'These are Ind'n lands'?"

"'Protect Sacred Lands'?" Rayanne said. "'Something something colonialism'?"

"Maybe the last one, if it were clever," Ester said.

"You see our problem." Rayanne handed over a wrinkled piece of paper. "Linda gave us a list. We haven't gotten around to it yet."

"I didn't know we had a list," Tommy said. He viewed his sign with renewed dismay.

"She knew without help we'd make a pile of signs that say things like: *Cake v. Pie, You Decide.*"

"That makes no sense," Ester said.

"None of this does," Rayanne said.

Linda's list had over thirty ideas on it. She'd once joked she majored in protests at college. If nothing else, she must have excelled at sign-making. Ester found a pencil and a ruler. After considering the list, she measured out the words: *Our voices deserve to be heard.*

"That's a good one," Tommy said. He'd taken Rayanne's offered blank board and kept it in front of him but didn't even pretend to work. When Ester finished penciling, she traded boards with him. He grabbed his paintbrush.

On the fresh board, she lettered: *City Hall ignores urban Natives.* They settled into a rhythm. Ester mapped out the lettering while Rayanne and Tommy filled in with paint. Tommy stuck with the black paint but Rayanne rotated through all the colors they had.

"What ever happened with your roommate's girlfriend?" Tommy asked.

"Situation continues. She's a mild annoyance. It could be worse."

"It could always be worse," Rayanne said. "Talk to Dennis."

"It's not that bad. I stay out of their way," Ester said. She stored her food in her room now, too. She got home from work, heated something in the kitchen, then hid in her room while watching TV on her tablet.

"It's his girlfriend, not him, though, right?" Tommy said.

"I guess. He doesn't have a clue she's a pain to be around," Ester said. "This weird thing happened last weekend where food was missing, but I could've misremembered what I bought."

"Sweetie, I'm worried about this," Rayanne said. "You're talking about your home."

"We don't know for sure. I don't want to accuse her. Theo thought I should put a lock on the door. That seems so confrontational."

Rayanne stuck her brush into the paint and sat up. *Oops.* Rayanne knew Theo had gone out to Warm Springs, but none of the rest of it.

Tommy, clueless as ever, said, "Locking up the room you pay rent for is not confrontational. In this case, confrontation is what the situation calls for."

"How did it come about that Theo weighed in on this problem?" Rayanne asked.

Ester's face grew hot. "Don't make a big deal about it." She had a hard time finding the right words. "We were out at the rez a whole day. It was a long ride in the car. It came up."

"You rode in the same car?" Rayanne said.

Tommy had a sense for the best time to duck out. "It's almost time for youth basketball so I'm gonna run. The four signs I made are drying."

Nothing could deflect Rayanne from this line of questioning. She smiled and waved him off.

Tommy said, "Ester, call me if you want. I can bring a lock by tonight after work and help you install it." He put on his coat and headed out the door.

Ester took her time rearranging his signs so they could dry properly. She pretended to wipe a smudge of paint from the corner of one board.

Rayanne hadn't moved.

"I can finish if you're done," Ester said.

"You've been mooning around here all week but I didn't connect it with your guy. What's going on?"

Ester was tempted to deny it but she was tired of holding it all in. "He's not my guy. He works a million jobs. He told me he didn't have much time but I thought I would at least hear something."

"Did you contact him?"

"I thought about it but I don't want to bug him."

"How did you leave it?"

"Vague. It's becoming a problem. I can't stop thinking about him. You know, like the sound of his voice and going over all our conversations. And…I don't know…his pants. The way they fit. The way he moves in them. The part at the top where the fabric ends and you can see his skin—"

Rayanne laughed. "I thought you said there was a problem."

It was a problem. Ester didn't have the same social ease Rayanne did. Even when uncertain, Rayanne could cover it up with a witty remark or a funny gesture. Ester forgot to smile. She forgot to talk. She couldn't use words to express what she intended.

"I'm not good at this. I thought he would find me."

"You might have to meet him in the middle."

"How do I know where the middle is when nothing is happening? What if I'm being the clueless girl with the crush on the guy who is too nice to say 'I'm not interested' to her face but is conveying that message by not calling?" Something in Ester's heart tightened saying those words out loud.

"That's a risk," Rayanne agreed. "But you're unhappy now. Wouldn't you feel better if you knew the truth?"

"I'd rather be unhappy with hope than unhappy without." Ester gathered the brushes together so she could take them to the restroom and rinse them out. She took her time closing up the paint containers and wiping paint drips from the sides.

"Whatever you do, don't invite him to the protest. That's going to be an exercise in humiliation."

Ester nodded, another worry added to the list.

16

_L_inda climbed off the bus to join the others. She'd recruited a handful of kids from the Native Student Association, and a few people from an inter-tribal counseling organization she'd been working to partner with. Audra convinced a few friends from a Native professionals group she wanted Linda to join. Everyone was instructed to bring friends. When they'd loaded the bus, they had a single unoccupied seat. A protest of sixteen. That was bound to make an impression.

Rayanne and Ester passed out signs and stacked the leftovers near the door in case others showed up later. Professor Stone had asked them to put out the call on social media. At least Linda succeeded in shooting that idea down. That's just what they needed, people who liked to protest for the sake of protesting to make the event more volatile.

"What a robust crowd we've assembled," Rayanne said.

"Don't start," Linda said.

Audra gestured for everyone to gather around. "A few tips for if you get arrested..."

An alarmed murmur went through the group.

"No one is getting arrested," Linda said.

"Better to have the info and not need it," Audra said.

Linda shook her head. "If it comes to that, exit in silence."

A woman with a camera waited at the corner outside city hall. "Is one of you Linda?" she asked. Linda offered the friendliest wave she could muster. The woman came over to shake her hand. "I'm Kathleen Stone. Arnie has told me so much about you."

Linda could only imagine what that meant. The woman had a friendly strident quality that must be useful in her field. She was also attractive, with a trim athletic figure that made Linda feel dowdy beside her. She spoke with confidence, which was what they needed for this project.

"The signs are great," she said. "No banners or flags? This is still good."

From the look on her face, she wasn't impressed. Linda didn't blame her after taking a closer look at their rag-tag group. Every one of them looked like they wished they were somewhere else.

She heard her name. Arnie ran across the street to join them, a huge grin on his face. "Like old times, eh?"

Linda couldn't help smiling back. "Let's hope this one goes smoothly."

"It's going to be fun. You got a name?"

"A name for what?"

"Who we're asking to see. I thought Paul Douglas gave you a name."

Linda bit back a sharp retort. He'd forced this crazy film idea on them and then left it to her to figure out how to make it work. "He gave me a few names."

"Say you're here for the mayor," Kathleen said. She touched Arnie's elbow. "Look at you all fine in a suit."

A look passed between them, not romantic but like people who shared a secret. A hot stab of irritation shot through her. She should have guessed. They were enduring this crazy circus of a plan so Arnie could impress a woman.

Arnie puffed up, the praise going straight to his head. "Gotta look professional to do the job."

"Can you join me?" Kathleen said, her head tilted to one side while she smiled at him. "You, too," she said, nodding at Linda.

Linda struggled to stay calm. She followed them as Kathleen worked her way through the group, transferring signs between protesters, and then arranging them the way she wanted them to walk to the building. Linda's staff slouched along with grim faces. She didn't encourage them to do different.

Kathleen moved Linda and Arnie to the back of the group. "I'm going to interview you two, and then we'll go in." She waved and an unsmiling Ester joined them, camera in hand.

"What happened to Theo?" Arnie asked.

"Good question," Kathleen said. "You don't mind if Ester helps?"

"Of course not," Arnie said.

Linda would have liked to hear what Ester wanted, but she had lifted the camera and waited while Kathleen smoothed Arnie's perfectly smooth collar. Kathleen moved back behind the camera.

"Can you tell us a little bit about what happened and why you're here today?"

Linda looked at Arnie.

"You first," he said.

"I'm the executive director of the Crooked Rock Urban Indian Center. Last year, after being approached by a city employee, we began negotiations to purchase a surplus building as a permanent home for our center." Even she could hear the lack of enthusiasm in her voice and she made an effort to brighten.

"What does the center do?"

"We serve the local urban Indian population. That can be anything from medical referrals to assistance with housing or transportation. We also host cultural events so Natives in the city have a place to go to connect with other tribal people. With a permanent home, we can expand the types of services we provide. For example, providing elder meals or conducting cultural classes."

"What happened?" Kathleen looked at Arnie.

Arnie stood taller and his bearing became more self-assured. "The center was invited to purchase the property. We went through an extensive process, getting inspections and environmental clearance. We had to seek funding. Purchasing a city building by raising private and public funds is no easy feat. We did everything we were supposed to do, but the city delayed and then cut off communication."

"We haven't been able to get any response from the city since then," Linda said. "We've asked for a letter or anything to explain what happened and we keep getting put off. Our meetings are canceled and our phone calls ignored."

"We're asking for basic respect," Arnie said.

"That's enough," Kathleen said.

She instructed them to walk to the building but take their time. Sometimes she hollered they should raise their signs. Other times she stopped them to change the camera angle. Ester followed her instructions, dashing around with the camera as if born for the job.

Arnie came up behind Linda and spoke in a low voice. "Remember the time we protested something at the dining hall? We joined another group, Future Leaders of Industry, or something like that. We camped out front. How long did we last?"

"Fourteen days. I didn't stay for the whole thing. I wasn't failing school for that."

Arnie laughed. "Remember the crazy guy who threw a textbook in the garbage can, poured vodka on it, and lit it on fire? The can was plastic and smelled so foul. I think that's when they made us leave."

Linda couldn't help laughing, too. "To this day, you can still find a greasy stain on the cement in front of the commons."

Kathleen waved to get their attention. "Don't joke around. You should look angry and defiant. Unconquerable."

"We should look how we look," Linda said.

"If you look at our history, we're not unconquerable," Arnie said. "This is us going to an extreme to get the city to pay attention to us." Here was the irreverent streak from the Arnie she remembered.

"Elaborate," Kathleen said. She had Ester bring the camera over and made a circling motion with her hand. Linda didn't understand what she was going for.

Arnie put his showman face back on. "We're willing to take risks if that's what's needed to earn the city's attention. We're serving citizens of this city, too, and we deserve the opportunity to be heard."

Kathleen gave him an enthusiastic nod. Linda wanted to knock their heads together.

At last they were at the building entrance. This wasn't their first trip to city hall. Back in the fall, Arnie dragged her over here hoping to shake loose official word on why the building purchase couldn't be finalized. That time, the only person who would talk to them was a poor assistant following orders from someone else. Linda couldn't imagine this going much better.

They walked up the stairs and crowded into the narrow, tiled hallway that led to a secured entrance. The security guards stopped talking and stared at them. Kathleen arranged them again before pointing at Ester. When the camera was on, she put her arm over her head and made a grinding motion with her arms. The corridor was quiet except for the sound of their footsteps and the echo of low voices.

"Does she want us to chant or something?" Linda whispered to Arnie.

"I'm not sure what she wants," Arnie whispered back.

After a while, Kathleen stopped waving. Linda heard a giggle behind her that she suspected came from Rayanne. She was afraid to look because she might laugh, too.

One of the security team picked up his radio. Two more security guards came around the security check and pointed at the camera.

"Ma'am, you need to put that away."

Ester put the camera down but Kathleen shook her head. "This is a public space. This is a public matter. Why don't you listen to what they have to say?" She motioned for Ester to continue. Ester gave Linda an uncertain look.

Linda nodded with confidence; then, feeling like Dorothy when she spoke to the wizard, she stepped forward. "We're from the Crooked Rock Urban Indian Center." The words came out garbled and she stopped to clear her throat. "We're hear to see the mayor to get an update on a business matter between the city and our organization."

The security captain nodded his head with weary patience. He spread his arms and indicated the group needed to step back. "Keep this area clear. This is for the public. They need to get through."

"You're the public, too," Kathleen said.

Arnie signaled they should move as instructed. They lined up against the wall, like poorly behaved school children.

The security captain headed back to his office or wherever he had come from.

"Will you let the mayor know we're here?" Linda called.

Without turning around, the man waved as if to say goodbye.

"Now what?" Linda said.

"We sit here," Arnie said. "Perhaps we should have strategized this better."

Linda refrained from wringing his neck.

Someone she guessed was from the Native Student Association came rushing through the door.

"Sorry I'm late," he said.

Ester broke into a radiant grin as she handed over the camera. This had to be Theo. Kathleen shooed Ester into the lineup with the rest of the protesters. Then she gave Theo what must have been an epic talking to. She was all impatient arm gestures and stony glare. Theo looked appropriately contrite.

While they stood there, a group came in, dressed in professional clothing. Linda couldn't tell if they had a meeting or worked in the building. They gave the protesters a curious look.

"What is it now?" one of them said, studying their signs.

"We're here about our building," Linda said. "We want to talk to the mayor, or anyone in facilities management." She didn't need Kathleen's approval for everything she said.

The person shrugged and then showed his badge to the security officer. The officer said something and they both laughed as the group went through.

"When does the part where people rush out to talk to us start?" Linda asked.

"Good question," Arnie said.

"We can't leave now or we'll look like we don't know what we're doing."

"That's accurate, though," Arnie said.

She couldn't decide whether she was furious or grateful that Arnie saw how ridiculous this was.

The afternoon wore on. Several of the protesters left to go back to work or school. Among those remaining, most sank down to sit on the floor, their backs resting against the wall, their eyes glued to their phones. The tile floor looked cold and Linda didn't want to seem settled so she remained on her feet. Stone kept busy setting up different angles. She interviewed everyone on the staff, asking them about other protests and why they thought tribal people faced bigger challenges than other marginalized groups.

Someone called from across the room. Everyone stood again. Linda craned her neck to see what was going on.

"Finally," Linda said. "They must be sending someone out. I thought this was a crazy idea, but whatever it takes." Several people gathered on the other side of the security point. They pointed at the group. A strange sense of relief flooded through her. All they needed was a straight answer, then they would know how to proceed.

The police came through the front door. At the sign of the first one, Kathleen grabbed Theo's shoulder and turned him to face the door. At first it looked like two officers. But more followed until there were ten officers lined up along the hallway.

"Wow, ten policemen," Rayanne said. "Must be a slow day for real crime."

Kathleen urged Theo to get the camera deeper into the mix.

"I need you to stand back," one of the officers said. Theo wisely complied. He had to know a big tall Indian would be the first one taken in if this protest went sour.

"Which one of you is in charge?"

"I am," Arnie and Linda said together.

Linda wasn't about to back down on this.

"I am," she repeated. "Are you arresting us?"

"No. You need to exit the premises. You can't sit in here." He pointed at the door as if directing traffic.

"You needed ten officers to tell us that? Are we that threatening, this group of poorly paid non-profit employees who are all of Indian descent?" She couldn't be certain but she thought she heard Arnie utter an encouraging, "Yes!" behind her.

The officer nodded with exaggerated patience. "Any persons loitering in public buildings may be asked to leave. We're asking you to leave." Linda's insides were boiling, leaving her shaky on her feet. Her heart hammered in her chest.

Arnie came to her side. "You getting arrested will make good TV," he said in a low voice.

Linda swiveled to meet his gaze and was relieved to see a humorous twinkle. She turned to look at Kathleen, who seemed to be hoping things would get more serious.

"Let's go," Linda said to her group. "We'll come up with a new approach."

17

The heat of humiliation crept into Ester's face. She kept her eyes on the ground as they filed out. She wasn't sure what was worse—having participated in the world's most pathetic protest, or having done it in front of a camera with Theo watching. They accomplished exactly nothing except waste a bunch of time and look like jerks in the process.

Theo came up next to her, his breath warm in her ear. "You have time to talk after this?"

Since he'd arrived, an ache in her heart had been building. Her gaze followed him as he scrambled to follow Professor Stone's directions, then looked away as if absorbed in the details of the protest. He looked as she remembered: well-worn jeans, filmy black T-shirt. The way he held the camera up made his biceps bulgier than she remembered. Whenever he caught her eye, his expression was chagrinned: *how did we end up doing this?*

"We're going back to campus on the bus," she said.

"I gotta go back, too. Can you ride with me?"

Ester's eyes flicked to Linda. Rayanne and Tommy stayed close to her side. All three of them looked defeated. What happened here today wasn't their fault but it would likely play out that way. They were all doing their best yet they still weren't moving forward.

"I'm not sure," Ester said.

"Do you want to?" Theo asked.

Ester connected with his gaze and a pleasant buzz thrummed through her. His eyes were searching and uncertain.

"I'm not sure I should ditch those guys." She indicated her colleagues. Tommy collected the signs. Several of the protestors left. The event had taken longer than planned. Linda and Rayanne had their heads together in conversation.

"I have to deal with the camera," Theo said. He stayed where he was, pinning her to the spot with his eyes. His ridiculous chest rose and fell with each breath.

"I'll ask Linda," Ester said.

"Good," Theo said, turning to go wherever he was going.

Rayanne waved at her, breaking the spell. She pulled her eyes back into her head and went to join her.

"Did you talk?" Rayanne said.

"He wants me to ride to campus with him," she said.

"Do you feel better now?" Rayanne said.

"If by better you mean tingly all over, then yes."

"Have you got three things?"

Ester made a face and pushed her toward Linda. Rayanne whispered something and Linda turned around and gave a thumbs-up, which should have been encouraging but instead she was mortified by the attention.

Before anyone else could leave, Professor Stone gathered the group together for some reason, probably to schedule the next big set piece. Maybe they would light something on fire and dance around it with their drums. Linda and Rayanne walked toward the bus but Arnie called them over.

Kathleen beamed at the group. "That was great. We've got good basic material to work with. Sorry there weren't more fireworks but that's part of the game."

"What is she talking about?" Linda muttered.

"I've got a number of ideas," Kathleen continued. "I'll arrange to meet with you"—this was directed at Arnie—"and discuss further. Great work, everyone." Professor Stone and Arnie walked off together.

"Good luck," Rayanne said to Ester.

"We're riding to campus, not negotiating world trade agreements," Ester said.

"Don't worry, I can cover for you if you're late." Rayanne winked.

A surge of anxiety gave her pause before she threw Rayanne a dirty look and went to find Theo. He knelt on the ground, arranging equipment to fit into two fabric bags. He piled the last of the equipment in and stood, yanking the straps with him. There was the sound of ripping fabric and clatter of gear. Theo waved the remains of a strap at her.

Ester laughed. "This day just keeps getting better." She squatted down and picked up a roll of gaffer tape and threw it into what was left of the bag. She gathered the bag into her arms. "Where to?"

"Professor Stone's SUV. That seems like our thing, carrying equipment to her car." He pointed down the block.

Ester walked at his side, happy to be with him again.

"I should have called," he said.

"It's okay," she said, the fretting and hand-wringing dismissed.

"I thought after we—"

"I know you've got a lot going on. You don't owe me anything." The words came out casually but her heart squeezed tight when she said them. She'd spent this entire time wondering whether that night meant anything to him.

"We should spend more time together," Theo said.

Ester's knees went weak. She stumbled and lost the gaffer tape again. Theo waited while she retrieved it.

"Me too," Ester said, not sure if those words expressed her thoughts.

"My schedule doesn't leave much room for..." He wagged his finger between the two of them, which gave her a bigger surge of joy than it should have.

"We could work on films together," Ester said. "You get your homework done and I get to do something I like." She blushed at the words.

"I saw you with your phone. Did you film some of that?"

She nodded.

"Yeah, let's do that," Theo agreed.

Arnie and Professor Stone were already standing at her car. When Professor Stone saw them, she opened the back door. Theo loaded in the bag in his arms before turning to take the one Ester carried.

"Ester, how do you think things went today?" Professor Stone asked.

"The protest was a bust but I can see how the footage could be useful for storytelling."

Ester wasn't sure if she made sense but Arnie nodded and said, "I had a similar reaction."

Professor Stone put her hand on Arnie's forearm. "Good. Glad we're thinking alike."

Ester didn't think any of them were thinking alike.

"I appreciate your help," Professor Stone said. She mock-punched Theo in the arm. "This young man has a problem with punctuality. Always an excuse."

"Same excuse every time: work. Jobs in the gig economy don't happen on a strict time schedule."

"All right," Professor Stone said, but her assent sounded phony, like she was being good-natured for Arnie's benefit.

"Am I done?" Theo said to Professor Stone.

"You are. See you in class."

As they walked away, Professor Stone said to Arnie, "Are you free for dinner? I'd love to talk more about the project." She couldn't hear what Arnie replied but his tone was warm. She couldn't sort out her feelings about the two of them being so cozy. Flirting out on the rez had made sense. This seemed like something more.

"Was that weird?" Ester said, nodding her head back toward Arnie and Professor Stone.

"I'm not surprised," Theo said. "They're grownups."

"I guess," Ester said.

"Fran has a yarnbombing event on Saturday. I'm squeezing the film class project in-between money jobs. You want to come with me?"

"Yeah," Ester said, a thrill in her heart. "That sounds fun."

$\mathcal{T}$heo picked up Ester and drove to the park where Fran's group was doing the yarn installation. A few wispy clouds drifted across the sky, but the sun shone through. After several days of rain showers, it was nice to dry out. The air was fresh and warm for early spring as they headed down the path.

Ester walked ahead with a funny, bouncing gait, like a kid nearing the entrance of an amusement park. She wore skinny jeans and an oversized sweatshirt. With her every step, it pulled up long enough to reveal the perfect curve of her butt. Her backpack swung off of one shoulder. She slowed until he caught up.

"Do you know where we're going?" She gazed up at him, her brown eyes searching his. She owned half his heart already.

"Fran said we'd know it when we saw it."

"This is a big park." She looked him over as if just noticing. "Shouldn't you have equipment?"

Theo held up his phone. "This is it. I signed up to use school equipment, but I missed my reserved time."

His school life had gone from tough to strained to unsustainable. The days blended together, rushing from job to job and cramming in homework while propping his eyeballs open. He made it to class, but it was tough to stay focused. If he made it through this quarter, it would be a miracle. "Half-assed like everything else," he told her. "Whatever I have to do to get through."

Ester looked at the sky and shook her head with mock-disappointment. "You need a tripod or a handheld thingy that keeps your shot steady. Fortunately, I have one of each."

"How do you know how to do all this stuff?"

Ester shrugged. "I figure it out."

"Have you told anyone about your project yet?"

Instead of answering, Ester uttered a gasp of delight and pointed. They approached a stand of tall trees. Each tree had a bright band of yellow, orange or pink yarn around the trunk.

Theo filmed Ester moving between the trees. She saw what he was doing and dropped her head before ducking out of the shot. She circled around from the side. "I only like behind the camera. When I see myself on a recording, I think my spirit animal must be clumsy flamingo."

"Maybe I like flamingos."

Ester made a dismissive noise and dug through her backpack. "You must stabilize. Trust me, you can see the difference." She pulled out a gadget that looked like nothing more than a sturdy handle.

"I got this used online. It's cheap and crappy but it works." She stood next to him and crossed her arms over his to show him how to clip in the camera. The shock of the casual touch brought an ache to his groin. Her head tilted forward, her mass of curly hair inches from his face. "That's it," she said, standing back. They stared at each other for a half-beat too long. She licked her lips and pointed at his camera. "I think it's secure, but keep an eye on it. Hold it like this."

He followed her instructions, holding the device in front of him while he walked. "Do I look like an idiot?"

"You can look cool when you're a bouncer," Ester said. "At the moment, you're a filmmaker." Theo couldn't help cracking up.

The trees led to a clearing with park benches and picnic tables. Every object was in some state of decoration, sometimes with strategically wrapped bits, others with elaborate wrappings. One of the park benches was decorated as a playful monster in shades of green with big white teeth. Ester pointed to bright yarn flowers attached to low tree branches. He walked through the installation, capturing it all.

"What were you planning on doing when your camera memory gets full?" Ester asked.

Theo hadn't spent one second considering the memory issues.

"You're lucky I'm here," Ester said. She sat on a bench and took out her laptop. He handed over the camera so she could pull the video off it.

"Tell me about it," Theo said, his eyes glued to her every move. She attached cables and tapped on the keyboard, then stared at the screen with her brows knit together.

"Hey, Theo." Fran waved and came over to join them. She gave Theo a hug.

"My friend Ester, who is saving my ass right now."

Ester smiled. "You can do the interview in a second."

"Your ass needs a lot of saving," Fran said. She grimaced. "Do I have to do this?"

"Yes," Theo said, indicating she should sit. "The knitting is pretty and everything, but it's not much of a film if we don't talk to the brains who made it happen."

"I didn't act alone," Fran said as she sat.

Ester handed him his phone. "What do you think about using a tripod?"

"Never question an Indian woman who knows what she's doing," he said to Fran.

Ester handed him the tripod and let him set it up himself.

"Did you prepare questions?" she asked.

"Nope," Theo said. "I'm winging it."

Ester twisted her mouth into a comic frown of displeasure. He wanted to kiss that mouth. She gestured he should go ahead.

Theo had worked out in advance what Fran was willing to talk about. She'd lived on her own since she was a teenager. She didn't elaborate other than to say her mom was unstable and men took advantage of her, so Fran left for the usual reasons young women leave home too early. She'd struggled on the street until she got it together, but she'd created a family out of this community. Public art was one way to share what they had.

"Why yarn?" Ester asked, when Fran had finished.

"Good question," Fran said. "It keeps my hands busy, and it keeps my mind focused. You know, sometimes you get stuck in your head in unproductive ways? You can talk or listen while you work. When we're knitting together we catch up, vent, solve the world's problems. Plus, yarn is fun to buy, too much fun. There's always a color or texture that's irresistible. I love showing off my stash and rooting through my friends' stashes. Online there are photos and videos of the stashes of complete strangers. And once you get how it works, you can do so many things. I like creative problem-solving. And when you're done, you have a physical object that may be useful. You ever try it?"

Ester shook her head. "I get the creative part but I think yarn would make me crazy."

Fran laughed. "It can. But it's fun. Let me know if you change your mind."

"What about me?" Theo asked.

"All are welcome," Fran said. "You have an interest in knitting?"

"Not at all. Thanks Fran," Theo said. "What happens next?"

"We'll come back next weekend and take it down. Some of it can be reused and some of it gets tossed. You want to film that part?"

"I'll figure out how to cram it in."

They said their goodbyes. Ester took the video off his camera before handing it back to him and putting everything away.

"I'll transfer it to a drive you can use when we get back," she said. "What next?"

"I'm writing out the voice-over. I can finish with what we did today."

"That's the part I need help with," Ester said. "The images are easy, the talking part is a challenge. I sound like I'm in front of a firing squad, reciting my last words, which were prepared by someone who doesn't speak English but ran the speech through an online translator."

"I can help you," Theo said. He glanced at the time. He needed to spend a few hours driving, but he wasn't ready to leave Ester yet. "You have time for a walk?"

She looked surprised. "Do you?"

Theo laughed. "A short walk."

"I'll show you the lake." She led him through the trees.

Theo expected a murky duck pond, but this was a wide stretch of blue-green water. If he threw a rock from the edge, he might hit the middle. Lots of folks were out, enjoying the good weather. The path was an endless stream of bikes and people with dogs and strollers. The tap and thump of a drum circle drifted from across the lake.

"I sent you Professor Stone's info on the film workshop. She said the staff is great and they want diversity. Did you look at it?"

Ester shrugged.

"It's perfect for you. If you're accepted, it's almost all paid for. You're more than—"

"I can't do a workshop," Ester said with finality. She picked up a flat rock and skipped it across the water. It bounced a half-dozen times before plunking in.

"Nice shot," Theo said. He searched for his own flat rock.

Ester said, "A few months ago we thought the center was shutting down and Linda introduced me around to other organizations so I would have a job. It made me think about what I want to do versus what I'm doing. I like my colleagues more than the work but I like the stability. I want to pay off the loans before anything else."

Theo picked up a rock and flung it over the water. It bounced three time before falling in.

"It's in the wrist," Ester said, playfully demonstrating. Theo's mind turned the gesture into something less wholesome.

They took their time walking back to the car. Theo kept his hands in his pockets but he walked close enough to brush against her. She didn't move out of his way.

Back at her house, she ran in to transfer his work to a portable drive. He waited in the driveway, going over his calendar, searching for any time they could be together again. It was always going to be like this. He had no time to do this like he wanted to.

Ester dashed out of the house as if exiting a burning building. She rushed up to him and handed over the drive. In the same breath, she stood on tiptoe and kissed him, then darted away.

"Wait!" His heart buzzed in his chest and a surge of longing swept through him. "Do that again."

Her dark eyes stared into his. She came back and pressed her hands to his chest, the gentle contact bringing more pleasure than it should have. She studied his lips before brushing her own across them. An involuntary groan came from the back of his throat. He dropped the drive on the hood and wrapped his arms around her. She leaned into him and he held her tight and kissed her hard, working his tongue into her mouth, lost in the sensation until she whimpered.

He let her go, and she took an unsteady step back. "Was that okay?" he asked.

"I think I passed out for a second," Ester said, the back of her hand pressed against her face.

Theo laughed. "We spent the night together, and we kissed. Now let's go on a date."

Ester nodded, still dazed.

"Professor Stone is screening her film for her students next Sunday. We'll eat noodles."

"I like noodles."

He kissed her one more time before he left.

inda knew better, but she scrolled down and kept reading, one comment after the other feeding her fury until her breath came out in short hot bursts.

"What are you doing?" Ester asked.

"The local weekly wrote an article about our protest." She bit off the last word with a scornful snort and kept reading. The article itself was mildly insulting, characterizing the event as poorly conceived and lamentably executed. The comments were soul crushing. They ranged from the ignorant—*don't these people get enough free handouts?*—to the irrelevant—*tribal basketball should get more news coverage*—to the outright vile—*the Indians need to face reality, their time is finished.*

"Are you reading the comments?"

Linda shook her head and kept scrolling.

Ester came over and took the mouse and closed the browser. "If you learn nothing else from our time together, it should be this: never read the comments."

"The thing that kills me is they're right. We put on a show for that woman's camera. We accomplished nothing except making fools of ourselves. I bet there's a memo circulating this minute about watching out for us if we enter a city building."

"It's an honor to be on a watch list with you," Ester said.

"I admit, I hated the film idea at first," Linda said. Hated was too mild for her reaction to Arnie's grand pronouncement they were doing this, but the more she thought about it, the more the idea gained appeal. A strong film could convince people of the importance of their mission. However, images of them standing around city hall holding signs was not what she envisioned. "I can see how it would be effective. But not contrived moments like last week." She groaned and hid her head on her desk. "I'm fatally embarrassed."

"It wasn't that bad," Ester said. "Just kidding, it was, but don't die. We'll give her suggestions. Her intentions aren't bad but she doesn't get us. At least not the way we want to be gotten. Does that make sense?"

"That's what worries me."

The door opened and Rayanne swept in, bringing a gust of rain with her. "One minute the sun was out, the next minute cloudburst. I ran from the parking lot. My treasure better be unharmed."

She pulled something from under her coat and set it on her desk. Then she peeled off her dripping coat and hung it by the door. Linda kept a towel at the office for moments like this. She tossed it over.

"Thanks. I'm glad it's just you two," Rayanne said, mopping herself off. She unwrapped the item to reveal a yellow box shaped like a treasure chest and brought it to Linda. "I'm ready to pass on one of my most valuable possessions."

"Your cardboard box?" Linda asked.

Rayanne tossed the towel over a chair. "I will have you know, I won this at a bachelorette party. I don't need it anymore. You guys are both dating. You need to be prepared."

It seemed strange to call her time with Virgil "dating." During their first meeting, she and Virgil sat at a dinky round table, in a room filled with people plugged into laptops. They drank coffee and talked about careers and people they knew in common. It had been pleasant. Next, they had dinner, the first half of the night retaining the vaguely formal air of a job interview. But after a glass of wine, they'd traded laughs. Later they walked to the bookstore, and he'd recommended a memoir she bought but hadn't read yet. Virgil was a good listener and polite. He was smart and challenged her ideas. She wanted to see him again. She turned to Ester. "You're dating Theo?"

Ester blushed and stared at the floor.

"Perfect." Rayanne lifted the lid. Inside was a collection of bright-colored foil packages. "I'm passing what's left to you two."

"Are those what I think they are?" Linda asked.

"It's a pirate's chest filled with condoms," Rayanne said. "Actually, it's only half full of condoms. And all the glow-in-the-dark ones are gone. Sorry."

"So thoughtful. Especially the part how you brought them to the office," Linda said, curious if there was anything in the bylaws that would forbid prophylactic exchange on work premises. "The board and any other person who we want to view us as responsible professionals will appreciate our preparedness."

"It is responsible," Rayanne said. She replaced the lid. "It's a cute little box. No one will even know."

"Fine," Linda said. "But you don't need to bring me condoms. We're still getting to know each other."

"What are you on, third date? It's only a matter of time," Rayanne said.

Linda tried to envision undressing with Virgil. He was one of those wiry guys who mentioned he did distance running. Probably had great legs under those work slacks.

"I'll take 'em," Ester said, sliding the box into her arms.

Linda shook a finger at her. "Put that back. We'll divide them up later."

"That's what I like to see," Rayanne said.

Linda spent her weekend going through archive boxes, searching for early contacts that might be rekindled. "Let's go over the private donor sources and make a calendar for applications. We can get started today."

The morning flashed by as the three of them put together a long-term plan for approaching donors. After lunch, they crowded around Ester's terminal, working together to complete online forms. Linda read figures off of a spreadsheet while Ester entered them in. Rayanne had a laptop open next to them to verify instructions.

Arnie came in. Even with the wet weather, he was decked out in his regular uniform: suit and tie plus a sharp raincoat. Even his boots looked good.

"Didn't know you would be here today," Linda said.

"Me either. Henry was supposed to help me write press releases, but he's too slammed with school."

There was a long pause. Linda leveled a stern eye at him. "Don't even think about it. No one on my staff is available."

"No one is asking for your staff," Arnie said, but from his tone she could tell that's what he wanted. "I can write them myself." He headed to the work station Ester had set up for him.

"What's this?" He pointed at the cardboard treasure chest on her desk.

"Nothing. Leave it alone." She got up to put it away, but it was too late, Arnie had it open.

He studied the inside of the box, a peculiar expression on his face. "Why do you have a treasure chest full of condoms on your desk?"

"It's only half full," Linda said. "And they're not all mine."

Ester used her hand to shield her eyes as if that would save her.

"I'm sure they could spare a couple if you're in need," Rayanne said.

"I'm good." He put the lid back on the box without smiling. "Glad you ladies are having fun."

Next he would make a comment about this sort of behavior at the office followed by questions about what they'd accomplished since he'd been in last. He'd act like a few jokes derailed them from their mission. But instead, he logged into his computer and got to work.

A long hour passed, a whiff of tension simmering in the air. Linda and the staff finished one application and completed half of another. At one point, Ester made a fresh pot of coffee and when she offered Arnie a cup, he shook his head without comment.

At the end of the day, Linda suggested, "We should talk about the filmmaker while Arnie's here."

Arnie kept his eyes glued to his work. "I'm in a time crunch. We've got press releases and so forth to write."

"Another time then," Linda said. She'd known Arnie long enough to leave him alone when he was worked up. She packed up, eager to get home and put on a pair of sweatpants and pour a glass of wine.

"Forget it. I can make time," Arnie said, turning from the computer.

So they were going to do this while Arnie was in a snit. No sense in sugar-coating it. "I'm concerned about the fallout over that stunt last week," Linda said.

She braced herself for a testy comeback, but instead he said, "Not the first bad idea we've had." His eyes were red-rimmed and his face washed out. She hadn't noticed it before but he was burned out. She hated to see him struggle, but she still didn't want to give up her staff. He rubbed his hand over his face. "You know how the news cycle goes. It will be forgotten next week."

"I'm concerned about the board."

He shook his head like she shouldn't worry about it—even after spending the last several months insisting that was her biggest worry.

"There are also worries about the filmmaker's approach, such as creating these events to film." Keep it in passive voice. No specifics, just concerns out there that they should think about.

"Let's give Katie a chance before blowing this off," Arnie said.

Katie?

"No one is saying anything about blowing it off," Linda said. "I'm worried about our image."

"We haven't seen what she can do yet," Arnie said.

"What if we end up invested in something we can't use?"

Arnie took his time putting his things away. He slung his bag over his shoulder. We're going to give it more time. That reminds me...the elder lunch. Can we fancy it up?" He had an aggravating way of asking a question that was really an order.

Linda straightened a stack of paper on her desk to keep from snapping at him. She couldn't guess what fancying up a luncheon meant.

Ester came to the rescue. "We'll talk about it. Did you know

Professor Stone is screening the film with the interviews from Warm Springs? I can get a better idea of what her work is like."

"The film is ready?" Arnie said. "I would like to see it."

"She's showing her students," Ester said.

Arnie smiled, as if remembering a private joke. "I'll ask her about it myself."

So, something was going on. An icy burst of jealousy shot through Linda's heart, followed by distress that after all this time he could still do that to her, make her feel inadequate by chasing after a competent woman. There had never been anything between them, yet there was always a part of her that felt overlooked by him. The guy you wanted to notice you who treated you like a sister. They were friends. They were colleagues. Whatever misalignment she was feeling was a figment that needed to die sooner rather than later.

"Let me know after you see it," Arnie said.

"Are you going with Theo?" Rayanne asked.

Ester smiled.

"I can't wait to hear what you both think," Arnie said. To Linda he added, "Trust me on this." He waited for her to respond. That was so like him, to push or demand and then pull back and ask for support.

"We will," she said.

20

$\mathcal{E}$ster ended up wearing a wool skirt, a gray sweater and tights with boots after enduring an endless lecture from Rayanne. The screening took place in a small theater on campus. The afternoon was chilly but there was no rain. Some of the trees showed tiny green buds, more hope for spring.

She hurried to keep up with Theo as they crossed campus. They had about three minutes before the film started and he didn't want to be late. They talked about work and Theo's film. Ester could hardly concentrate on the words, instead her energy focused on keeping her heart from exploding out of her chest. Whatever tentative thing they had started, she was prepared to take it forward. She had on the matching bra and panties that Rayanne took her to buy. The potential was endless.

She studied Theo out of the corner of her eye. He wore jeans and a gray hoodie and probably didn't spend three seconds thinking about his underwear. She wondered what kind of underwear Theo would wear. Probably boxers in soft flannel.

He caught her eye. "What are you thinking about?"

"Nothing," she said. "Films. Editing. Voice-over. The normal things people think about. Did you do the voice-over for your film yet?"

"I wrote a draft. I'll show you later."

About three dozen students sat in the screening room when they arrived. They settled in their seats and Ester's attention stayed fixed on Theo's physicality. The way he sat back in his seat, sexy-lazy, with his elbow on the armrest, poking over on her side.

He leaned over to whisper, "You warm enough? It's cold in here."

She wasn't warm but she didn't see any solution other than crawling into his arms in the uncomfortable wooden theater chairs. "I'm fine," she said.

Theo folded his hands in his lap and that's where Ester's eyes wanted to rest.

Professor Stone acknowledged them with a nod as she stood at the front of the theater. She talked about the film and her process along with techniques and choices she made for a film about family connections. She asked the students to compare what they saw with what they'd learned in class. Ester took out her phone to type notes. If only she could take a class like this.

"I like the way she teaches," Ester whispered.

"It's still a work in progress," Professor Stone said. "I'm counting on you to have comments and insights into the process of filmmaking."

The lights dimmed and Ester smiled because she sat in the dark next to Theo. Every move he made caused something to vibrate inside her. As soon as they'd planned this date, she knew she wanted more, but she wasn't confident she knew how to make it happen. She had one film and one plate of noodles to figure it out.

As the images flashed up on the screen, she understood what Professor Stone was doing: an extended family celebrated a quinceañera, the kitchen staff of a busy restaurant hustled during the dinner rush, a wealthy family of four lived in a huge house where each person had their own room, a family of little means played board games together on their kitchen table, and a halfway house welcomed individuals recently out of prison. The interviews and images explored the question of how people find family.

Ester loved the way she organized her shots and cut the interviews with imagery. She had to figure out a way to get better at this. She could ask Professor Stone to recommend a path for self study.

She recognized an outdoor shot from the trip to Arnie's. It was the view from his brother's place, a wide vista of knobby trees and rolling hills in pale winter light. The camera lingered on the most run-down houses she would have seen during the trip and then cut to the inside of Mike's house, crowded with family. A cold finger of doubt ran down her spine. The edit made it seem like Mike's family was crammed on top of each other in that little house. The interview was well done, highlighting comments from each generation, but the camera paused on anything broken or run down. A chip on the mug as grandma sipped her coffee, the splintered leg of a chair the kids had broken when they were chasing the dogs. Whatever joy had been in the room was muted by an emphasis on what was worn out. And where the kids had hung back, shy around her, the framing made it appear they were shrinking away as if frightened.

Arnie's grandma shared a joyful memory of her grandparents moving into their first tribal home, but as she spoke, the camera cut to the unfinished home on Arnie's road and the little boy on the ground crying. Ester tried to push back her disappointment. The scene switched to a college dorm common room and a group of young people with their laptops and tablets.

When the lights came up, Professor Stone started the discussion. The students had questions and comments about the way she'd done her film. No one mentioned the tribal piece. Ester wasn't sure about speaking up, after all she wasn't a student. She loved the film; it was just the bit on the rez with its emphasis on what was broken that bothered her.

At last the questions wound down and Professor Stone wrapped up the event. She waved them over. Ester followed Theo, uncertain what to say or how honest to be. Arnie was hell-bent on making a film for the center, so she should keep her disappointment to herself.

"What did you think?" Professor Stone asked.

"I like how the diverse viewpoints lead to the same conclusion," Theo said.

Professor Stone nodded in agreement. "How about you, Ester?"

Ester held her hands up as if she were too overwhelmed to think. "I'm still sorting it through."

"Fair enough," Professor Stone said. "We'll see you next week at the lunch for the elderly."

"Elder lunch," Ester said.

"Ester does film-making," Theo said. "I told her about the workshop you've been talking about." She knew he meant well, but she couldn't take herself seriously standing next to this woman.

Professor Stone gave her a polite smile. "Doesn't hurt to apply."

Ester was embarrassed that he brought it up. She'd intended to ask about classes but her confidence faltered. She barely heard the rest of the conversation, something about Theo's final project and something about Arnie. She kept her expression agreeable and was relieved when Theo touched her back and they headed for the door.

THE EVENING WAS Theo's reward for a long week. During all the crazy working hours and absurd amount of time on homework and Professor Stone's final project, he'd reminded himself he had this night with Ester. He tried not to think about how little sleep he'd been getting. Spring break was around the corner, and he could sleep then. For now, his problems were set aside and he was enjoying breathing the same air as Ester. She calmed him. It was like he was juggling chainsaws and he couldn't go on but it was too dangerous to stop. Then he'd remember Ester's crooked frown before she said something funny, or the warmth in her eyes when she listened to him. Her company filled him with longing to let this grow into something bigger. The notion was impossible, but it was getting tougher to resist.

He carried two plates of noodles to the narrow counter that ran along the window. Ester set down their beers and crawled up on the seat next to his, her dark curls hanging in her face.

He waited for her to try her food. "What do you think?"

145

"Spicy, I like it," she said. She studied her plate. "Do you come here a lot?"

"I usually eat at home. Tell me, what did you really think?"

Ester sighed. "Did you see the way she did our part? It was like everything was framed to reinforce her idea of what rez life is like."

Theo sat back and reviewed the footage in his head. The wide outdoor shots and the family together, laughing through the interview. "I thought it was a good film."

"It is, but think about what it was like when we were there."

She meant while they were on the rez but his memory flew back to the motel and their bodies pressed together in the tiny room. He wanted more of that.

"Sure," he said, taking a swig of beer.

"How would you describe our time with Arnie's family?"

"It reminded me of visiting my grandma on the rez at home," Theo said. "Chaotic but happy."

"Did you get that out of the film clip?" Ester asked.

Theo closed his eyes, thinking back again to that part of the film. The image of the kid crying in the front yard, the window screen hanging off the frame, Mike's house crowded and squalid...

"The images made everything small and dingy," Theo said.

"Exactly," Ester said. "I don't know what to do. Should I say something to Arnie or wait until they see it for themselves? Linda and them might like it."

He wanted to wipe the frown from her face. He was the one who had introduced her to Professor Stone, perhaps he could fix this. "Professor Stone invited written comments if we came up with anything. Let me think about it. I can diplomatically say something."

"This film isn't the real problem," Ester said.

Theo held back from clearing his plate in three bites. If he wanted this evening to last, he had to slow down.

"What worries me is using that angle to make a film about the center. The idea isn't to make us pitiful."

"Tell me what you think the idea is," Theo said.

Ester dragged her fork through her noodles. "We're preserving culture and traditions. We're tribal people and we're creating a tribe here, in the city. It's like she has the right idea, but the wrong execution."

"But think about the target audience."

"You probably have a point but I'm not ready to hear it," Ester said. "Do you go to your rez often?"

"Nope," Theo said. "The last time was two years ago. Planes make my mom nervous, and she asked so I drove her down there."

"Oh, wow," Ester said. "That's a long drive."

"It is," Theo said. "The trip that changed everything."

"What changed?"

Theo tried to figure out the best way to tell the story. "I was a pain-in-the-ass kid," he said. "The kind who skipped school, drank beer. I disappointed everyone."

"Ooh, a bad boy."

"You're not supposed to be impressed," Theo said. "I have an older brother. Similar story."

"How did you get it together?" When Theo paused, she said, "You do have it together?"

She teased but he shouldn't have brought it up. He'd convinced his dream girl to have dinner with him and now he was explaining all the reasons she should run.

"That's the image I'm attempting to project," Theo said.

When he was silent, Ester made a rolling motion with her hand. "What happened on the trip?"

"I saw how happy my mom was, being back. She kept talking about how home smelled, as soon as she got out of the car, the plants, the dirt, the sky. She wanted me to understand what the place meant to her. My grandma kept telling me how proud she was I'd turned out so well. Keep in mind I dropped out of high school and was doing labor jobs to get enough money to run around with my friends getting high." Theo and his friends chased girls, too, but he left that part out. "I can't figure out what she was so proud of. It was like being proud of me amounting to nothing was worse than telling me she was disappointed."

"How come your mom left?" Ester asked. There was a half plate of noodles in front of her but she had her hands in her lap. She saw him looking and pointed at her plate with her chin.

Theo smiled and pulled her plate on top of his empty one. He forced himself to look away from those eyes.

"She met my dad, and he was a good guy. If she wanted a family, she needed a good, stable man. When he moved up here, she came with him. It took another year, but I realized my choices disappointed two incredible ladies who weren't giving up on me. So I dumped my friends and got my GED and now I'm at school, killing myself to keep a promise."

Ester met his gaze with incredible strength and compassion. He wanted to put his head on her shoulder.

"Professor Stone seemed happy enough with your work," Ester said.

"I'm not so sure." He finished the last of the noodles. Both of their beers were finished. A surprising tug of urgency burned in his belly. He didn't want the night to be over but he had no idea what else they could do. There weren't a lot of options and she had to work in the morning.

Ester shifted around in her seat. Maybe she was too polite to ask him to take her home. He didn't want to be the one to suggest it first.

"What's on your mind?" he finally asked.

And to his great surprise, Ester shrugged and said, "You could show me your place."

2 1

$\mathcal{E}$ster gave him her best vixen-y smile, although she wasn't sure that was getting across. People who liked each other did this all the time. She needed a script to get there because the hidden powers of the matching underwear were not manifesting as promised.

She decided to be that woman who asked for what she wanted instead of the one who went home alone and kicked herself for the rest of the night. But after she asked, he said, dumbfounded: "You want to see my place?"

He crumpled up his napkin and threw it on his plate, then sat back like he was ready to wrap things up and this suggestion had caught him by surprise. His expression was either amused or annoyed. The noodles churned in her stomach.

She swallowed. "Sure, you've seen mine." She tried to sound like she didn't care either way.

Theo said nothing. This matching underwear was a giant fail. He got up and threw their plates in the trash and they headed out the door. He wasn't even mentioning it. He was so embarrassed he was pretending it didn't happen. Stupid underwear.

The silence was excruciating and grew more awkward by the minute. So, he didn't want to. She could turn it into a joke. There were lots of excuses. It was a school night. He probably had homework. She had work in the morning. They could do it some other time.

Do it some other time. Ha!

They passed a boisterous group headed for the noodle shop. Ester focused on the sound her boots made on the concrete walkway out to the parking lot.

They reached the car. Theo opened her door for her. "It's a chair, a table and a bed. Not much to see."

Ester shrugged as if to say: *It was a silly idea. Forget I mentioned it.*

"We can stop by, if you want," Theo said.

Ester exhaled more air than a person should hold. While Theo walked around to get in the car, she lifted her collar and whispered encouragement to her bra strap.

Theo lived close-in to downtown. She was still preparing herself and already he was driving slowly down a car-lined street.

"Parking in this neighborhood is a giant pain," he told her.

She'd set them on this course, but her confidence wavered. She was aware of every move he made, the way he turned the steering wheel, the turn of his head before taking the car around a corner. All the heat and manliness that rolled off him made it hard to sit still. She shifted in the seat, warmth pulsing in her belly.

He parked the car, and they got out. His street had lots of tall leafy trees and a mix of homes and apartment buildings. Ester was out of things to say. Theo had his hands in his pockets but he walked so close to her that his elbow brushed against hers. The longer she remained silent the more nervous she became.

From behind a wall of shrubs, a dog growled, then barked. She gasped and leapt to the side, her heart beating like crazy again.

Theo put his arm around her shoulder and pulled her along again. "We're good," he said, his voice calm.

"Are you a dog person or a cat person?" she asked.

"I guess neither," he said.

"I like dogs," Ester said, grateful to have found a topic to fill the quiet. "Someday when I have a house, I'm getting a couple of dogs. Rescue dogs. I try not to picture them because I want to be ready for whatever dogs need a home the most. But I don't like really little dogs or super hairy dogs. But I'm open-minded. Any dog could win me over."

"Dogs are good," Theo agreed. "This is it."

Ester gulped.

Theo lived in an old two-story brick building. He unlocked the main door and let her in.

"I'll give you the tour." He used his chin to point at the bank of mailboxes. "Mail." Then he indicated a box on the floor that had a single rubber boot, a miniature basketball hoop and a grease-stained sweatshirt. "Lost and found." He nodded at the staircase. "Stairs. I'm on the second floor."

Ester walked up the stairs with Theo following behind her, her emotions in a confusing tangle of terror and joy. At the top of the stairs was a small landing with four battered doors. A trio of pizza boxes leaned against the wall next to one door.

"Like living in the dorms," Ester said in a low voice.

"I never did that. Guess I didn't miss much." Theo unlocked the door and let her in first before closing the door behind them.

His description was accurate. There wasn't much there. The entire space seemed to be bed. There was no place to move without getting closer to the bed. It was the motel room all over again, only Theo lived here and she'd asked to be here.

"It's not that bad," Ester said, taking off her coat. She wasn't cold now. The walls were bare except for a tribal flag. He didn't have a single photo on display. There was no bookshelf or any kind of shelf for that matter. Just a cheap table with his school books piled on it and a single chair. This room revealed nothing about him, except he didn't mind living in a sparsely furnished place and if he had guests, they didn't need a chair.

The sheets were well-worn navy-blue flannel with a navy comforter, no doubt soft and comfortable. Simply standing in that small room with him and a bed set her entire body throbbing.

"Not at all," Theo agreed. "I like a small place. I can fit everything I own in my car and be out of here in an afternoon."

He pulled the chair out and offered it to her. She stayed where she was.

"You brag about that?" She'd meant it to come out light-hearted, but it sounded like a cut.

"Not really." He sat down in the chair himself. "You want something?"

"Do I want something?"

"To drink? A snack?"

Ester shook her head and tried to guess what Rayanne would do at a moment like this. Ester sat on the bed and looked at him expectantly. She studied his face. Whatever lustful gaze she wanted, this wasn't it.

"Something you were thinking about?" Theo asked.

Ester's mind raced. What sort of come-hither thing would Rayanne say? Nothing—she wouldn't have to say anything because any guy would be all over Rayanne in a hot second. Ester reviewed her options. She could keep playing this game with him and die of anxiety before she ever got to touch his abs.

She patted the bed next to her. He raised an eyebrow and came over to sit down. As soon as he was seated, she got up and crawled onto his lap, facing him. Then she held his face in her hands and kissed down the side of his face and along the crease of his neck.

Theo groaned. "You're killing me, Ester."

"That's what I'm trying to do," she whispered, "kill you."

Ester stopped to trace her fingers over Theo's face. Now that she'd touched him, she couldn't stop running her fingers across his eyebrows and over his cheekbones.

Theo's eyes were closed, and he wore the most peaceful expression on his face. "What are you doing to me?"

Ester pondered the meaning of that question. "I'm getting to know you," she murmured.

"There are more interesting places to touch," Theo said.

"I disagree," Ester said. "This is the most personal place." She kissed him on the mouth again.

Theo sat up and wrapped his arms around her and kissed her hard, his tongue working into her mouth and stroking over hers. When he came up for air, he said, "You surprised me when you kissed me the other night. That was quite a wind-up."

Ester hid her face. "Once I made up my mind, I didn't want to chicken out."

"I'm not complaining. You can kiss me all night, Shoshone."

"That's what I want to do," she said.

Theo stopped and shifted in a way that made her uncertain. Her heart sank. He waited for her to look at him.

"I want you to," Theo said, "but you understand my situation here. I'm not boyfriend-material. I have to pass these classes. School is the most important thing. I have to keep up with work. If I fail, I go home."

"I understand," Ester said, wondering if she seemed desperate.

Theo pressed his forehead against hers. "I don't want us to start something here without you knowing there's not much potential here."

"When something starts, no one can be sure how it will end up," Ester said, her voice calmer than she felt inside. She kissed him again.

"Give me a second. I gotta see if I can find a condom. If there is one Indian cliché I would like to avoid, it's the one about the unplanned pregnancy."

"I have condoms," Ester said.

"I'm not worthy," Theo said with a surprised smile. He lifted Ester off his lap. She got the condoms out of her purse and put them on the pillow. Meanwhile, Theo switched off the overhead light and turned on the desk lamp, leaving them in low golden light. "That's the best I can do for mood lighting," he said.

Ester wasn't sure what to do next. She sat back down and yanked off her boots.

Theo's eyes never left her and she worried about meeting his expectations. He held out his hand. She took it and he pulled her into an embrace, his face sinking into her hair. It seemed like he was trembling. He tilted her face up and kissed her hard. He pressed his body against hers, his hands moving down to cup her ass and grind her against him.

"Let me show you the idea I had for a work around, if we didn't have condoms." His voice had fallen into a lower register that made her tingle down to her toes.

Several things happened very quickly. Theo's hands slid around her waistband and the skirt dropped to the floor. He slipped the tights and panties off together. Before she'd even stepped out of them, her sweater was being peeled off over her head and her arms were still caught in the sleeves when the clasp to her bra came undone. She let the bra drop to the floor.

Theo's gaze was pure hunger. At least he was taking charge of things now.

"The bra and panties match," Ester murmured.

"Sexy," Theo said. "I'll pay better attention when you put them back on tomorrow."

She shivered thinking about being naked with him until morning.

He backed her up until she was at the edge of the bed and pushed her down. She tried to quiet the trembling of her limbs. Now that they were here, she was unprepared. Things should be unfolding slowly, but already she was naked and sprawled across the bed. She put a hand on her stomach, willing her nerves to calm.

Theo still had his clothes on and stared down at her. "You're gorgeous," he said.

"When do I see you with your shirt off?" Ester managed to ask.

"I'm going to show you my thing, first," Theo said.

"I don't see your thing," Ester said.

Theo smiled and kneeled at the side of the bed. "I'm demonstrating the thing I have been thinking about since this conversation started."

"With your shirt on?" The anticipation was making her lightheaded.

"You women, you're all alike." He grabbed her by the ankles and slid her toward him. Without taking his eyes off her, he grabbed a pillow and jammed it under her hips.

"Shouldn't we be warming up with more basic stuff?" she said, mostly to herself.

"This is the warm-up." Theo threw one of her legs over his shoulder and used his lips to caress her inner thigh before working his way down. Her eyes fluttered open long enough to admire his muscular arms in the pale light, and then there were too many sensations to process at once. No one had touched her like this before. His hands stroked along her hips. His tongue made lazy circles that made her center pulse and quake. He exhaled with quiet moans that would be amusing if she weren't so distracted by lust. Her body settled into the unfamiliar state, damp heat and rising tension.

"Okay, I think this exactly—"

Theo stopped with his mouth but moved one hand and did something clever with his fingers. "If you can talk, I must not be doing it right. You want me to try something different?"

She intended to say something in the affirmative but what came out was a high-pitched gargle.

"Was that a good squeak or a bad squeak?"

She tried again, and it sounded more like she was clearing her throat while singing a high note.

Theo kissed her inner thigh again. "Do you want me to stop?"

She said no but it came out like an exhale of surprise. She wiggled her hips until he nestled back down and returned to what he was doing.

She exhaled slowly, every cell in her body on fire. Theo's mouth was warm and persistent, working in a steady rhythm. Whatever shyness or uncertainty she'd brought with her when she'd entered the room, was long gone. She tried to find an orderly way to organize the sensations. Body, mind, skin, breath. Pieces of her drew into the center while other pieces grew further away. Her heart pounded everywhere at once and it was Theo doing this to her. Everything crested and came undone at once. She let out a noise that would have been embarrassing in any other circumstances.

Theo squeezed her thigh and kissed a line to her knee. He pulled the pillow out from under her and moved her up on the bed. Ester's eyes were half-closed, her mind tied up in a dreamy place as she rode the last of the sensations.

From somewhere far away, Theo said, "I'm taking my shirt off."

"Too bad my brain has stopped working." She opened her eyes. He whipped his shirt off and dropped his jeans just as swiftly as he'd removed her clothes. His skin was golden brown in the dim light. She wanted to touch him everywhere. She gestured him closer.

"You'll do," she said. Ester gave what she hoped was a sexy grin, but she was so addled, she probably looked deranged.

His boxers were puffy, pale-blue cotton, like something a grandma would buy as a Christmas present. If you looked like him, you wouldn't need to worry about your underwear. He stepped out of them and there was his thing.

He rolled on the condom and took his time crawling onto her. His chest was perfectly sculpted muscle. She would have to remember to ask him how he kept that up when he didn't have time to sleep. She reached up to stroke his belly and his breath caught. She wanted to say something about how sexy he was, except her mouth couldn't make the words her head was thinking. He raked his teeth across one of her nipples.

Ester gasped.

"Good, you're still in there," Theo said. He nibbled on her lower lip. "How're you feeling?"

"Delicious," Ester said.

"Ready for more?"

Before she answered, he slid in and filled her up. Once again, her mind and body were a blur of sensation and electric heat. She stroked her hands down the muscles of his back and over the curve of his butt. The unexpected sounds of their bodies slapping against each other heated her up again. Theo's breath rasped in her ears. She opened her eyes and tried to see his face in the dim light but it was hidden in the crook of her neck. She sensed the moment when he lost control, bucking against her, groaning in her ear.

He rocked his hips slowly against hers before his lips brushed the side of her face. It took a minute before his breath slowed down and he moved off of her.

"I'll be right back."

Ester made a little singing noise in the back of her throat that made him laugh. When he returned, he pulled her against his chest, his heartbeat steady against her cheek. She floated in a blissful haze, her fingers tracing over his chest.

"This time I get to hold you properly," Theo said.

"This time?" Ester said. "Oh. The motel night was nice though."

"The motel was torture," Theo said. "I had to jerk off in the shower."

"You had a funny expression on your face when you came out of the bathroom but I thought it was your rush to get home."

"It was about you," Theo said. He nuzzled her neck. "You know, I noticed you before, when you came to the computer lab."

"How come you didn't try to talk to me?"

"I wasn't in a position to start something so I didn't see the point."

"And yet, here we are," Ester said. She was glad her pleased smile was hidden from him.

Theo kissed a spot between her neck and shoulder, and she sighed happily. "You sleepy?"

"Unfortunately," Ester said. "I'm not used to staying up late on school nights."

"What time do you have to be at work tomorrow?" Theo said.

That was a splash of cold water on the afterglow.

"Ugh, work," Ester muttered.

Theo's lips brushed across her temple. "I'll set my phone alarm to get us up by ugh."

"I can't go to work in my date clothes. Rayanne will tease me to death," Ester said, half-heartedly trying to push herself up. "I'm too young to die." She hated to do it but Theo could drop her off.

Theo pulled her back. "I'll get us up early enough to go by your place so you can change. I don't want you to die, either."

2 2

The bed was empty when Theo woke up and he felt a twinge of disappointment until he heard Ester in the bathroom. He pretended to sleep while she tiptoed out and slithered back under the covers. Through half-closed eyes, he admired the beautiful body he'd fondled the night before.

Before she settled, he reached for her and lined her body against his. He put his hand on her belly and pressed into her, his lips on a tender spot he'd discovered under her ear.

"Sorry, did I wake you?" she asked with feigned innocence.

"I had to get up, anyway." His hand snuck up to play with one of her nipples. She jerked in surprise. He kept his lips brushing her neck.

"Something you were thinking about?" she asked.

"I'll show you." It didn't take him long to put on the condom and then roll her on top of him.

"My, you're acrobatic," she said with an irresistible laugh.

She stared down at him, flushed cheeks and dark lips. She pressed the back of her hand to her mouth, her eyes shiny. He urged her to lean down and he kissed her mouth.

"No one's ever said that about me before," he said.

He held her hips until they found the same rhythm, then let her take over. She leaned over him, her face twisted in bliss. She ducked her head and her hair tickled his chest. He felt it everywhere in his body. This had already gone too far and now he couldn't stop it if he tried. He memorized the way her shoulder slumped forward as if in a perpetual state of mild embarrassment, and the whimper in her breath when he stroked her inner thighs. She bounced faster until at last she gasped his name and something seized in his heart. He grabbed her hips again and pumped into her until he finished, too.

Afterward he dragged her into the shower with him.

"You are a terrific host," Ester said later while he towel-dried her hair. "It's been a long time since I've been so thoroughly scrubbed front and back."

"Leave a good review online," Theo said, wishing they didn't have to leave. "Let's see the matching underwear."

Ester's shoulders hunched forward, but she found her bra and panties and put them on while he watched.

He kissed her shoulder. "I'll think about this view all day."

"But none of the other part?" she asked with half-smile.

"I need to function," he said. "We've got about thirty minutes to get to your place and then to campus."

They hurried out of there and pulled onto campus barely five minutes late.

"My work schedule isn't etched in stone. It'll be fine. What do you usually do in the morning?" Ester asked, looking about as happy to be ending the date as he was.

"Normally, I catch up on sleep—not complaining—I thought I would go in with you and catch up on homework."

Ester's mouth dropped open, but no sound came out.

"Ester?"

"You want to come into the office with me? Everyone will know." Her voice rose in panic.

"No, they won't. Besides, you're crazy-hot. Why wouldn't you be getting any?"

"But that's why I wanted to go home to change clothes," Ester said.

"Do I embarrass you?" Theo asked. He tone was serious but his eyes were not.

Ester didn't smile.

Theo got out and opened her car door. He held out his hand. "No one cares. Let's go."

Ester blushed and took his hand. "Try to act normal. Let's come up with three things."

"Three things?"

"It's this thing Rayanne tells me to do when I get nervous about talking. I'm supposed to think of three things I can say."

Theo could barely hide his amusement. "We won't need three things. We met early to have coffee with Professor Stone."

"That makes no sense," Ester said. "What did we talk about?" She squeezed his hand with a mighty grip.

"No one is going to ask," he said.

When they arrived, the only person in the office was Arnie, whose reaction to the two of them arriving together was, "Theo! You can save me."

"Save you from what?" Theo said.

"I have a job for you," Arnie said.

"Arnie, let him study or he'll never come back," Ester said. She went straight for the coffee pot and poured them each a cup.

"Another time. I need to finish homework," Theo said, imagining the job Arnie would have. It was either moving furniture or carrying heavy boxes.

"Where is everyone?" Ester asked.

"They are at the longhouse discussing elder lunch. They said, and I quote, 'Tell Ester to get her tardy ass over there if she wants to live.'"

"Rayanne?" Ester asked.

"Who else? Linda would never say something like that."

"She wouldn't," Ester agreed. She gave Theo a nervous look. *You okay with this?*

Theo recalled the sight of her bouncing on top of him, her head lolling back and forth. He held her eyes until she blushed and backed out the door.

Arnie waved him over. "Let me show you." He fanned out a packet of documents: newsletters, printed webpages, meeting minutes, everything related to an inter-tribal government conference. "I have no staff and I need this now. My nephew is too busy. Katie said you are a terrific writer. I'm adequate but slow. I need a press release and an article we can put online."

"You want me to write things?"

"You're good at writing things," Arnie said.

He'd already met two Arnies. Family-man Arnie on the rez and then public-executive Arnie at the protest. This was another Arnie, a man who accomplished things. He needed something done and he would find someone to do it. He was asking but he would make it tough for Theo to say no. "Do you have samples?"

Arnie pulled a couple of sheets out and slid them over. "Plain and simple."

"When do you need it?"

Arnie chuckled. "Last week? National Association of Tribal Governments is meeting in our city soon. I'm overextended and then some."

"I can relate," Theo said. The issues were unfamiliar. He had no experience with tribal government, but he could follow the format easily enough. He checked the time. If he took care of Arnie's project, he'd be underprepared for class, again. However, he couldn't help being pleased that Arnie had asked.

"I'll give it a try," he said.

Arnie sighed with relief. "Thank you." He packed up his bag and put on his coat. "I have to run. I almost forgot to ask. Did you two see the movie?"

"We did," Theo said, not sure how much to say. "She's a good film-maker but Ester and I had a few questions."

"Great," Arnie said as he headed out. "She's showing it to me when I can get a minute. Tell Linda the good news."

So this must be Arnie the aggravating communicator that Ester had described. Theo didn't work for the center. Let Ester tell her about the film.

The door popped back open and Arnie stuck his head in. "You're getting paid, by the way. Keep track of your time."

Getting paid for writing. That was a new one. He immediately got to work on the article. By the time Ester and the others returned, he had finished what Arnie asked plus turned the material into one of his articles for class.

"I heard Arnie got you," Linda said, sounding genuinely apologetic.

Ester studied the screen over his shoulder. "What did he make you do?"

"Press releases. I enjoyed it. He asked you to send those to him. I gotta run. Can you walk me part way?"

He didn't miss the *I want to know everything* look Rayanne shot Ester as they headed out. He took her hand when they were outside.

"You don't mind I did a job for Arnie?"

"Why would I mind?"

"This is your place. I wanted to run it by you."

"No reason you can't be part of the place. He paying you?"

"He is. He told me to get his contact info from you. If he has more work, I'm interested."

Ester squeezed his hand. "Good. You'll be around."

They arrived at the media building. He pulled her close. "I'm always around for you. It's going to be tough figuring out when we can spend time together. This quarter is almost finished, but until then I'm buried."

He leaned down to kiss her. She tangled her fingers in his hair and pulled him close, rubbing up against him until he had to break away. "Hold that thought, I like it," he said.

"Next weekend?" Ester asked.

"Come hang out at Frenzy's. My place after."

"I don't mind dancing around by myself," Ester said. "But what if I get hit on? I don't get hit on a lot but when I do, it's always the creepiest goofball in the bar."

"I won't let anyone hit on you," Theo said.

"You'll be working," Ester said. "Can you do a weeknight?"

"Yeah, but then we gotta get going early. It would be nice to wake up on a Saturday morning and do morning-after activities." He held her chin and kissed her.

"I remember morning-after activities," Ester said.

"More relaxed. Make breakfast, fluff up the pillows, that kind of stuff."

"Next weekend," Ester said.

23

The Native professionals' mixer took place in the lobby of a new building downtown. Linda crossed the polished floor and stopped to admire an intricate light-fixture, like a fishing net spun from copper and frozen in midair. Miniature light bulbs hung like water droplets from the structure. Networking events weren't terrible but the tall sheets of tinted glass that made up the walls and church-door-sized abstract art pieces made her feel like she was in the wrong place. A temporary bar stood in one corner and about two dozen people milled around the room.

Audra spotted her and brought her a name tag.

"You made it," she said. Audra had on a business suit, heels and red lipstick, all looks Linda had tried and failed to pull off. She'd worn her same blue dress. She had a closet full of frumpy, and this one dress. Curse Rayanne for making her self-conscious about her wardrobe.

Audra wrote out Linda's name. "How do you spell your nation?"

"Y-U-R-O-K."

"Is that the same as Rayanne?"

"Nope. Downriver."

Audra laughed. "I'm sure that means something to you." She handed over the name tag. "Virgil will be here."

"We're still seeing each other," Linda said, but she understood Audra's caution. One of the pitfalls of setting up friends was if things didn't work out, the inevitable run-in.

"I wasn't sure," Audra said, seeming cheered by this information. "How are you two getting along?"

"Fine. Does it have to be all planned out or can we get to know each other? Can we enjoy not eating alone?"

"You can do whatever you want. Just making conversation."

"Sorry," Linda said. "Rayanne's been attentively quizzing me. She's a lovely girl but when she has an idea in her head, she can be ruthless."

"Share as you wish," Audra said.

They grabbed a glass of wine at the bar. There was another table with cheese and crackers and fruit but Linda never figured out how to balance a plate of food and eat while she had a glass of wine. "We talked about a trip to the coast for the weekend," she said.

"We're still talking about Virgil?"

"Yeah. I love the idea of getting away and having some nice dinners and wandering around on the beach."

"But not long nights alone with him?"

"It feels soon. But then I haven't done this dance in a while. Maybe I'm too uptight."

"Or he's the wrong person," Audra said."

"I can't figure it out tonight."

"Did I tell you I saw Arnie Jackson looking cozy with that film-maker the night of the protest?"

Linda caught her reflection in the glass. She looked unfinished, or like a person resigned to defeat. Something quick and cold squeezed her heart. When she answered, she was ashamed by the quaver in her voice. "Really?"

"You didn't know?"

Linda forced a laugh. "I got that impression but I don't keep up with Arnie's social life." Now that Audra confirmed it, she wondered why she'd doubted.

"Does it bother you?" Audra said.

"I don't care if Arnie is dating," Linda lied, bothered by how much she cared. "The entire time I've known him he's run around with women like her. Do I think it's a good idea he's canoodling the woman working on our film? No. But he's always had a way with ladies, he knows what he's doing." She reminded herself that she was wearing matching underwear and had a perfectly nice man waiting for her.

A random memory popped into her head: Arnie in college. One night he'd had a few too many beers and tracked her down at her dorm room where she was wearing sweatpants and reading for class. He talked her into walking over to the plaza near the student center to study the stars. From anyone else it might have sounded like a line, but she knew him well enough to understand he needed to talk. That didn't stop a little bit of hope from growing in her heart during their walk across campus.

The plaza was empty. He pointed to a park bench and they lay head-to-head, watching the sky. Arnie never stopped talking. He told stories about home, the rez, his grandma. He talked about his favorite dogs and what it was like picking huckleberries with his cousins. He had a favorite swimming spot, and he missed hunting with his brothers. He spoke as if these were things they were going to do together someday.

The night had been clear, and they were far enough from the light pollution to get a sense of the stars and haze of the milky way.

"What are things you miss about home?" he wanted to know. She'd known he meant her tribal place not her parents' place. She told him about hiking down to the river on a hot day and sitting with her grandpa and counting buzzards circling high up in the sky on a sunny afternoon.

"That's why I had to find you," Arnie said. "I didn't want to be around someone who doesn't understand what it means to be truly homesick."

It was going to be a long painful life if she was going to pine about Arnie while she was working with him. If she couldn't put it behind her, she had to pretend she could.

"Virgil is here, I'll leave you alone," Audra said.

Virgil crossed the room to join her. "Nice to see you," he said. He had an honest smile and had a sweet manner, like he would be terrific with kids or puppies. He wore suits. She liked a man in a suit. He was a good man, but there was no denying it, there was no spark. She wished for more certainty, but then, they were still getting to know each other. This was how people did that.

She tried to imagine herself as the kind of person who went off to the beach with a man she'd been out with a handful of times. He had a nice mouth. Strong jaw. Maybe.

"Nice to see you, too."

"Let the mixing begin," he said, rubbing his hands together. Linda was comfortable at networking events, but Virgil was a pro. He steered her through the room, introducing her to folks he worked with. She recognized a few faces and made a point of talking to them, too. The evening flew by. By the end of the event, she had a number of contacts, new ideas for funding, and a couple of possible inter-tribal promotions. Plus she'd met several people who would be great for the center if she ever got it running the way she wanted. She would drag her entire staff to the next get-together. Rayanne could bring Henry and Ester could bring Theo. Everyone would benefit from more connections in the local Native community.

At the end of the night, she stood at the bar with Virgil. Audra came and found them.

"Did you ever get a name from Paul Douglas?"

Linda shook her head. "Nothing we could use. I've given up on Paul Douglas. He's getting the run around, too. I need a new plan."

"Did Virgil tell you about his meeting?"

Virgil shook his head. "Listen to this, I have a tribal client. They mentioned this week they had a similar issue to your organization. They were supposed to collaborate on the use of a park located on officially city land but was once tribal territory. The city disappeared in the middle of the negotiations. No correspondence exiting the negotiations, they simply stopped answering calls."

"What does that mean?" Linda said.

"It means playing nice and patient is a worthless strategy," Audra said.

"We know that," Linda said.

"I'm not familiar enough with your organization to be certain," Virgil said, "but a snarly intent to sue letter might shake something loose."

"But if they ignore the letter then we need to follow through," Linda said.

"I think we have a decent argument they are in breach of contract," Audra said.

"Decent argument," Linda repeated.

Virgil smiled. "Decent argument is pretty good."

He had a nice smile.

"I'll give it some thought," she said.

"I'm saying goodbye to some folks. Meet you at the front door," Audra said.

She'd spent the last couple of hours at Virgil's side and had warmed to his company. He had a goofy charm to him.

"I'm traveling the next couple of weeks. Let's grab dinner when I get back," he said.

"That sounds great," Linda said. A couple more weeks to sort out her feelings.

he line for Frenzy's stretched down the street and around the block, much earlier than usual, no doubt due to the milder weather. Theo contacted Pete on the radio in case he wanted to swap spots earlier. Most evenings Theo didn't notice the time but now that he waited for Ester, his eye kept scanning the block, looking forward to seeing her curly hair and funny walk headed toward him.

Pete came out and took the radio. He would let her in when she arrived. The entire time Theo had worked there he'd never asked to let someone in. Pete promised he'd keep an eye out for her.

He took his time walking through the club. It was business as usual except for a shrieking bachelorette party that waved him over and insisted on taking his photo with the future bride. One of them tried to give him a twenty with instructions for the DJ.

"The DJ would rather talk to you than my ugly mug," he said, pushing the money back into her hands.

Fran worked the back bar, and he made his way to her. She rang up a customer and cleared the counter of empty bottles. When she finished, she plunked a glass of water in front of him.

"What's going on?" she said.

"I'm close to finishing the film project," he said. "You want to see it?"

"I don't know. Do I come off like a weirdo?"

"Not even close," Theo said. His kept his eyes fixed on the main door, willing Ester to arrive even though he knew she wouldn't be there for another hour.

"I recognize that look," Fran said. "But not on you."

"There is no look," Theo said, doing his best to adopt his all-business bouncer face.

"Your friend is more than a friend." It wasn't a question.

"Could be," Theo said with a small smile. "Why do you say not on me?"

"You meet tons of women but you never pause over a single one. Now you have an elated shine coming off you like you won the lottery. You really like her, the one from the park?"

Theo leaned forward. "She's smart. She's sweet. She's funny. And she's red like me."

Fran laughed. "I didn't realize that was important to you."

"I didn't either. She's way too good for me but I will enjoy it as long as it lasts."

"Why wouldn't it last?"

"I have nothing to offer. Not even time. No way to make it work."

"People who like each other figure out how to make it work," Fran said.

"It's not that simple," Theo said.

"It never is," Fran said.

Theo didn't elaborate. "She's coming in tonight. Can you keep an eye on her while I work?"

"Does she need keeping an eye on?"

"Let me try again. Can we save her a seat so she can hang out at the bar and not...?" He made a motion with his hand.

"And not get swept away by some other dude with shiny shoes and a slick pick-up line?" Fran had a playful look on her face but he wasn't in the mood for jokes.

Fran picked up on it. "You got it bad. She can sit back here if she wants. Why don't you bring her to Pete's tonight? She can hang out with the group."

Theo gave it one second and then shook his head. "We don't get to spend that much time together. We're gonna pass."

"You mean, you're new. You can't keep your hands off each other," Fran said. Before he responded, she said, "I get it. I'm envious. You still owe me for the film. Can you bring a couple buckets of ice back?"

Theo followed orders.

ESTER TOOK the bus downtown and walked to the nightlife area. Every other doorway was a restaurant or bar. Different music drifted out from open doors and smokers stood out front puffing into the night. She walked around the block to Frenzy's.

The line was huge and Theo wasn't the bouncer at the door. She stood on the sidewalk, not sure what to do.

"Ester!" The other bouncer was Theo's friend, Pete. He moved from his place at the door and flapped his hand at her. Everyone in the line turned to look at her. These were all the cool people with their fine outfits and intelligent use of accessories. She wore black pants and a bright blue ultra-soft sweater Rayanne had picked out and her usual ratty coat. It didn't matter because the goal was to impress Theo, not these people.

She walked to the front of the line. Pete nodded at the door without saying another word.

Ester went in with the sound of dismayed voices rising behind her.

It was strange walking into the club alone. The vibration of the music grew stronger as she walked down the dark hallway. She recognized the song and hummed along, a bounce coming into her step. She came into the packed main room. A smoky haze hovered over the crowded dance floor. The place hadn't been so busy on Jack's birthday. She waited for her eyes to adjust to the murky light.

Now what? *Meet me at the club,* he'd said. She hadn't considered what to do once she got there. She pushed her way through the crush,

PAMELA SANDERSON

hanging on to her backpack. The main bar was jammed, so she
changed course, thinking a corner upstairs would help her to get her
bearings.

Then Theo was there, his lips to her ear. "Hey, gorgeous. I was
worried you changed your mind." He pulled her bag off her shoulder
and grabbed her hand and took her to the smaller bar at the rear of
the club where it was incrementally quieter.

There was a bar stool at the side with a jacket on it. Theo helped
her take her coat off and draped that over the stool as well and she
sat down.

"Remember Fran?"

"You keep a yarn stash back there?" Ester asked.

"I wish." Fran took Ester's bag from Theo and stowed it behind
the bar.

Theo rested a big warm hand on her leg. His face was inches from
hers, a lusty gleam in his eye. "I'll check in on you when I can. You
dancing?"

"Unless someone can stop me," Ester said. Already her shoulders
were shimmying in time with the music.

"I look forward to that." And he was gone again.

Fran set a frosty glass of beer in front of her and winked. The back
bar was crowded too, and she was fascinated to watch Fran work. She
always seemed to be doing three things at once, taking a drink order
while pouring into the glasses lined up in front of her, then running a
card, and tossing a napkin down to mop up a spill.

Ester sipped the beer and turned her attention to the dance floor.

Fran stopped by and said, "If you want to dance, go ahead. I'll save
your corner."

Ester jumped off the stool and made her way to the dance floor.
She had danced by herself before but not in a place like this. She
danced her way into the middle of the dance floor like she owned it
and bumped along with the beat.

Rayanne liked to say it was hard to make sense of the Ester who
was quiet around strangers when she became a flailing dancing queen
the minute the music started. But she liked the sensation of finding

172

the beat and following it with her body. She danced until she was breathless, threading through the crowd pulsing to the music. When she returned to her bar stool, it was open as Fran had promised.

The crowd at the back bar had eased a bit. She scanned the room but didn't see Theo.

Fran brought her a fresh beer. "Someone got unruly. Theo had to walk him out. Most everyone backs down when they see him."

Talking to the tall blonde women made Ester nervous but hearing her talk in the park about her troubles made her seem like a friend.

"How long have you known Theo?"

"We worked together a little over a year but it took a while to get to know him. He's so…" She used her arms to indicate tall and wide, then crossed her arms and made a mean face. "He terrified me at first." She laughed. "Now he's a good friend."

She couldn't help asking, "Has he had lots of girlfriends?"

Fran shook her head as if the thought was absurd. "You're the first one who's done a number on him. He's got it bad for you." Fran covered her mouth with her hand as if she'd said too much. She went down the bar to serve a customer.

Ester had it bad for him, too, which Fran had already figured out. Ester kept alert, hoping for Theo to reappear. Hanging out at the club alone was fun at first but now she was ready for the next part of the night to begin.

Someone stopped at the bar. She assumed it was a customer, so she paid no attention until he said, "You waiting for someone?"

"More or less," Ester said. A guy about her age stood next to her. It was too early to tell whether he was creepy, but he was unsteady on his feet.

He moved closer. Whatever magic line divided personal space from too close, he was teetering over it. "You're not sure?"

"My boy— My friend—" Her mind garbled over her status with Theo. They hadn't talked about what they were. "I'm here with someone," she said.

"Sure," the guy said, unconvinced. "You mind if I get a drink while I wait for my friends?"

Nope, he was creepy.

"Do whatever you want," Ester said. Unfortunately the guy took that as encouragement.

～

THEO LIKED the idea of having Ester at the club, but now that she was there, he couldn't stay focused on the job. His eyes would scan the room and then drift until he found her. He wasn't sure how much time he spent watching her do her thing on the dance floor shaking her tail with her arms pumping up and down. She would have caught his eye even if he didn't already know her. Later she'd stayed back in the corner, pushing her hair out of her face. She sipped her beer and laughed at something Fran said.

Then she would glance around the room.

He'd invited her to come to a club filled with people trying to hook up, and asked her to sit by herself or dance by herself. It didn't seem like such a terrible idea at the time.

He got called to escort someone out and then there was a scuffle on the sidewalk. By the time he took care of that and returned to the main room, there was a guy talking to Ester at the bar.

Something fierce jabbed at him and he crossed the room in a flash. He stood next to her with his arm behind her on the bar, giving the guy a cold stare. In seconds the guy backed up and disappeared into the crowd.

"Oh no, you made him forget his drink," Ester said, her eyes teasing. "I should go find him."

"He can come back if he wants it," Theo said, nuzzling her as much as he dared at work.

"Told you," Ester said. "It's always the creeps and goofballs who talk to plain girls like me."

"You're not even close to plain, Ester."

"With crazy hair and gangly limbs," Ester added.

"Your limbs are perfect," Theo said.

"You have to say that. I let you touch them."

174

"And only me," Theo said, surprised by his protective impulse.

"Look at you. All worked up and chest-thumpy. Do I need to worry about that?"

"Never. You are free to leave with anyone you want or go home alone."

"Good to know." She pretended to scope out the room. Then she grabbed a handful of his shirt and pulled him close and said so that only he could hear, "I'm going to be very aggressive with your man-thing later."

Theo's man-thing stirred at the words and hot breath in his ear. "I can't wait."

Fran caught his attention and pointed across the club. There was a woman crying and pulling another woman's arm.

"I'm needed," he said. "Leave a note if you decide to leave without me."

Ester put her finger to her mouth as if to think about it.

As PACKED as the club was when Ester arrived, once it was last call, things wound down quickly. Theo cleared people out from upstairs. Fran put away freshly cleaned glassware and wiped down the bar. The music changed over to classic rock. The houselights came on and everything magical about the club disappeared.

Fran returned her backpack and she pulled her coat back on. The sweatshirt on the stool belonged to Theo, and she hugged it to her.

Theo came and found her. "Lucky me, you're still here."

"I didn't get a better offer," she said and handed him his sweatshirt.

Fran came out from bar. "Invitation stands. Pete's for burgers and beer. You want to join us?"

Ester hoped he wouldn't ask for her vote. Fran was so nice, it might be rude to blow them off.

"Nope." Theo put on his sweatshirt and took Ester's hand and led her out the door.

"You didn't ask me if I wanted to go," she said.

"Do you?"

"No."

"We're out of here," Theo said.

The trip back to his apartment happened in a rush but once they got there, everything slowed down, like the plan for the evening had changed and no one bothered to tell her. Theo yawned and fell back on the bed. He put his hands behind his head and watched her with sleepy eyes.

"You ready for bed?" she asked.

He nodded. She kicked off her shoes and sat on the edge of the mattress.

"You're sleepy?"

He nodded again. Disappointment flooded through her. At least cuddling was better than nothing. "Should I turn off the light?"

"Do you want to do it in the dark?"

"I thought you wanted to go to sleep."

Theo grinned. "What were you thinking?"

"You have done this before?" she teased. She took her time pulling off his shoes.

"Not like this, with you," Theo said.

"What's like this?" Ester said.

"I never bring anyone here," he said.

Ester stopped. "What do you mean you never bring anyone here?"

"I've never brought anyone here. No friend, family or other person has seen where I live. Except for you."

Ester's heart cracked open another level. She crawled up to him and hugged him. "That's kinda sad."

"Sometimes you need to stay focused on getting through the day," Theo said, his hands still behind his head.

"This tender moment is nice and everything but I've got some itching I'd like scratched," Ester said.

"I'm waiting for you to get aggressive with my man-thing," Theo said.

Her eyes traveled to the place where his man-thing was, currently hidden in his pants. "I said that, didn't I?" She didn't want to admit she was uncertain. It was obvious what she wanted; it would be nice if he got things going.

"Change your mind?"

Ester shook her head. She ran her fingertips along his forearm, tickling the soft skin at the crease of his elbow. "I thought you'd work your moves," she whispered.

"Anything particular?" Theo said. "Maybe you can think of three things."

Ester's cheeks went pink. "I can think of more than three things," she grumbled.

Theo lowered his face to hers and bit her lower lip. Her heartbeat pounded down to her feet.

"Tell me what you want," Theo said.

"More of this kind of thing," Ester said.

"You can do better than that," Theo said. He gazed at her with steamy lust, but his hands stayed put.

"I want you to rub your man-bits all over me," Ester said.

Theo broke into a lazy bad-boy smile but didn't laugh. "That's a start." He pulled her on top of him so she straddled the man-bits. "Anything else?" he asked.

Ester rocked her hips until his breath hitched. She made a rolling motion with her hand.

Theo narrowed his eyes. "You want to change the sheets?"

"Finally. You guessed," Ester said, pretending to be cross. "I hung out at a meat-market by myself all night and now I'm sitting around some cute guy's apartment because I want to help him with the sheets."

"You think I'm cute?"

"You're okay," Ester said. She leaned forward, her hair swinging into her face and after the briefest hesitation to make sure she lined their lips up, she kissed him. His lips were warm and soft and tasted like sunshine on a warm summer day. She kissed him again, this time stroking her tongue along his lower lip.

Theo groaned.

"Oh yeah?" Ester said. "Hold that thought." She flipped off the overhead light and switched on the desk lamp. She grabbed a bunch of condoms from her backpack and threw them on the pillow.

"I have some of those this time," Theo said.

"Good for you," Ester said. "We don't need to get all of them out at once."

"We might."

"Stay there and look pretty. I'm about to have my way with you," Ester said.

Theo cracked up. "About time."

"If you're laughing, I'm doing it wrong," Ester said.

"No, you're not. You're doing it perfect. I watched you in the computer lab and you were so quiet and methodical. And now you're here with me and you're wide open and amazing."

"The sweet-talking will get you nowhere," Ester said. She yanked at his sweatshirt until he pulled it over his head, then pushed his shirt up until he peeled that off, too.

∼

THEO COULDN'T THINK straight with Ester stroking her hands across his chest, that intense look on her face, like she was defusing a bomb. Her cheeks were flushed, and her breath came out in short, hot bursts. A trembling in his knees surprised him; this woman had that much effect on him.

He reached to catch her mouth, but she ignored him and, instead, kissed a trail down from his collarbone—skipping a huge swathe of skin to bite down on his nipple.

"That was a manly grunt," Ester said. "Do you need me to stop?" She flicked her tongue over it while she waited for him to answer.

Theo mumbled a sound that he hoped she could interpret. He put his hands back behind his head and forced himself to keep them there. He was about to burst out of his pants. He thrust his hips forward until she noticed and shifted her attention. She lightly stroked the back of one hand over the front of his jeans.

"Ester," he gasped, his hands reaching for her, "I can't wait any

178

longer."

He pulled her sweater off and unclasped her bra while she tugged at his waistband. In short order they were both pantsless, bodies entwined.

"Give me a sec, Theo."

She put on the condom then squirmed beneath him. Just the sound of his name in her scratchy voice made him crazy. They moved together, a blur of heat and sensation. He couldn't get enough of her mouth, her tongue sliding against his. He slid one hand down to her ass and angled her pelvis up to his. The sounds that came out of her urged him on faster, the bed thumping beneath them. He shook everywhere at once, all the waves cresting in one place—mind, body, and spirit in the same place at the same time. He came down from it slowly, his face pressed into her neck. Her legs remained hooked around his waist.

Ester sighed. "Wow, it's been a long time since someone did that to me."

Theo propped himself up to look at her.

She grinned. "Just kidding. Only you." She tangled her fingers in his hair and kissed him.

He rolled over to his back and pulled her onto his chest and stroked his hands along her back.

"Are we a thing?" she asked.

"What's a thing?"

"You know."

"I don't know. Is there some official thing we're supposed to do?"

Ester sighed. "Yes. Theo Dunne, will you be my boyfriend?"

Theo's heart sped up, all the protections he'd laid there went creaky. All the stories he'd told himself about why this shouldn't happen were forgotten. "I am your boyfriend. Will you be my girlfriend?"

"I have to think about it," Ester said.

She joked, but the sentiment was the correct one. He wrapped his arms around her and held her tight, imagining he could feel her heart beating against his. "Tell me when you decide," he said.

25

*E*ster was still weak in the knees after Theo dropped her off. She watched his car drive away, ticking off all the morning-after things they had done. Fooling around when they woke up. Check. Fooling around in the shower. Check. Tidying up the disarray of the bedclothes and fluffing the pillows. Check. Making cow eyes and kissy faces over a bowl of oatmeal. Check.

She could get used to this boyfriend thing.

As delightful as advertised, she would tell Rayanne when she saw her.

She floated into the house in a blissful haze, remembering the sense of his skin brushing against hers. The way he spoke, his voice soft when they were intertwined together. The way he whispered her name. He had spent so much time hanging back and now it was like he didn't want to let her go, always a hand on her hip or his fingers searching for hers.

Inside the house, the door to her room—which had been firmly shut when she left—was ajar. Inside, nothing looked out of the place, but she had so much crap stacked around there was no way to be sure.

She emptied the dirty clothes from her backpack and pulled out her laundry. She sorted out enough for a load and headed to the basement. At the bottom of the stairs, she found MacKenzie dumping dirty clothes into the washer.

"Oh, hi. You must have just gotten home."

MacKenzie could do laundry anytime. She could do it at her own damn place.

Ester turned around to go back upstairs, determined to hang on to her euphoria.

"You going to be around all day?" MacKenzie asked.

"I live here," Ester said.

"No problem," MacKenzie said, as if it had anything to do with her. "I wondered since you have a boyfriend now."

Ester went back upstairs. Dennis's bedroom door was wide open. On the bed sat the hard-to-miss silver and blue shopping bag from Big Stop Outdoor Store, the same store of her missing gift card. Next to the bag sat pair of winter boots. Not a pair of make-do, get-you-through, practical boots. No, these were fancy leather boots, with a fuzzy trim.

"You like those?" Dennis said, finding her. "She had a gift card and picked them out at the end-of-winter sale."

"They're lovely," Ester said, picking one up. The tag had one of those goofy high-tech names: WinRTech Performance Boot with breathable lining. "Did you give her the gift card?"

"I have no idea where she got it," Dennis said. "Listen, I don't want this to be weird but she thinks you don't like her."

Ester put the boot back down, wondering if now was the time to say something like, *Does your girlfriend steal soup?* Instead she said, "I didn't mean to give that impression."

"She thinks you hide when she's around, like you're avoiding us."

Ester did avoid them but perhaps it wasn't their fault. Maybe she needed to try harder to get along with MacKenzie. The Big Stop Outdoor Store was a popular store. The boots didn't prove anything, but it was hard to ignore her suspicions.

"I'm glad you found someone," is what finally came out.

"I'm glad you found someone, too," Dennis said. "We're going out this afternoon but we'll be home tonight. Will you be at Theo's?"

Ester shrugged. "He has to work. I have a work thing tomorrow. I planned to watch movies."

"That sounds fun," Dennis said. "We can do like the old days and have a theme. Initiate MacKenzie into movie night."

"That sounds great," Ester said, wishing she meant it.

She went back to her room and closed the door. The spy cam was back in its box since she'd discovered Tommy's mournful presence in the office late at night. That was enough unwelcome discoveries. Dennis liked his girlfriend and wanted them all to get along. But she wanted to be sure. She set up the camera in her room.

26

---

*A*rnie showed up at the address she gave him, a new bistro in one of the trendy restaurant rows. Inside, the light was buttery yellow. The tables were small and cozy, with cloth napkins and piano music coming from the speakers. He'd dressed for it, but this place signaled a get-together more serious than the one he'd signed up for. The plan was to go over elder lunch. Here they were with heavy cutlery and stemware.

Katie stood and waved from a cozy table in the corner. Little black dress, hair pinned back in a fancy 'do, lipstick. Somehow he'd ended up at a meal different from the one he prepared for.

"Hey," he said when he reached the table. "Hope you haven't waited long." She offered her cheek, which he kissed quickly and dryly. She smelled good, and the dress displayed a peek at intriguing cleavage. He could adjust his expectations.

"How was your day?" she asked.

"I was at home this morning. I cleaned up weather debris around Grandma's place. She sent me over to another aged relative who needed a clogged drain cleared. I'm out there doing the important work."

A server came over to pour water and give them menus. "This

looks interesting," Arnie said, scanning the entrees for choices that resembled red meat and potatoes. His nephew gave him grief for his narrow palate but a man liked what a man liked. "How about you?"

"Movie done. I spent the entire day working on it. It's ready to submit to festivals. I'm looking forward to celebrating tonight," she said.

"What an accomplishment," Arnie said, trying not to get hung up on the word *celebrating*.

"I have ideas for expanding your film. We should create a story with the festival circuit in mind."

"Not *my* film," Arnie said. He could already hear Linda's protests, her voice taking on a wavering pitch that meant she was annoyed with him. She would worry about who was paying for it and how would film festivals build the relationships they needed. "Crooked Rock is a group effort. My contributions are minor."

"Perhaps you see it that way," Katie said. "You pick the wine."

Arnie picked up the wine list and did a double-take when he saw the prices. If it had been up to him, they would have met at a brew pub and had burgers and tots.

"Sure," he said, trying to remember what he'd learned about wine. His sister liked the red with the silver lion on the label, and that was all he could come up with. When the time came, he confidently chose the third-cheapest bottle.

Katie folded her menu and set it on her plate. "How do you manage all the back and forth?"

Arnie laughed. "I'm not sure I am managing. My mom says I do too many things poorly instead of one or two things well. She's entitled to her opinion."

They paused while the server poured the wine. Arnie raised his glass to hers. "To your film."

"And to our film," she said, tinking her glass against his. "You don't get along with your mother?"

"We get along fine. You know how moms are. To get to your question, sometimes, the time on the road wears me down, but for now it's necessary."

"Theo's piece on you was interesting. His insight was the conflict between your ties to your home place and family, and your commitment to the work that needs to be done."

"He nailed it. My offer to help is serious; he's a smart kid."

"He is a frustrating student, but he's got a lot going on."

"He said he works a lot. I hired him to write for my committee. The pay isn't great but better than delivering pizzas or whatever he's doing."

"There must be others who can do it. Why him?"

"That's the mission. We want our people working for our people."

She considered that for a moment and he waited for her comment. Instead, she steered the conversation to local restaurants and favorite foods. She didn't get out a lot but when she did, she liked to try new places. She talked about the challenges of teaching and asked questions about politics on the rez.

By the time the entrees came, his doubts had faded. She made a joke about a local politician Arnie had dealt with and made him laugh. This was exactly the kind of woman he was attracted to, the kind he chased after when he'd had more time for chasing. Or more like the kind who used to chase after him. It was nice being chased. Her confidence was attractive. He admired her brains and ambition.

She'd ordered fish with a fancy sauce she convinced him to sample and teased him about the vegetables he left on his plate. The food was delicious, and the conversation was easy. He couldn't remember the last time he'd been out for fun. Except he wasn't. This was a business dinner. The servers cleared away the dinner plates and Katie ordered a single dessert and two forks.

Arnie asked, "My team will murder me if we don't discuss elder lunch. How do we make the film part go smoothly?"

"What events will unfold?"

"Elders come in and get served lunch," Arnie said. "The staff arrives early to work in the kitchen. You could show how they make it happen. They are a fun group. The center has a bus and Tommy will go pick up folks to bring them over."

Katie thought about it. "Is there anything cultural?"

"The whole thing," Arnie said. "If you want specifics, there will be a group of veterans. They always make for good stories."

"What about dancing or singing?"

Arnie shook his head. He'd suggested Linda add entertainment to the event, but she said with the small staff, they needed to stick to the basics. He didn't push the issue with her. "Not for this."

"Oh," she said, making no effort to hide her disappointment. "People associate certain images with Native Americans. I want images and sounds they will grab onto."

"I understand where you're coming from," Arnie said. But he understood Ester's concerns, too. Katie wanted to rely on a particular image to tell their story. Well, they'd hired an experienced filmmaker, they needed to trust her.

"You'll have plenty to use," he said.

The servers took away the last of the plates and brushed the crumbs from the table. Arnie paid the bill and walked her to her car, still uncertain what his move would be.

"Where do you stay when you're in town?" she asked with exaggerated casualness.

Arnie smiled. He always appreciated a direct approach. One benefit of dating as you got older, there didn't have to be so much guesswork.

"I stay with my sister, Tildy. Her place is between downtown and the road out to the rez."

"She expecting you?"

"She is," he said, wavering on his commitment to going over there. He needed to stay professional. Linda would not approve. "And tomorrow, I need to be up bright and early."

"Me too," she agreed, gazing into his eyes. She came over and kissed him softly but with promise.

"Next time," she said.

---

27

*E*ster used her phone camera to zoom in on hands forming meatballs.

"Henry is giving us lessons in handling his balls," Rayanne said. They were in the longhouse kitchen prepping for elder lunch.

Ester laughed. "I might want to use this for something. Keep it clean."

"Our hands are perfectly clean for ball-handling," Rayanne said.

Tommy held up the meatball he was working on. "Is this how you like it, Henry?" He took his time caressing the meatball with his fingers.

Ester collapsed against a stainless steel counter, shaking with laughter.

"That's enough," Linda said, although she was smiling, too. "Technically, this is sexual harassment although I'm not sure who the victim is."

Henry put his hand to his heart and pouted.

"Toughen up, pal." Linda checked the time. "Food going out when we said it will? We can't have elders rioting."

"Close enough," Henry said. "Time to get the sauce going. Rayanne wisely suggested we use store-bought bread product so that part will be a snap."

"No frybread?" Tommy and Ester said together.

Rayanne made a face.

"The elders will complain if there's no frybread," Linda said.

"Hard cheese," Henry said. "They can have toasty garlic bread or plain white rolls with butter. Or they can eat at home."

"A pox on those frybread-yearning elders," Ester said.

"Green salad and a berry cobbler for dessert," Henry said.

"That's kind of boring," Tommy said.

"They are coming for the company," Linda said. "You did great, Henry."

Ester caught Henry's pleased smile on camera.

Someone knocked on the main longhouse door. Linda washed her hands before going out to open it.

Ester peeked out the kitchen doors. "It's them," she hissed.

"They came in together?" Rayanne said. She hurried to watch over Ester's shoulder. "What do you think?"

Arnie carried the big camera case and had a bag on his shoulder. Professor Stone carried an additional bag. They both looked freshly showered and cheerful but their body language didn't scream sex happened.

"Inconclusive," Ester said.

"What's going on?" Tommy said.

Rayanne put her hand to her lips. "Arnie had a date with Professor Stone last night."

"So?" Tommy said.

"Don't tell Linda," Ester said. "I want this to be a good day for her."

"Why would Linda care if Arnie—?"

Ester gave him a look. Must be nice to go through life so clueless. Linda returned to the kitchen with them. Professor Stone eyed their meatball production line with a bland smile.

"Morning," Ester said in a loud voice. She put her phone away.

"My, aren't you cheerful?" Arnie set the hard case on the floor and dropped the bag on top of it. "Didn't you used to hate mornings?" He patted Ester's shoulder as he walked by to get to the coffee.

Ester caught Rayanne's eye and smirked. "Depends on the kind of morning it is."

Rayanne choked back laughter.

"Katie?" he asked, holding up a cup. She nodded.

Linda washed her hands again and dug into the pan of meat as if making meatballs was her last chance to save the world.

Arnie brought the cup to Professor Stone. If they'd been doing it, they would exchange a loopy grin. Nope, they stayed all business. If Arnie had stayed with her, they would have already had coffee at her place. Unless they fluffed the pillows and had to rush to get to the longhouse on time.

Ester pulled out a big box of paper napkins and fumbled to open it. Arnie pulled out a pocketknife and slit it open.

He mimicked her knowing tone. "Where's your friend, Theo?"

Oops. Lesson learned—don't underestimate Arnie.

Ester blinked before blushing with the force of a second-degree burn. *I didn't have THAT kind of morning,* she wanted to protest. Instead she grabbed a pile of napkins and folded them in half with the precision of an engineer.

"Where *is* Theo?" Professor Stone asked, taking the coffee from Arnie.

"I have no idea," Ester said. "I haven't talked to him since yesterday."

"He hasn't contacted me at all," Professor Stone said. "Ester, I'd like you to give me a hand today." Much as she enjoyed working with Professor Stone, elder lunch would be busy for the staff and she didn't want to abandon her friends.

But Linda nodded that it was okay. "Henry and Rayanne can holler for you when they need you."

Professor Stone picked up her bag and Ester grabbed the other. Arnie dragged the case out into the main room. The staff had set up the tables but hadn't decorated them yet.

"How many are showing up?" Arnie asked.

"We invited thirty elders so we're prepping for ninety," Ester said.

"Sounds about right," Arnie said.

"Why?" Professor Stone said, a questioning look on her face.

Arnie laughed. "You must be new to Indian Country."

Ester helped Professor Stone get out the equipment she wanted and stashed the rest out of the way. They walked through the table set-up and talked over how the event would unfold. Ester had a few ideas but chickened out when Professor Stone explained how she planned to work. As the morning progressed, delicious smells filled the room. Ester's stomach growled as she decorated the tables. A few people had arrived already.

She checked her phone but still no word from Theo. Something had to be wrong.

Arnie disappeared but about the time she was ready to grumble about it, he returned. He held the door open and a diminutive elder hobbled in using a rolling walker.

"Margie!" Ester called. She used her phone to film Margie's progress into the room. Arnie tried to take her elbow, but she jerked it away.

"I can move fine. Let me be," she said. "You young men can't keep your hands off me."

Arnie laughed and backed away.

Ester skipped across the room to give Margie a hug. "I've missed you," she told the elder.

"I miss you, too," Margie said.

They had a special table reserved for VIPs and Ester guided her to a seat.

A loud engine rattle announced the arrival of the bus. Ester searched for Professor Stone but she was busy talking to a group of veterans. Ester ran out to get clips of Tommy helping the elders climb off the bus.

"Gus!" she called. She ran over to hug Rayanne's grandpa when he was safely off the bus. "You here with the band?"

"You bet," he said, hugging her back. Gus was part of an elder inter-tribal drum group. "Where's my granddaughter?"

"Making food," Ester said. She stepped back to film a shot of the others as they got off the bus, and then ushered them into the long-house. She would offer the clips to Professor Stone later.

In the midst of everything, she saw Theo run across the parking lot.

～

THE MOVING JOB had taken twice as long as scheduled. Theo returned to a dead car battery followed by an endless wait for a jump. Then an accident had the freeway backed up and by the time he figured out the problem, he was stuck in it.

Ester standing outside the front of the longhouse was the best thing he'd seen all day.

"Did I miss anything?" He reached for her but she pulled away.

"You're late," she said.

"I'm aware there's a problem," he said, trying to take her hand. "The moving job ran late—"

"You took a moving job?"

"I'm not getting paid for this. You know how it is for me." Ester's ire was an unexpected jab when he was already on edge. "The last thing I need is you on my case." The words came out angrier than he'd intended.

She blinked in surprise.

He took a deep breath and tried one more time. "I could use a hug."

"Sorry you're having a bad day," Ester said. She put her arms around his waist. He pulled her close and inhaled her sweetness.

"Things going okay in there?" he asked.

Ester made a dismissive grunting sound.

"You here to work?" Professor Stone called from the door to the longhouse.

"She's mad," Ester whispered.

He would have been shocked if she weren't. "On my way," he said.

He pulled a thumb drive out of his pocket and handed it to Ester.

"For me?" she said with exaggerated delight. "You shouldn't have. People will talk."

Theo kissed the top of her head. "I'll explain later."

Inside the longhouse, Theo found another version of the chaos he'd experienced with Arnie's family, except here they had more elders and no dogs. Kids tore around long tables filled with visitors. Bursts of laughter floated from every corner of the room. The food smelled incredible.

Ester followed him with a finger crooked into his back pocket. She said, "I'm doing a lap with a pitcher of drinks. There's a plate of food for you in the kitchen when you can get away. I have a lot to tell you." She gave him a quick kiss on the cheek and slipped through the crowd. He watched after her with longing.

"Focus, Dunne," Professor Stone said, her mouth a hard line.

"Sorry, I—"

She held up her hand. "It's not important. Let's get the work done."

The next hour passed in a blur. The relaxed and informed film-maker who'd shown up in Warm Springs had turned into a person who misunderstood the room. When Professor Stone spotted an elder she wanted to talk to, she pushed into the conversation. Theo would move in and talk about the film and coax them into answering a few questions. The elders were more inclined to talk to Theo, which only intensified Professor Stone's irritation. She communicated with abrupt hand gestures and two-word orders.

They got through a brisk interview with Linda and then a longer back and forth with Arnie, which earned the only genuine smile from Professor Stone all day.

Theo sighed with relief when the crowd thinned. As people began to make their way out, Ester found them again.

"Professor Stone, would you like to interview Margie? She founded the center and now she—"

"We can interview Margie," Professor Stone said.

They followed Ester to a tiny gray-haired woman with bright eyes.

"Margie, this is Professor Stone. She's the one helping the center with the film. And, uh, this is Theo."

Margie shook Professor Stone's hand. She gave Theo a careful once-over before nodding approvingly at Ester. Theo wanted to make a smart remark but not in front of Professor Stone.

They set up the equipment for the interview. Ester stayed out of Professor Stone's sight, filming on her phone.

"What were you hoping to accomplish when you founded the Crooked Rock Urban Indian Center?" Professor Stone asked.

Margie gestured at the room. "This. Bringing our people together. Some folks get lost when they're in the city. We want them to have a place where they're welcome like home."

"Can you speak specifically about programs the center offers that address problems in the Native American community?"

"I thought that's what I was doing," Margie said. There was no mistaking her impatient scowl.

Professor Stone closed her eyes. She took a deep breath. "What about mentioning specific programs? For example, addressing alcoholism or unemployment? What issues do Native Americans face living in an urban area?"

"When our people are away from home, they feel like a piece of them is missing. This is a place for them to fill the empty spot. The programs enable us to stay together."

Ester tucked her phone away and gave Margie a hug. "We thank you for it every day." Margie smiled and patted her arms. Theo's heart opened up at the easy affection that passed between them.

"Thanks, Margie," Professor Stone said. To Theo, she said, "I'm ready to pack up."

"Got it," he said. "Nice to meet you, Margie."

"I'll see you again," she said with a flirty smile.

Theo traded a grin with Ester before going off to put the gear away.

Professor Stone worked with him, winding up cables and stowing them away. "What about you?" she said. "Do you feel less lost?"

She'd been so pissy with him since he'd arrived, he misunderstood her question for sarcasm, but when he looked at her, she was sincere. Theo thought about it. The first time he'd seen Ester with her friends at the club, he'd admired their camaraderie. Then there was the day with Arnie's family and again here in the longhouse. He was surrounded by Indian people and there was a sense of something he couldn't articulate. With Ester, he thought of it as peacefulness. Here, with the group, an unfamiliar sense of belonging expanded in his heart. Out in his everyday life, on campus or his endless jobs, a part of him stayed wary. That part turned off when he was here.

"It sounds goofy but yeah, I do."

"It doesn't sound goofy," Professor Stone said.

Out at her car, they loaded up the equipment. She slammed the back door shut. "I need to talk to you," she said.

"Sounds ominous," he said, but he knew what was coming.

"I've given you so many chances. So many last chances..." She glanced up at the sky, searching for words. "Do you care about this?"

"I'm doing the best I can," Theo said.

"I know you're in a tough position," Professor Stone said, "but I can't reward someone because he means well. You missed most of the day."

He wanted to speak, but her look made him stay quiet.

"I want my students to succeed but I'm feeling taken advantage of."

Theo stared into the distance. Making up for missed schoolwork by working on her film had always been a fragile proposition, but he thought he could balance the time. "Honestly, I want to pass this class."

"You have to pass the class, otherwise you have no financial aid. You haven't done the work. Your final project was lazy, thrown-together work."

That was like a cold punch in the gut because it wasn't true. He'd put a lot of work into his final project. He'd spent time with Fran's knitting friends in the yarn shop and at their get-togethers. He'd researched other yarn art projects around town. He didn't have a lot to work with due to his time constraints but he'd put together a story, as the assignment called for.

"Sorry, Theo, being smart but lazy can only get you so far."

"Am I failing your class?"

"I don't see what choice I have," Professor Stone said.

Any number of arguments came to mind, but the set look on her face made clear the time for negotiation had passed. He'd done his best and failed.

"Thanks for giving me a chance," Theo said. He looked her in the eye and shook her hand and then returned to the longhouse. Everything was about to change quickly and there was no way to stop it.

~

"YOU'RE POOPED," Ester said as she dragged Theo into the kitchen. She slid an extra paper plate under the soggy one heaped with the lunch she'd saved for him and pushed the food into his hands. She guided him to an empty sliver of counter space and handed him a plastic fork. "Sorry, the meatballs are kinda stingy." She turned to Rayanne. "No ball jokes, please."

"Thanks, Ester," Theo said, gloomier than she'd ever seen him. She guessed Professor Stone was on his case. She wanted to be the one to make the troubles go away.

"This is delicious," Theo said. "Thanks, guys."

"Anytime," Henry said. "Join us for beer after this?"

Theo shook his head. "I'm driving tonight."

Off of Henry's questioning look, he explained, "Rideshare. That's one of my side gigs. Another time, for sure."

Ester sprinted around the cramped kitchen with the rest of the staff, anxious to finish the clean up. Even Arnie had his sleeves rolled up and wrestled with the sink nozzle and a big metal dish.

Theo sat hunched over his plate, shoving forkful after forkful into his mouth as if he were in a contest for joyless eating.

Ester's heart sank. She found a pitcher of punch that hadn't been dumped yet and poured him a glass.

"Something happen with Professor Stone?"

Theo shook his head and stabbed another forkful of spaghetti. "Let me enjoy being here with your friends."

"They're your friends, too," Ester said. She gave him a quick squeeze. "More hugs later."

Theo nodded, something like defeat in his eyes.

PAMELA SANDERSON

"Looked like the filming went well," Arnie said, oblivious to their quiet moment. "Did she get what she wanted?"

"If you like clips of elders getting interrupted while they're eating, then yes—today was a win," Ester said.

Arnie's expression turned to annoyance. He dropped the clean dish on the counter with a clatter.

"What do you think, Theo?" Arnie asked.

"I missed most of it, which is why I'm in big trouble with the professor." He offered a regretful smile. "She has a specific idea of what images of Indian people will convey a message. Whether those images will help with what you're trying to do, I don't know."

"I'm sure it's better than you think," Arnie said. He dried his hands and rolled his sleeves back down. "I'm driving back to the rez tonight, so I'm out of here."

Rayanne and Linda traded a knowing glance. Henry and Tommy started trading dumb jokes, so Ester took her phone out to get a few last shots of the gang cleaning up. Theo laughed along with them a few times, but mostly he kept quiet, his eyes on his plate. Ester pushed back the creeping uneasiness.

They finished mopping up and carried out the trash. Linda locked up the longhouse while Henry urged them to go to the bar one more time.

"You should join them," Theo said. "I'm not good company right now. Don't sit out on my account." His face remained blank, his voice emotionless. Whatever was going on, he was keeping it to himself.

"I'd rather hang out with you," she said, reaching for his hand.

"Not tonight," he said, pulling back.

The words froze in her heart. "Will you drive me home?" She didn't know what she would do if he said no.

"If you want."

Ester waved goodbye to the others. She unlocked her bike and wheeled it beside her as they walked to his car. The campus was quiet. The only sound was the soft click from her bike.

"Did I do something?" Ester asked.

"This isn't about you." Theo rubbed the back of his neck. "Professor Stone is failing me."

The heavy knot in Ester's stomach loosened. She suppressed a huge sigh of relief. "Because you were late?"

Theo chuckled. "More than that. This isn't the first time I was late. She gave me many chances."

"But you caught up on all your work. You turned in your final project."

"She said it was lazy work."

Theo's gait grew faster. Ester struggled to keep up with him. "That can't be the end of it. Can you do it over?"

"No," Theo said. "Even if she would accept it, which is unlikely, she thinks I've been disrespectful, and maybe I have although not intentionally. I don't have time to do it over."

He was ahead of her now. His car sat in the middle of the parking lot. She waited for him to open it so she could load her bike but instead he turned around and leaned against it. He radiated a dangerous mixture of frustration and anger.

"You can finish the other classes. Try to do better next quarter," Ester said. She wanted to hug him but his body was not inviting.

"Remember, if I fail, no more financial aid."

If Theo lost financial aid, he was out of school. If he left school, he would go back home. The heaviness returned along with an odd sensation of falling.

"What happens now?" she asked.

Theo rubbed his face with his hands and heaved a weary sigh. "I don't know what choice I have."

"You're going home now, just like that?" Ester said. He was smart and worked hard. There had to be another chance, plus they had this thing between them.

Theo's eyes went dark. "Not *just like that.* I've busted my ass trying to make this thing work. I've done everything I can."

"You said school was the most important thing."

"It is. It was. Not every story ends with everyone getting what they want."

"Maybe this is one of those decisions you're not thinking through." Ester tried to keep her voice calm.

"I tried my best. I wasn't good enough. What's the matter, you don't want me if I don't finish school?" Theo's voice rose louder.

If she wasn't so sure of him, she might be afraid. "I don't want you if you're going to give up so easily on something you said was important to you," Ester said, the words coming out in a sob. He wasn't just giving up on school, he was giving up on them. She cleared her throat and met his gaze so he wouldn't think she was crying.

Theo's face was dark with outrage. "Who are you to get on my case about giving up easily? At least I showed up and tried. You hide in your sad little room with your stuff piled in boxes and let your roommate's girlfriend push you around. You could kick her ass. And your film work is a million times better than *Katie's*, but instead of doing something about it you bury yourself in a job you don't like because you're terrified of putting yourself out there. Oh no, what if I end up living in a car? You survived."

Luckily she had her bike to hang on to because her knees went watery. His words stung not just because they were true but because of the cold delivery. "Why are you picking on me?" she said, her own voice rising with outrage. "You finally have a...a tribe here and people rooting for you and you're ditching us."

He shook his head. "I have to get out of here. I told you from the start this was never going to work. No point in dragging it out."

Ester opened and closed her mouth, not sure what to say. She didn't want him to leave, but she didn't want them to keep yelling either. It couldn't be ending like this.

On the inside she was still falling, only faster now. He got out his car keys and opened the door. She waited for him to say something, or for the right words to come to her, but there was nothing.

The world moved in slow motion. He didn't say goodbye. He got in the car and drove away.

28

$\mathcal{E}$ster parked the bike in the garage and entered the house. MacKenzie called to her but Ester headed straight for her room and closed the door. She curled up on the bed and replayed the conversation in a dark loop in her head, trying to pinpoint the moment when the conversation shifted from *this is what happened* to *this is over*. Where might she have said something different to change the outcome? She shouldn't have yelled at him.

They were finished, and he was packing up his tiny apartment. Then he would be gone. She closed her eyes. A painful surge of desperation flooded through her. She should have told him she didn't want him to leave. *Don't leave.* Those are the words she should have repeated over and over until he changed his mind. She pressed her hand to the aching spot in her chest. They couldn't be finished. They were barely started. And he had to finish school.

She opened her eyes. The door to the closet stood ajar, and a sweater had fallen into a heap on the floor. She sat up and studied her room. Her laptop was on the dresser along with a stack of library books. The metal tin that once held chocolates and now held loose change sat next to them.

The shower caddy with her toiletries hung off the back of a chair.

But something was missing. Her eyes flicked around the room several times until she realized what it was: the condom treasure chest was gone. Linda had let her take it home and she kept it next to her bed.

Ester grabbed the laptop. The spy camera was supposed to reassure her that nothing was going on. Dennis wouldn't let his girlfriend steal from her. But when she pulled up the footage, MacKenzie wandered through her room, methodically opening and closing drawers. Ester's blood boiled watching her poke around her closet before opening the funny little box and leaving the room with it.

Her body knotted up in a mixture of fury and betrayal. She grabbed her wallet and rode her bike to the hardware store. When she returned, Dennis was back, his car parked in the driveway.

She grabbed a screwdriver from the toolbox Dennis kept in the garage and stomped into the house. MacKenzie read a recipe off of her phone while Dennis stirred something on the stove.

"Hey, Ester," Dennis said. "How did the lunch thing go?"

"It sucked and I have a problem with your girlfriend," Ester said. She went back to her room to replace the doorknob.

Dennis and MacKenzie carried on a muffled conversation in the kitchen, most likely Dennis wondering what the hell was going on and MacKenzie telling him that she would deal with it. MacKenzie came to the hallway to watch her.

Ester had a hard time getting the screws out with her hands so shaky. She took a deep breath and kept at it.

"I don't think that's legal," MacKenzie said.

"You know what's not legal? Stealing," Ester said.

"We might have to charge your damage deposit when you move out," MacKenzie said.

"I didn't make a damage deposit and I don't rent from you," Ester said, her voice rising. She took the old parts and dropped them into the bag from the hardware store.

Dennis came from the kitchen in time to see her fasten the new doorknob to the door.

"What's going on, E?"

"Your girlfriend steals my stuff," Ester said, closer to tears than she would have preferred.

"Oh come on," Dennis said, his tone light. "There has to be a mistake."

"Is there? Have you seen any frizzy-hair products in your bathroom? Because I can't find mine. Have you enjoyed any Aunt Barbara's soup? Because four cans disappeared from the kitchen. How about that bag from Big Stop Outdoor Store? I had a hundred-and-fifty-dollar gift card from my parents for that store because I need a new coat. The card vanished."

"Those are all common items. If you lost them, it doesn't mean I took them," MacKenzie said.

"Mac, could you let us talk alone for a sec?" Dennis said. He and MacKenzie spoke in low voices before MacKenzie left them alone.

Dennis shrugged. "I don't know what to say. She says she hasn't stolen anything. She has her own money. There's no reason for her to take your stuff."

"Did she recently come up with a yellow cardboard box shaped like a treasure chest with condoms in it?" Ester asked.

A strange look passed over Dennis's face. "Mac?"

"It isn't even full," MacKenzie said, returning to the hallway. "I've had it forever." She'd been eavesdropping the entire time.

Dennis looked more uncertain.

Ester finished tightening all the screws and then shut the door and tested the key. She shut the bedroom door and handed Dennis the bag with the old parts.

"I have video of her snooping around my room," Ester told him, every word precise. "The video shows her walking out with my condom treasure chest, which was a gift from my friend Rayanne who won it at a bachelorette party. I would show you the clip now but I want to set it to a moody song first."

"She's never liked me," MacKenzie said. "She's making trouble between us so we don't kick her out."

Ester pushed down a fresh burst of rage. An argument with that woman wouldn't accomplish anything.

Dennis stared at MacKenzie with dismay and confusion. Ester didn't envy him. He really liked his girlfriend but the spy cam didn't lie.

Ester unlocked her door and packed a backpack. She had no place to go, but she'd figure it out later. When she went back through the house, MacKenzie sat on the couch, sniffling into a tissue. Dennis wasn't around.

"Are you getting your boyfriend to beat me up?" MacKenzie folded her trembling hands in her lap.

"Wow, you're sure invested in being the victim," Ester said.

MacKenzie wiped her sleeve across her eyes.

"Let me guess, you're afraid of him because he's brown. Theo doesn't beat-up women. And he's not my boyfriend."

She found Dennis in the backyard, scraping the barbecue grill with a cheap, long-handled tool.

"Sorry," she said.

"Don't be sorry," he said, chipping at the crust. "I'm the one who should be sorry. I had no idea that was going on. She's good to me. I wish—" The scraper's plastic handle snapped, and he threw both pieces across the yard. His shoulders slumped forward and he hung his head. There was nothing to say.

"I'm leaving. I'll be back tomorrow." She walked on the outside of the house so she wouldn't have to see MacKenzie again. She got on her bike and rode away.

heo took the stairs to his apartment two at a time. Since the day he moved in, he told himself he could be out in half a day. The clock was ticking. Once inside, he was distracted by the sight of the unmade bed. It had been a long day and he'd only gotten a few hours of sleep between the time he got home from Frenzy's and the time he had to take off for the moving job. He'd been fighting off a bone-crushing weariness all afternoon.

He needed to rest, except the minute he stopped moving he would think about Ester and the ache in his chest. The boxes from the move-in were broken down and stored behind the dresser. He got them out, then searched for the packing tape.

The words he'd said to her replayed in his head. He couldn't shut them out. He'd run himself into the ground and, when it went wrong, had taken it out on the best thing that ever happened to him. He was alone again.

The meal she saved for him sat heavy in his gut and left a sour taste in his throat. This reminded him of all the worst things he'd done in his life, like dropping out of school or wrecking his mother's car or taking money from her wallet when money was tight. It made him sick to remember how bad he'd been to his mother.

He reconstructed the first box and pulled clothes out of the closet. He was tempted to shove everything in as fast as he could but he needed to use care to make it fit in a single car-load. What had Ester said about this place...*kinda sad?*

He rolled his clothes into tight bundles. When he'd moved in, the pared down approach seemed advantageous. Now, all he could think about was Ester's look of pity when he told her how easy it would be to move out.

No matter how great their thing was, this ending was inevitable. Ester was never going to end up with a guy like him. She thought he was okay now, but it was only a matter of time before she realized how little he had to offer.

He checked the time. He needed to call his mom and tell her what was going on but hadn't figured out what to say. She would be crushed to learn he dropped out. He'd done his best, and this was how it ended. Any ideas for the future were drowned in the thought of everything he was running out on. His lease wasn't up until summer. Jess would be left without his most reliable mover. Frenzy's would need a new bouncer. Plus, quitting school now meant he was giving up the classes that he was actually passing.

He filled the box in front of him, then pushed it aside and assembled another.

He spotted a scrap of black fabric balled up on the floor and grabbed it and shook it out. A pair of Ester's panties. Any other woman and he would assume she'd left them on purpose, but not Ester. Now she had one less set of matching underwear.

He paused with them in his hand, not sure what to do. He couldn't throw them in the trash. Tossing them in the laundry didn't make sense. He threw them on the bed; he would figure it out later.

He was shoving things into box number three, when his phone rang. There was no one he wanted to talk to, and it was too late in the day for a moving job. It was a surprise to see Arnie's name on the display.

"This is Theo."

"Bad time?" Arnie said.

It's all bad time, Theo wanted to say but instead he said, "Not really. What do you need?"

"I'm in a pinch. It's not a great job, but the pay is good."

Theo had no interest, but he asked anyway, "What is it?"

"I need an intern coordinator."

Theo tried to imagine what an intern coordinator might do and what skills Arnie thought he had that would lead him to call. "You called me?"

"You did great with the other work. It's National Association of Tribal Governments. It's a great networking opportunity for you," Arnie said.

It was like Theo had stumbled into someone else's conversation. Arnie had the wrong idea if he thought Theo was a guy with something to network about.

The unpacked boxes leaned against the bed, ready to be filled and loaded into the car. "I can't—"

"The timing is terrible, I know. You've got school and all your jobs. It's enough money to cover some of your jobs. It'll be a time sink during the conference but we can accommodate for school as needed. School is the priority."

Those were Ester's words. *School is the most important thing*. When she'd said it, he'd taken it like she was scolding him. When Arnie said it, it was a bitter reminder of what people expected from him.

"I appreciate the thought but I wouldn't have the first idea how to—"

"You think I know what I'm doing?" Arnie laughed. "I've been faking it for over a decade. Common sense and confident words can take you far. There's an intern meeting tomorrow night. I'll text you the details. All you need to do is show up."

"You're not going to let me say no," Theo said without humor.

Arnie laughed again. "I'm not. See you then."

Theo stacked the packed boxes against the wall and put the unassembled boxes back behind the dresser. Arnie bought him some time to figure out what to say to his mom. Maybe he could make some calls about job training so he would be set up when he got there.

His books still sat on the kitchen table. In his head he'd already given up on school, but now that he was going to be in town, might as well finish the quarter.

30

---

    *E*ster rode her bike in a slow circle around the neighborhood, regretting her decision to take off. The sky had grown dark and she had no money for a motel. She didn't want to bother Rayanne, and Margie would give her a place to stay but Ester wasn't in the mood for explaining. She thought about hanging out at a coffee shop all night. She could worry about the rest later, except she didn't want to be in a coffee shop. Elder lunch had produced some great film clips and she wanted to work on her film. She rode to the office. Campus was deserted for the night. She spotted two people on the path from the library but otherwise it was quiet.

    Once inside, the florescent lights glared bright at the late hour. While her computer booted up, she considered making coffee but didn't want to keep herself up all night. Instead, she heated a pot of water. Linda always kept tea in her desk and she searched around until she found a packet of something fruity that said no caffeine.

    She glanced at her phone. She and Theo had gotten into the habit of talking on Sunday nights. He would call and tell her about his rides and how much homework he'd caught up with. She would tell her the latest on MacKenzie or talk about her progress with her film.

    "I am not thinking about him," she said. Her voice sounded small and shaky in the empty room. The phone battery had dwindled, so she dug into her backpack for her charger. Instead she found the thumb drive Theo had given her. He'd never told her what was on it. She stuck it in her computer and found an audio file.

Her finger hovered over the mouse button. She wasn't certain she wanted to hear it, whatever it was. What kind of sound file would Theo give her? She left it on the desktop and opened her film project. If only the computer lab were open at night, it was so much easier to work on the better equipment. She fussed with new clips from lunch, uncertain about length and the best places to cut. Theo always had good feedback when she needed a fresh pair of eyes.

"Don't think about him," she said, saying the words out loud to solidify her determination.

She added the new clips to the work in progress, weaving comments Linda had made about the center with images of the elders. She waited for long stretches while the software ground away on the old computer. She talked herself through the process, explaining her choices and acting like it was normal to be at the office late Sunday night with nowhere to go and no one to talk to.

When she could no longer resist it, she clicked on the file Theo had given her.

"I did a couple of versions to give you some ideas," Theo said on the recording. Then, with a different inflection, he began:

Community. Family. Tribe. Home.

Everyone wants a place to belong.

We gather for support, culture and identity, finding comfort in a place filled with our own.

A single tear slid down her cheek and she wiped it away. He'd taken her description of the project and arranged the words into a story. His warm and familiar voice was reassuring as he talked about the center and all the things they wanted to do.

She listened to both versions before bringing her film back up, her eyes glued to the work. She broke down each step down, and reviewed each cut and effect. It was tough to resist the urge to listen to his voice again.

The office door rattled with a key. She practically jumped out of her seat. Tommy stood at the door.

"What are you doing here?" he asked, his expression troubled.

"What are *you* doing here?"

Tommy shook his head. "I asked you first."

She started to make a joke and say, *Problems at home,* except the words choked at the back of her throat, so she shrugged and made a pointed look at the computer as if that would answer his question.

"Do you need a ride home?"

The image of MacKenzie rooting around in her closet and drawers made her stomach flip. She shook her head. She mustered every bit of calm and sincerity she had in her. "I'm fine."

"Is there someplace else you would rather go?"

Ester nodded and then the tears came. "Sorry," she said, trying to hold back.

Tommy came over and touched her arm. He wasn't usually demonstrative and her heart was wound up so tight, this gesture of tenderness took her by surprise. She sobbed for real. "Sorry," she repeated.

"It's okay," Tommy said. He patted her on the back with the awkward sort of pats that you'd get if you burst into tears in front of a doctor or a UPS driver.

She gulped a few times and calmed herself. "I know you hate dealing with this."

"Not true. I grew up in a family of alcoholics. This is nothing. You're coming with me." Ester was too upset to object. She saved her project, and they sat there while the computer creaked and hummed.

"It's slow," Ester said, wiping her hands over her face.

"I know how it feels," Tommy said.

He waited for her to pack up, then he led her to a beat-up Toyota with the back crunched in.

"Did a giant truck use you to stop?" she asked. Her throat hurt and she ached with exhaustion, but she already felt better now that she was with someone she trusted.

"Something like that," Tommy said. "The trunk won't open so put your bag in the back seat."

"I always picture you driving the bus now," Ester said, once inside. The car smelled like old coffee but it wasn't messy.

"I love the bus, but the fuel gets expensive," Tommy said. He turned the radio to something quiet and Ester relaxed. Tommy didn't ask any questions. Friendships that didn't require a lot of talking were underrated.

Tommy lived in a shabby duplex just off a busy street. Inside, he sat her on the couch and gave her a fleece blanket with a cartoon character on it. He returned from the kitchen with a glass of apple juice. "Do we need—?" He pretended to dab at his eyes.

"Are we talking now?"

"Only if you want to." He set a box of tissues on the arm of the couch.

"What's at the office late on a Sunday night?" Ester asked. She'd still never told anyone about seeing him on the spy cam.

Somewhere in the apartment a door opened, accompanied by a sound like weeping.

"That's why," Tommy said. "My cousin."

"I had no idea you lived with anyone."

Tommy ran his hand through his hair. "I don't."

A creaky voice came from the other room. "Do you have a friend over?"

"Excuse me," Tommy said, rising from his seat. Two hushed voices came from the hallway but she couldn't make out what they said. The other voice rose in distress but eventually quieted again.

When he returned, Ester said, "Is everything okay?"

Tommy sighed. "I'd like to keep this private."

"Who would I tell?" Ester said.

"Work. Everyone would be supportive but I want to keep it to myself," Tommy said.

"Keep what to yourself?"

"Tommy's halfway house," He tried to sound upbeat as he swept his arm around the room. "I shouldn't joke. Not long ago my uncle wanted to sober up, and since I've been successful, Mom suggested he stay with me. She doesn't understand why that's a terrible idea. Sobriety is more than not drinking. But, surprise, he succeeded, so then he sent his daughter. Her case is a little more serious. Sometimes, when I need to be alone, I go to the office and watch movies on the computer."

"Isn't it good, you're helping people?"

"Do you want to be the sober house for your family?"

"I guess not," she said, trying to reconcile this Tommy—serious and responsible—with the guy who had carved out a job where his main duties included playing basketball and driving a bus.

"What happened to you?" he asked.

"I got proof Dennis's girlfriend steals from me; our dumb job— what are we even accomplishing?—and now it's show-time with Arnie and Professor Stone's movie like that's going to save us; I'm always stressed about money; oh, and I got mad at Theo and he broke up with me." She choked back a sob.

"It's okay not to be fine, Ester."

"It's exhausting."

A quiet moment passed. Tommy's apartment was surprisingly normal. He had a big TV and a gaming console. A tall bookcase with a full shelf of Tony Hillerman in hardcover stood in one corner. Another shelf bowed under the weight of giant cookbooks.

"Those all yours?" she asked.

Tommy's gaze followed hers. "Yeah."

"All this time I pictured you living in a tree house or a secret bunker. Something mysterious."

Tommy smiled. "Keep thinking that."

"How did you do it? Quit alcohol. You were so young."

Tommy fiddled with his sleeves, pushing them up to the elbow and then pulling them back down again. The cuffs were stretched out like bell-bottom pants. "It's hard to explain," he said. "If it was easy to change, to quit, to stop destroying yourself, people would do it. But that's how it happens. You get to the point where you decide. You decide to ask for help. You decide not to fight the help you think you don't want. You decide you're tired of feeling miserable and disappointed in yourself. Yeah, I was young but I could see my future and I didn't want it. So I did one thing, then I did the next thing. Parts of it were miserable."

"You decided. You don't have a box of magic here somewhere?"

"I do," Tommy said. He left the room, and when he returned, he presented her with a closed fist.

"Nothing alive?"

"No," Tommy said. He opened his hand to reveal a smooth gray stone. "This is a sacred rock of my people. It will give you whatever you want. Well, in the realistic realm of the world you live in and the problems you have to solve."

"That's quite a qualification for a magic rock," she said, taking it from him.

"It's not magic, it's sacred." Tommy sat back down.

"You're making this up," Ester said.

Tommy shrugged. "Talk to the rock and see what happens."

"I am. For science." Ester yawned so hard it hurt her face. "I'm sleepy."

"Me, too. I want you to sleep in my bed," Tommy said. "Lock the door."

Ester couldn't hide her alarm.

"She won't hurt you but she might come in and try to talk to you. She has trouble sleeping. If I stay out here on the couch, she's more likely to pester me."

"When we joke about how mysterious you are, I envisioned it as being something more fun," she said. "Thanks for rescuing me."

When she got to his room, she set the rock on his bureau and told it, "More courage. For all of us."

31

Theo hiked through the conference center, searching for "Manzanita." The rooms didn't have numbers, they had names like Cedar and Ponderosa, which didn't help when everything was beige walls and brown doors. As soon as he found Arnie he was out of there. Arnie would just have to deal with it. The more he thought about it, the more ridiculous the proposal sounded. He had no idea how to coordinate people, especially for a big event. It was better to show up as a grunt worker and follow instructions while the rest of it was up to someone else. Arnie needed to find someone better suited for the job.

He rode down an escalator and walked under a banner welcoming people to a convention for the flooring industry. A hand-lettered sign that said "NATG," directed him down another hallway.

Ester would have made a joke about the Ind'ns being an afterthought stuck into the worst corner of the events center. He couldn't stop thinking about Ester. Something that great shouldn't have ended so badly, but dealing with disappointing people was wearing him down to nothing. He still hadn't told his folks or his grandma he was leaving school. Ester was supposed to be his refuge, not another person to let down. She'd said the words: she didn't want him. It was best to leave it alone.

He should probably talk to Professor Stone, too. For what it was worth, she was right. She had given him a chance. Lots of chances. It wasn't her fault his situation was so precarious. That was his own decision.

"Theo!" Arnie's shout echoed down the corridor. He struggled through a heavy door with a crummy hand truck, one arm looped around a stack of boxes that wanted to slide off. Theo ran over and grabbed the door until Arnie pushed the cart through.

"These things come out of the factory half-broken." Arnie kicked the wheels with the toe of his boot.

"It's overloaded," Theo said, picking up the top box and hoisting it onto his shoulder.

"Story of my life." Arnie reset the rest of the boxes and pointed ahead. "I'm glad you're here. I forgot how squirrelly college kids are. You get a half dozen in a room and their hormones go ballistic."

"I'm a college student," he said automatically. Soon that wouldn't be true.

"You don't have a squirrelly bone in your body," Arnie said. "You're going to be the one to reel them in."

"I wanted to ask you about that," Theo said.

"One sec," Arnie said. He nodded at another door. Theo held it open while Arnie pushed the cart. Inside, four young men and five young women waited. Once again, Theo found himself in a room full of Indians. He set the box down on the table.

Arnie said, "You all have better things to do, so we'll make this quick. Theo, these are nieces, nephews and friends from the rez. Guys, this is Theo. He's the one in charge of wrangling you. Introduce yourselves later. You all are the latest in a long history of successful interns who began their careers making packets." Arnie gestured to the stacked boxes. "One of each item per folder. Put the finished folders in the empty boxes. Start now, while I talk. Tomorrow morning there will be more people to help finish them up."

Arnie searched his pockets with growing frustration. Theo

reached into his front pocket and pulled out a pocket knife, which he held up with a questioning eyebrow.

"That's it," Arnie said. "I must have left mine somewhere."

Theo set two tables end-to-end and then cut open each box and lined up the conference materials on either side, assembly-line style. It didn't take long to catch on to what Arnie meant. The guys sized him up one way and the women in another. The ladies elbowed each other until one of them went to great pains to catch his eye. This was Arnie's family. Theo made a point of returning his most paternal smile and gestured they should come up and get started. They assembled packets while Arnie talked about the days ahead.

"Once the conference starts, we'll be in this entire half of the convention center. We've got Ind'n leaders from all over the country. Your job is to help people find their meeting rooms, answer questions about the city, and assist presenters as needed. Theo will hold the schedule and tell you where to go."

The packets came together quickly. Theo didn't miss the nudging and whispering among the interns. He tried to remember if he'd ever been like that.

Arnie lectured them on proper behavior, appropriate dress, and how to network. "What's the point of being an intern if you don't get anything out of it? If you plan to work in Indian Country, this is a great place to meet people."

Theo tried to imagine all these leaders who were so eager to meet a bunch of college kids. He had nothing to say to someone like that. He needed Ester's three things.

Arnie wrapped up the meeting and told them when to be back. Theo packed up the completed folders for distribution in the morning.

One of the women came over to him. "A bunch of us are going out after this."

He appreciated the gesture. Until he'd hung out with Ester, he didn't realize how much he missed having friends and doing things with other people. But he saw the interest in her eyes. She was pretty, but even if she weren't connected to Arnie, she wasn't his type. At the moment his heart was still tied up with an Eastern Shoshone with big brown eyes and messy brown hair who was busy forgetting about him.

"Maybe another time."

"I'll keep that in mind," she said with a smile before hurrying back to her friends.

Arnie had his phone to his ear. He waved at Theo. "Do you have time to go to dinner?"

"Is there any point in saying no?"

Arnie laughed. "We're on our way," he said into the phone. They headed toward a steak house across the street from the convention center.

As if sensing his unease, Arnie said, "Don't worry. My treat. You got something to wear to the conference?" Arnie had on a suit that probably cost two weeks' worth of moving jobs and ride sharing.

"I don't have a suit," he said.

"Slacks and a shirt with a collar?"

He'd had a similar conversation with Pete when he interviewed for the job at Frenzy's. "I clean up good."

"Just checking. It's not for my benefit, it's for yours," Arnie said. "This is a good event for you."

Theo didn't have the heart to explain he was headed back home to live with his folks. Once there, he would ponder the options that would put his aptitude for physical labor to good use.

Inside the restaurant, Arnie waved to someone in a booth. "I got another job for you. My cousin works for a regional timber association."

Before Theo could object, he was shaking hands with a short man with skinny legs and a round belly.

"This is Derek," Arnie said.

"You're not what I thought," Derek said. He used one hand to shield his eyes as if looking up to a great height.

"I get that a lot," Theo said.

"Who's your people?" Derek asked.

"Jicarilla Apache."

"I haven't been down that way," Derek said.

"It's a long way from here," Theo said.

"That's how it is in the west," Derek said as they settled into their seats. "Meat and bread going to be okay?"

"Any food is fine," Theo said. "Thanks for taking care of me."

They put in their orders and talked about sports and local issues. Arnie and Derek went back and forth about a family dispute that involved Auntie June's chickens and the use of a shed. Theo had no problem finishing everything set in front of him, even the green salad, before they finally got down to business.

"Our organization needs conference coverage," Derek said. "We want you to act as a reporter. Summarize what's going on for our website. Short, sweet bites. Short film clips. Later you can write it all up for the tribal paper."

Theo gave Arnie a questioning look.

"You'll have time," Arnie said.

Theo didn't think Arnie had a clue about how much time it would take, but this was exactly what Professor Stone's class had trained him for.

"Try to talk to some of the speakers, if you can. Get behind-the-scenes nuggets." Derek folded his hands in front of him. "We got budget to pay you."

"I'd be getting paid for two jobs at the same time?" Theo said.

"You're a natural," Arnie said. Derek laughed.

"We can introduce you to others in the association. We could use someone regular," Derek said.

"One thing at a time," Theo said. He'd left the house planning to get out of this so he could finish packing and get all this behind him. But he liked these people and the work sounded okay, too. He let the idea roll around in his head. Derek and Arnie discussed various tribal issues and the upcoming conference. They spoke about forestry and policy goals. He tried to follow.

"What do you think of all this?" Derek said with a grin. "You work with tribal organizations before?"

Theo exhaled. "No. I get called when they need muscle. Not..." Theo made a vague gesture. "It's a lot to take in."

"Anything here work for class?" Arnie asked.

"What do you mean?" Theo asked.

"Like when you interviewed me, can you work some of this stuff into a class project?"

"Class is finished," Theo said.

"I thought Katie said you had another week or two."

"Not for me," he said. Off Arnie's questioning look he added, "I'm not passing her class. I was already on iffy ground with my financial aid so I'm done."

"I'm disappointed to hear that," Arnie said. His concern sounded genuine, which somehow made Theo feel worse. "Is there anything I can do?"

"Like talk me up with my instructor?" Theo said, raising an eyebrow.

Arnie traded a quick look with Derek, then laughed. "That's complicated."

"I don't need to know," Theo said.

"I'd like to hear," Derek said.

"Later," Arnie said. "Don't say anything to Ester. I don't want everyone gossiping about something when I don't even know what it is."

"Not a problem. The thing with Ester is finished, too," Theo said.

"Wow, you're having a bad week. Ester's a good one. I'd fix it if you can. You find a good Native woman, don't screw it up."

"He would know," Derek said.

"I am the reigning champion of missed opportunities," Arnie agreed. "Don't give up on school. It might not be as bad as you think. Were you planning to transfer to the university in town or go somewhere else?"

Theo shook his head. "I hadn't planned for that at all. You know, the whole financial thing."

Arnie brushed the statement away. "There are all kinds of scholarships. We can get you taken care of."

"They don't give money to people like me," Theo said.

"People like what?" Arnie said. Derek made a face as if he were offended.

But it was obvious, he was a big brown guy who intimidated people by walking into a room. No one looked at him and thought, *This guy is good scholarship material.*

"You're serious, aren't you?" Arnie said. "You're smart, you're hard-working. That's the kind of person who wins scholarships. Derek's organization gives out scholarships. Kiss his flat brown ass."

"No, don't," Derek said.

Arnie paid the bill and stuck the receipt in his wallet. "Don't give up. We'll talk more about it. I'll see you when the conference starts."

The only reason Theo had shown up was to tell Arnie he had the wrong guy, and somehow he had two jobs and a crazy notion that school could work out. If there was one thing he wanted to learn from Arnie, it was how to trick people into doing things they had no intention of doing.

32

*T*ime dragged when your heart was torn in two. Every time she closed her eyes she saw his apartment stripped bare and his silver car driving away. Every once in awhile she'd tap out a text to him that she'd just as quickly delete.

Back at the house, she and Dennis spent their evenings in different rooms, both of them shuffling around in their own miserable haze. She slogged through the work day thinking about new programs with no idea what the future held. In the evenings she worked on her movie, adding in Theo's voice-over and fine-tuning each scene because it kept her mind focused.

Rayanne wanted to talk but she wasn't up for it. She kept Tommy's secret and felt closer to him after that. With NATG in town, the week was packed. Linda fretted about their presentation and Professor Stone's film, which would take place in a few days. Arnie said at least twenty local tribal leaders planned to attend, but Professor Stone still hadn't produced a final film, and everyone was tense with so much riding on this one thing.

"It's here," Linda called from her desk. "I almost gave up. It's downloading. Ester, can you set this thing up?"

"I'm on it," Ester said, squishing Linda aside to work at her keyboard.

Linda texted someone on her phone. The phone chimed back and Linda exhaled in an angry huff.

"Boss?" Ester said.

"Nothing. He's watching it with her," she said in an unhappy voice. "We'll do a conference call with them after we've seen it."

"We're ready," Ester said. She expanded it so it filled the computer screen and the four of them crowded around the monitor.

An Indian flute trilled. The blurry picture slowly came into focus on a cluster of high-rises downtown under a cold winter sky. A series of images: a tree with an overflowing garbage can next to it, a lone bicyclist riding along the river path. There was a big fountain in the park by the river and a shawl dancer twirled in slow motion with a line of city buildings behind her.

"Who is that?" Linda asked.

"The dancing looks good," Tommy said.

Rayanne patted Tommy's arm. "You're adorable. What does that have to do with anything?"

"She's setting the stage," Ester said. "The tone. A tribal person, alone and contrasted with the urban landscape."

The flute music rose and fell and then drums came in. The dancer moved mournfully around the fountain. Linda stared at her keyboard as if there were a solution there.

"Watch, boss. You need an informed opinion," Ester told her.

"I have an opinion," Linda grumbled.

The scene dissolved and the next scene showed the room where they were currently sitting, all four of them bent over computers.

"We look good when we're working," Linda said.

"Well, that's the message we want to convey," Rayanne said.

The film did a series of cuts with the rise and the fall of the music. An elder sitting by herself gazing sadly at something out of sight. The same shot of the crying kid with the dirty face in Warm Springs that she'd used in her personal film. An unflattering angle of Linda sorting through a stack of paper at a harried clip.

"Do I really have that many chins?" Linda said.

"No one has that many chins," Ester said. "It's a terrible shot."

By the time the film faded, a gloomy shadow had parked over the room.

Linda squeezed her forehead as if staving off a terrible headache. "Is that what an outsider sees when they visit our organization?"

"I hated it," Rayanne said.

"You need to make it constructive criticism when we talk to Arnie," Linda said.

Ester sorted through her impressions. The film itself was fine. She'd done a lot with what little she had, creating a story about urban Indian people. But it wasn't working. Why were they all sharing this reaction?

The office phone rang and Linda picked it up.

"It's them," she mouthed. "We just finished. Hang on, let me put it on speaker." Linda muted the phone. "I think Professor Stone is with him so be diplomatic."

Rayanne made a face.

"We're all here," Linda said, taking the phone off mute.

"It's a great piece of filmmaking but not in the spirit of what we need," Ester said.

Now it was Linda's turn to make a face.

"What? That was diplomatic," Ester mouthed.

Arnie chuckled. "Thank you, Ester. I want to hear what Linda thinks."

Linda took her time before she said, "I'm still processing what I saw. It covered a lot of ground image-wise but a few bits of narration could fill in."

"That's along the lines of what we thought. Pretty pictures but the message isn't getting across," Arnie said.

Linda traded puzzled looks with Rayanne and Ester. Tommy flipped through a sports magazine.

"Who's we?" Rayanne asked.

"Oh, sorry," Arnie said. "I'm here with Theo."

Ester's stomach flipped at the sound of his name. Tommy set the magazine aside. They all looked at her. "Where are you?" she asked, a slight waver in her voice.

"Conference center," Theo said. "Someone tricked me into doing work I am completely unsuited for."

"I thought you left town," Ester said, a painful mixture of longing and hope stirring her up inside.

"Plan changed."

Ester had so many questions. She realized the others all watched her, and she shook her head and sat back. For now, Theo was in town and working with Arnie.

Linda leaned toward the speaker. "I'm not sure it does what we need, but we've booked a room and promoted a movie."

"You could do it without if you had to," Arnie said. "You're great in front of a group."

Linda gave the phone a disgusted glare. "Let's work with what we have. Are you, uh, talking to her?"

"Conference is keeping me busy. I have to go. I'll see you at the session," Arnie said. Ester noticed he didn't answer the question.

"Talk to you then," Linda said, ending the call. "I can't believe him sometimes. The film screening idea was his."

"Do you want to use it?" Rayanne asked.

"We have to, otherwise we have nothing."

Ester was tired of overthinking so she stopped thinking. She went to her backpack and got her external drive. She plugged it into the computer and clicked a few buttons.

Her film started with a clip of two elders speaking in their native language, their expressions animated before they broke into laughter.

"Sounds like the Beat Braves," Rayanne said when the music started, a contemporary mix of Native singing and drumming with guitar.

"Used without permission," Ester admitted. "A placeholder."

The camera moved through the room, catching snippets of laughter, elders being served food, the staff in the kitchen joking around while they filled plates.

"Is this what you've been working on?" Tommy asked.

Ester smiled.

"This is terrific," Linda said, eyes glued to the monitor.

"This is from the clips I've been collecting for months. I did online tutorials to put it together. I'm still not sure about a few parts..."

"Is that Theo?" Rayanne asked when the voice-over started.

Ester didn't respond.

The film showed their previous office in the strip mall and the school building they'd planned to buy. She had clips of Tommy playing basketball with a group of young people, kids doing traditional dancing, and Linda sitting next to Margie, their heads bent together while they talked.

Linda pressed her hand to her chest. "You're really good at this. Why didn't you show us before?"

Ester shrugged. "You've seen what I put on social media for us."

Linda got up and gave her a hug. "This is better than that. You need to keep up with this. The only bad part is we have to tell Arnie we don't want his friend's film."

Now that Linda wanted to show it in public, Ester's confidence flagged. "It needs more work. There are effects that came out stupid and I had a funny clip of Tommy parking the bus I wanted to add."

"It's perfect," Linda said. "We need to get you some classes and better equipment."

Linda had never encouraged Ester to do anything except spreadsheets and number-crunching and normally she would have been pleased, but instead all she could think about was...Theo was still in town.

33

*L*inda found the conference center endlessly confusing. Clusters of small rooms and then huge cavernous rooms. Sometimes the huge cavernous rooms were broken into smaller rooms or sectioned off into areas. She wandered the wide hallways with Ester and Rayanne.

Her cellphone rang and she checked the display. Audra. Her heart sped up. "Do you have news?"

"Immediate response. Three people from the city will meet with us. They gave me several dates. I said I'd check with my client. Have you talked to Arnie yet?"

"Haven't had a chance," Linda said. She'd found Arnie's pocketknife in the longhouse and she turned it over in her pocket. The smooth bone handle reminded her of her grandfather's knife. "He's going to be furious."

"But we got what we wanted," Audra said.

"He doesn't like to be kept out of the loop," Linda said.

"You know him better than I do," Audra said. "He'll be fine. I'll email you the dates and times and you work out with him when we're going to sit down. Congratulations. We're moving forward."

"Thanks," Linda said. She shoved her phone back in her bag. Now she had two critical pieces of information Arnie needed and didn't have because, other than their conversation the day before, she couldn't get ahold of him.

They found the check-in desk and an intern pointed them down another hallway. Their city had a large tribal population and Linda was around Natives all the time, but there was something special about walking through the concourse busy with Indian people, some wearing traditional accessories, some dressed in professional clothing, all ages and genders. She grew more optimistic about their mission.

Ester said, "What did Arnie say, room B? Actually, 'room number B' is what he said. Shouldn't it be room letter B?"

"Yeah," Rayanne said, "but which room B? There is room B Alder and room B Cedar and, if I understand this map correctly, there are two more room Bs if we go up a level."

Hearing his name gave her a tremor of nervous energy. Arnie had disappeared. He didn't return calls, emails, or texts. She'd considered leaving him a message to give him a clue, but his lack of communication had inspired a mutinous streak. If he wanted open communication, he needed to keep up his end.

Linda checked Rayanne's map. "He said that when you get out of the parking garage elevator, stay to the left and you'll see it. Is there more than one parking garage elevator?"

A spike of cold-nerves tickled between her shoulder blades. She tried to tell herself it was the pressure of the event, but she worried about Arnie. When they'd started working together, she confirmed to him they would be a team and not work at odds to each other. She wanted to blame him for dating their filmmaker and making this transaction awkward, but that didn't excuse changing the films without warning. She didn't want to surprise him. At the same time, ever since he'd joined their organization he made her question her judgment. This was her decision; she didn't need him to confirm.

"I recognize those guys," Rayanne said, indicating a group ahead.

Audra stood in the concourse with several people Linda remembered from the mixer.

"We're ready," Linda said, sounding like she didn't believe it herself. "Have you seen Arnie? I have information he needs."

"Never standing still," Audra said, walking with them to their room. "I've been here all week. You know how these meetings are. Day one you are fully invigorated by how amazing working in Indian Country is. Day two you're still getting a lot out of it but you're tired of the coffee and blasting air conditioning. Day three you're hanging in there but tired of people standing up and giving longwinded talks that aren't even on point and you will punch someone if you have to eat one more deli sandwich."

"That brings us to day four. Show us this damn presentation so we can all go home," Linda said.

"They wouldn't have stayed if they didn't want to hear it," Audra said.

The room could have held sixty and was only about one-third filled. An ice-filled tray at the front table held pop, and a platter of brownies sat next to it.

"Promising food helps," Audra said.

Virgil was there, and she went over to say hello. Seeing Virgil gave her a different sort of nervous pang. He'd had a busy travel schedule, and other than periodic texts with photos of generic meeting rooms and the words "guess where I am today?" they hadn't been in touch.

"Nervous?" he asked.

"No," she lied. She liked speaking and she recognized a number of tribal leaders from other government meetings, but these were the local folks she needed to win over if the organization was to continue. Ester and Rayanne set up the movie while she introduced herself and encouraged everyone to grab a treat and sit down.

Ester gave her the signal, and she headed for the front of the room. "This will be quick because I know you've had a long week and want to get home. I'm not sugar-coating it, we're in trouble. You all have plenty to deal with on your home reservations, but I want you to consider the Ind'n people who end up here in the city. They struggle. They're far from home and their support system. We're here for social and cultural contact, and bigger things such as housing, healthcare, transportation, and ideally, education. This short film shows a little bit of what we do and what we're up against. We need strong tribal support for the work we do. I'll be here afterward if you want to ask questions."

She nodded at Ester to begin the film and found a place where she could keep one eye on the movie and the other on their guests. From this spot, she could see whether they connected with the message or stared at their phones. The uneasiness about keeping Arnie out of the loop persisted but he still hadn't shown up. Maybe his priorities had shifted.

The lights in the room dimmed and the movie started. Ester had stayed up half the night fiddling with the music. That girl was such a perfectionist. She needed a whack over the head so she would recognize her own talents.

A phone rang and the man who answered got up and left the room. Her heart sank to lose even one pair of eyes. Two others talked in the back. Rayanne sat at the front with her eyes on the screen. Ester chewed her fingernails and stared at the floor.

The door opened again but instead of the man who'd left, or maybe a few later comers, Arnie came in and he had Professor Stone with him.

ARNIE'S NIECE found him as he headed to the movie. "Can we stay at Aunt Tildy's? A few of us want to go out tonight."

"If it's okay with her, I don't care. What are you guys going to do?"

"Dance club. Theo is a bouncer."

"Sounds like fun. He'll watch out for you," Arnie said, hoping he hadn't misjudged the guy. "Thanks for your help," he said, but already they'd rushed off.

He spotted Katie coming down the concourse. He was uncertain about having her at NATG with him. This conference was from eyes open to eyes shut, all business. He had to keep track of the interns, work with his tribal council, and stay on top of his own meetings and agenda. He'd even been too busy to respond to Linda's pings, antici-pating a break to carve out a few minutes and then getting hauled off to talk to someone or solve a problem. Katie wouldn't drop the idea of seeing the response to her film so he welcomed her to it.

She wore nice slacks, a snug blouse and long beaded earrings. For one heart-stopping second he thought she was going to kiss him. Whatever had developed between them, he wasn't ready for a PDA at his big work meeting.

Whether he misunderstood her body language, or she understood his, she didn't kiss him. She gave him an affectionate pat on the arm. He'd planned on taking her straight to the meeting room but on the way they ran into a couple of folks from one of his committees who wanted to talk. He'd introduced Katie, who'd charmed them with her curiosity and playful questions. She was intelligent and a good listener. Yeah, he could see something happening between them.

"I'm not sure how many folk we have here," he told her. "If you expect a room full of people, you're going to be disappointed."

"I won't be," she said.

The door to the room was closed. They'd missed the start. Inside, the lights were dim. He guided her to the first empty seats he found. He looked around the room to see if he could identify how many folks were there and who showed up. They had a bigger crowd than he expected. He recognized a couple of tribal leaders that had already expressed an interest in being involved. He spotted his tribal chair-man. Linda stood against the wall near the front. He tried to catch her attention but she kept her eyes on the screen. Then he spotted Audra and Virgil seated near the front. Did Linda think he would be both-ered by Virgil? Of course not.

Katie's hand landed on his knee, more familiar than he'd expected. "That's not my film," she whispered.

Arnie returned his attention to the front. He'd only seen the film once and at first he thought she must be mistaken. These were scenes from the elder lunch. His confusion could be from seeing it on a larger screen. But the music was different, too. Katie's version used flute music and she had done the voice-over on her film, but this

229

speaker was male. The camera lingered on different images and showed more interactions between tribal people.

Katie patted his leg to emphasize her words. "That's not my film."

"I don't know what's going on," Arnie said. His eyes found Linda again, and she studiously avoided eye contact.

Katie transformed into a bundle of disappointment and confusion. "That's Theo's voice. Did he make this?"

"I'm not sure," Arnie said, taking her hand and squeezing it. The film on screen was very good; if Theo made it, he shouldn't be failing her class. He knew better than to suggest that, though.

He couldn't understand why Linda would screen a different film without telling him. That was so like her, to make an executive decision without even a hint. If he'd known, he could have at least saved Katie from embarrassment.

"If she didn't want it, she should have said so," Katie said, biting off each word. Arnie stroked her hand, trying to convey a sense of calm he didn't feel. As soon at the film finished, she said, "I'll meet you outside." She slipped out the door before he could stop her. He had a mind to chase after her, but he needed to talk to Linda first.

The lights came up. A half dozen of the guests lingered. Linda worked her way through them, thanking them for coming, answering their questions. She excelled at this part, conveying her message and giving people her attention. He'd always liked that about her.

Ester came over. "Blame me. It was my idea."

"Is that your work? I assumed it was Theo. Ester, that was amazing. But it doesn't matter whose idea it was, I could have used a heads-up."

"She tried. We thought you would be here earlier, and um..." She glanced at the door where Katie had exited.

"I need to work this out with your boss," Arnie said, finding that the more he thought about it, the angrier he became.

Virgil Harris came over to shake his hand. "Hey, Arnie, I guess congratulations are in order."

This was the guy Linda was dating. Arnie had run across him at meetings but they'd never worked together.

"Nice to see you, Virgil. Congratulations for what?" Arnie ticked through the week of meetings and tried to figure out what Virgil was talking about.

"I'm surprised she didn't tell you," Virgil said. A pang of irritation rose hearing him refer to Linda so casually as if they had something in common.

"I wasn't aware the film had been changed, if that's what you mean," Arnie said, but he already suspected Virgil was talking about something else. Linda had made another decision without telling him.

"Our intent to sue letter worked. We have a meeting with the city next week. We've got names. They're appointing an action committee to work with us. We might get you guys into the Chief Building after all."

"What intent to sue letter?" Arnie said, the air rushing out of him. He glanced over at Linda. She was in the middle of an animated conversation with a tribal leader from a tribe with a prominent community charity funded with profits from their gaming operation.

Virgil's smile was completely genuine. "Audra drafted it and sent it out on behalf of the organization. Linda wanted to shake something loose, and it worked."

He knew it was silly but Arnie chose to see something spiteful behind it—Linda letting Virgil give him a tremendous piece of news about an action he knew nothing about and wouldn't have approved of if he had.

Arnie did his best to smile back. "Linda hadn't given me the news. That's great. I'm glad your strategy worked. Can you excuse me?"

He had to get out of the room. He didn't trust himself right then, and he didn't want to ruin whatever remained of his friendship with Linda.

34

Theo had to find Arnie before he left the conference for good. He had a thumb drive and there were a few leftover boxes of packets that needed to be dealt with. The conference food had grown tiresome and he needed a power nap before he had to be at Frenzy's. Some of the interns wanted to go to the club but last he'd heard they were still looking for a place to stay.

The plan was to get out of there before the Crooked Rock presentation. Ester would be in the building, and after the rush of emotion at hearing her voice during the conference call, he didn't think he could handle seeing her again. Not even to say a proper goodbye. Unfortunately, time got away from him and he had no choice but to search for Arnie at the screening.

He headed through the now empty concourse, hoping he'd find Arnie and would be able to slip out before anyone from the center saw him. He was surprised to see Professor Stone rush out of the room as if she couldn't get out of there fast enough.

He called to her and her head snapped up, her face a mask of fury that she struggled to hide when she saw him.

"Theo," she said with forced cheer. "Why weren't you in there? You and Ester did a lovely job."

The sound of their names together brought up a lonely ache in his chest. "I don't know what you mean."

Arnie burst out of the door with the same flush of anger that Professor Stone had exited with seconds earlier. What was going on in there?

Arnie pointed at Theo. "Did you know about that?"

Theo shook his head. Whatever the meltdown was about, he wanted to get out of there as fast as he could. "I know nothing. I came to tell you I'm done." He handed Arnie the thumb drive.

Arnie took a big calming breath. He exchanged a look with Professor Stone that Theo didn't understand.

"The Crooked Rock film," Professor Stone said. "They screened it for some tribal leaders to attract supporters."

Theo's confusion must have shown on his face.

Professor Stone nodded. "They didn't tell you, either? That was you on the voice-over, wasn't it? You must have known about Ester's version."

"I didn't know she made something for today," Theo said, pleased that Ester finally showed them what she could do. He wished he had seen it with her. Then it occurred to him that if they used Ester's, they hadn't used Professor Stone's. He didn't know what to say.

"It's fine," she said, as if she were still thinking it through. "I missed my own message about taking advantage of a unique perspective. You two are better suited for the job, which would have been nice to know before I did all that work. Not your problem. Did you have something for me?"

Talking to Professor Stone while she was worked up wasn't the best idea, but it was now or never.

"I worked for Arnie this week using everything you taught us in class. I did short interviews for the web, things like that. I know you were disappointed with how I did in class but I wanted you to see the work I did. I learned a lot from you. If I send it, would you take a look?"

He was prepared for her to lecture, but she smiled at him. "You did great in the other class. I still have hope for you. Send what you have, I'd like to see."

"Derek's happy with it," Arnie told her. "You'll be pleased."

To Theo, he said, "Sorry we don't have more time to talk but now I have a situation to deal with." His expression turned sour. "I meant everything I said. I have resources to get you more money for school. You've got a place here. We can keep you busy. If not, good luck. Send me an invoice, sooner rather than later. And don't be shy about bugging me if you don't get paid."

"Thanks for the opportunity," Theo said, wondering if it was a mistake to rush out of town.

"And one more thing," Arnie said. "Watch out for my nieces."

"Not a squirrely bone in my body," Theo reminded him. Hopefully inviting them out wouldn't turn out to be a bad idea.

Arnie took Professor Stone's elbow. "You ready to get out of here?"

Stone had her purse tucked under her arm. "Did we have plans?"

"Let's go to dinner."

An unmistakable tension flared between them. Theo backed away, wishing he hadn't seen it. He averted his eyes and turned around in time to see Rayanne and Ester come out of the meeting room, their faces bright with success. Ester's eyes widened and her smile disappeared when she spotted him. Rayanne nudged her and then walked over to Theo as if there were no question they were going to say hello.

"How's life as Arnie's intern?" Rayanne asked.

"Busy," Theo said. "I learned a lot." Ester wouldn't look at him.

"The film came out great, you guys did a good job," Rayanne said.

Theo nodded at Ester. "She's the talent. My job is to follow orders." The attempt at humor fell flat. Ester turned to look at the exit as if she couldn't wait to get out of there. This might be his last chance. He had to say something.

"Ester, could we talk for a minute?" He raised an eyebrow at Rayanne.

"Sure," Rayanne said a little too loudly. She pulled the computer bag off Ester's shoulder. "I'll take your things to the car. Text if you don't need us to wait for you."

Ester gave her a sour look.

Rayanne walked off, leaving them alone in the middle of the concourse.

Ester took a deep breath and met his eyes, and he was lost. He wanted to leave things less confusing and angry but he couldn't find any words.

"I used the voice-over you made," Ester said. "I should have asked."

"I did it for you."

"People liked it," she said.

"Everything else okay?" he asked.

Ester shrugged and shook her head as if she couldn't believe she had to deal with this.

"I didn't know they were using your film," he said.

"I showed it to Linda yesterday after we saw Professor Stone's. She decided."

"Sorry I missed it."

"I can send you a URL."

Whatever he wanted to say, or hoped to accomplish, it was too late. Some hurts you couldn't get past. "You're talented. I wanted to tell you that," he said, his chest tight. That was barely a start of the things he wanted to tell her, but it would have to do. He turned around and dragged his weary ass out of there.

ESTER WATCHED Theo walk down the concourse, unable to sort out all the emotions churning inside of her. She wanted to throw herself at him, she wanted to throw something at him, she wanted to tell him about the film, she wanted to ask about his week with Arnie and whether that changed anything. She hated seeing the sadness in his eyes. She hated all the unfinished things between them.

"Theo?" His name came out in a strangled croak. Either he didn't hear or he was ignoring her.

She took a couple of steps after him. "Theo?"

He still didn't turn. Running after him seemed desperate, so she walked as fast as she could. His legs were twice as long as hers and he walked fast so it took a minute to catch up.

"Hey, Theo!" she called.

He stopped, his face fixed with the same infuriating blank expression he had when he was breaking up fights at Frenzy's or coaxing a response out of a reticent elder during an interview. The teasing smile she wanted was not forthcoming. Now that she had his attention, she didn't know what to say.

"Thanks for helping me," she said.

Finally. His mouth curved into something resembling the Theo smile she remembered.

She had more to say but couldn't get her head to untangle it into words.

"You headed to the parking garage?" he asked.

She nodded.

"You want to walk with me?"

That would be enough time to figure out what to say. She caught up beside him, remembering all the times she'd had to keep pace with him. This would be the last time unless someone said something. She searched his body language for clues that he would be willing to try again.

The silence stretched out between them. If she'd known she would see him, she could have come up with three things. They could have a conversation but she needed a place to start.

Two young women called his name and ran over breathless.

"We have a place to stay," one of them said. Her eyes grazed Ester for split-second before she returned her attention to Theo. "We can go to the club with you."

So this was what it felt like to be so embarrassed you could die. She would have turned to dust and disappeared if that were an option.

Theo barely reacted, no doubt to save her pride. He kept his voice low. "Get there early when I'm working the door, otherwise there's a cover and you'll have to wait outside. Pete is the other bouncer. I'll tell him you're coming."

"We'll see you tonight," they said, their eyes shiny.

Ester swallowed the lump of despair in the back of her throat. "I guess you're still at Frenzy's."

"Until the end of the month."

He still planned to move. Her heart sank into her feet. If she felt hopeless before, this was worse. She searched for something that would make it sound like her life was moving forward in a spectacular fashion, but not much had changed.

"I'm moving, too," she told him.

"Away?" he said.

"From Dennis. I set up a camera in my room and caught MacKenzie stealing from me. He broke up with her but it's time to find something else."

"Good for you, I'm glad you—" She could tell he was about to say "stood up for yourself" but he cut himself off. "Good luck finding a place you like."

"Thanks," she said.

The concourse stretched on forever. She never wanted to say goodbye but couldn't wait to get it over with. Having him standing so close to her again was waking up all these terrible emotions that she'd stuffed down and convinced herself didn't matter.

"You still driving?" she asked.

"Yes, and moving for Jess," he said. "I retired from the muscle-for-hire app since working for Arnie."

They arrived at the parking garage elevator. Theo pressed the call button.

"Was it a good week?" she asked, not sure what she meant.

Theo shrugged. "It was only an okay week."

The elevator doors slid open, and they stepped inside. Theo pressed 2. Ester pressed 4. This was the last time she would be standing this close to him. She wanted to do something. Hug him? That didn't feel right. The elevator doors slid open at the second floor.

"See ya, Shoshone," he said.

"Bye, Theo," she said, the tiniest catch in the back of her throat. She rode up to the fourth floor and found Rayanne waiting at the car.

"Everything okay?"

Ester shrugged and wiped away a tear.

"Did he say anything?"

"I don't want to talk about it now," Ester said.

"I've never seen anyone built like a linebacker look so haunted, like someone stole his kitten."

Rayanne tried to hug her, but she shrugged her off.

Linda came charging off the elevator a few moments later, wiping her own eyes. "That went great," she said, half sobbing. "Three of the tribal leaders gave me handshake commitments on the spot. Two more want me to talk to their Councils." She took a deep, shuddering breath. "And we got our meeting with the city."

"The suing letter worked?" Rayanne said.

"What did Arnie say?" Ester asked, not understanding what went wrong.

Linda wiped her hands across her face again. "I never had a chance to talk to Arnie about the intent to sue letter. Virgil told him we were successful, and he stormed off."

"I'll drive," Rayanne said.

Linda didn't protest. She crawled into the passenger seat, fastened her seatbelt, and stared straight ahead. "He's furious with me. He'll never forgive me. I said I would always be straight with him and first I yanked his girlfriend's movie and then I did this behind his back. It's not Virgil's fault. I shouldn't have kept it from him."

"He'll cool off," Rayanne said. "You guys have a lot of history."

Linda gulped a few times before regaining her composure.

Ester understood why Linda sent the letter without discussing it with Arnie but not why Arnie would be so angry, if they got what they wanted. The day's drama was catching up with her and all she wanted was a hot shower, a good cry, and then sleep.

35

*S*aturday morning, Ester rode her bike to the office. The sky was clear and pale blue with true spring in the air. Daffodils bloomed in the campus flowerbeds. The office was a mess after the crazy schedule of the conference and she spent a few minutes tidying up before she got to work.

She plugged the drive into her desktop computer and finalized the long version of her film. Jack had given her permission to use the Beat Braves music she wanted, and she added that to the mix. Then she swapped a couple of scenes around and fretted over several edits. She watched the final version one last time, with Theo's golden voice telling the story she wanted to tell. His words remained steady and familiar over the images.

Every time she heard his voice on the film, her heart stuttered and her eyes dampened all over again. That was it. They said goodbye. She had to stop thinking about it.

She'd already filled out the form for the filmmaking workshop. All she had to do was upload her film and hit send. If she thought about it too long, she wouldn't do it, and the deadline was coming up. She hesitated over the application and what it meant to get in. If she succeeded, she'd need time off from work and she'd have to take a break on her aggressive student loan repayment plan. If she failed, she could put this silly distraction behind her and recommit to being a spreadsheet wizard. She could sign up for advanced courses in data crunching for nonprofits. There was nothing stopping her from making movies for fun on the side.

She hit the button.

The act of doing one small thing for herself boosted her higher than she would have guessed. She couldn't imagine getting over Theo, but the sadness had to go away, eventually. Linda had secured local support and a meeting about their building. The center still wobbled but not from such a dire place.

On the way home, she rode her bike past a house with a room for rent. It was a newer row house in a line of boxy buildings painted a shade of beige so drab, the builders had to have purchased it on clearance. From the street, each unit seemed to consist of a big garage door with a square window above and brown front doors dividing each unit. A cheap plastic sign was fastened to the wrought iron fence out front with the number to call.

This was early reconnaissance. It wasn't like she had to call, but at least it was an idea. She stopped and dug out her phone so she could save the address and number for later.

There was a missed text from Theo.

Could I talk to you again? I messed up yesterday. I'm ready now. I've got three things.

Her heart thudded faster. She considered her response, her fingers hovering over the touchscreen. After a minute, she got back on her bike. Theo's place wasn't far. She took off in that direction. She locked her bike up in front of his place and tiptoed up the stairs. When she got to his door, she heard him speaking to someone.

She froze. He did have those plans with those women from the conference. He wouldn't expect her to stop by. Too late now.

Her hands shook. She almost changed her mind, but she tapped on the door.

Theo went quiet when the door inched open. "Gotta go. I'll call you back."

"Hi," Ester said, hoping this wasn't going to be an embarrassing mistake. "Did I interrupt?"

"Talking to my mom. I'll catch up with her later." He still hadn't opened the door all the way. "You're here."

"I was in the neighborhood. Is there someone in there?"

"You're the only one who has ever been in here," Theo said.

Ester shrugged and allowed a playful note into her voice. "You know what they say, once you jump out of an airplane, it's easier the second time."

"No one says that," Theo said, a half-smile on his face. "Will you come in?"

Ester hesitated before stepping inside. Boxes lined one wall and the closet was in disarray. His laptop sat open on the kitchen table with his notebook open beside it.

"I brought the movie." She had a hard time meeting his eyes. She was afraid he would be angry or annoyed or emotionless. She finally took a peek. His eyes were sad, haunted, like Rayanne said.

He gestured at his computer. "A copy for me or do you want to watch it now?"

"Later. You have three things?"

He let out a heavy sigh. "I have a hundred and three things."

The apartment walls closed in, smaller than ever. A car alarm went off on the street somewhere outside. She couldn't figure out what to do with her hands. She took a deep breath. "What's one?"

"Will you forgive me?" Once Theo started, the words came out quickly. "I shouldn't have gotten angry at you or said any of those things. All the working and worrying, I was worn to nothing. Except for you. You were the only thing that was right and I shouldn't have walked away. I don't like to disappoint the people that I love."

Ester swallowed and played those words back in her head. That was the longest speech she'd heard from him since she met him. He had the same inconsolable look on his face that she'd been wearing since their falling out.

"I shouldn't have said I didn't want you," she said, her voice barely a whisper. "That's not true."

He smiled at her hopefully. "Can we fix this? Ester Belle Parker, will you be my girlfriend again?"

Ester smiled back. "Is that your second thing?"

"It is."

She let her eyes travel around the room. They stopped on a wad of black fabric on the bed. She was still processing his words, which sounded like... "Are those panties?"

Theo winked. "I sleep with them under my pillow."

"They're mine, right?" Ester said, mildly embarrassed she hadn't noticed they were missing.

Theo laughed. "Of course they're yours." His body shifted, and he reached for her hand.

She looked at it and then at him, his eyes filled with the same longing that she felt. She let him pull her into his arms and hugged him tight, her cheek pressed to his chest. "I want to be your girlfriend."

There was a long quiet pause while they settled into each other, their future less uncertain.

Theo said, "I did some work for Arnie's cousin, and Professor Stone said she'd take a look at it. I could pass all my classes after all."

"We blew off her film without telling her," Ester said. "She's probably not in a great mood when it comes to Indians."

"If I fail, I fail. Arnie is convinced he can find some scholarship money and the timber association has more work for me so I think I'm going to be okay."

"I thought you said you were moving?"

"I'd rather stay here with you."

Ester squeezed him again. "Good. I applied for the film workshop."

"You did?"

"You were right, I was a big fat fraidy cat," Ester said. "I sent off the application this morning."

"I would have been disappointed if you didn't," Theo said.

They hadn't loosened their embrace. Ester couldn't help but be comforted by the sound of his heart in her ear. "Did you have a third thing?"

Theo leaned over and picked up something from the kitchen table. He showed her a key. "I was going to give you this earlier."

"For here? When earlier?"

"When the plan was to leave, I thought you could stay in my place. Lease isn't up until June."

"You thought I might like to stay in the empty apartment of the guy who ran screaming into the trees at the first sign of disagreement?"

"I don't agree with that characterization of events," Theo said.

"Withdrawn. You thought me and my broken heart might like to stay in your empty apartment?"

Theo put the key back down and hugged her again. "It wasn't a well thought out plan. Not like the rent is paid until the end of the lease."

Ester mock-sighed. "Well, I have learned that every plan doesn't have to be well thought out."

"Good," Theo said. "I want you to have it now."

A mixture of joy and fear clutched in Ester's belly. They were solidifying something.

"This place is too small for both of us in the long run but we can find a bigger place in June," Theo said.

Her heart jumped in her chest. "We just had a big bad thing, and now you want to move in together?"

"Don't you?"

"Shouldn't we give it some time?"

"You mean think it through? All the pros and cons and make a list of what could go wrong? And then sit down and talk about it? You run it by Rayanne. I run it by Fran. We do research online and find other couples who moved in quickly and tally the results—"

"This seems like the kind of thing a person would think through," Ester said.

"I have. I can't imagine fitting better with anyone else than the way I fit with you."

Ester dared her wheels to spin faster. "Could we put things on the walls?"

Theo chuckled. "We can put our names on the mailbox, too. If you want to get fancy, we'll buy furniture. If we find a house, we can get a dog."

"This sounds fast," she said.

"Does it? It's not until June."

Ester kissed his cheek. "Do we have to decide this second?"

"Only if you don't want to leave me hanging."

"It's the least I could do," Ester said, kissing along his jaw.

"I love you, Ester," Theo said. "You feel like home to me."

Ester froze, lips in mid-nuzzle.

Theo wrapped his hand in her hair and tilted her head up to his. "I wouldn't have said it if I wasn't sure."

Ester smiled. "First a key, then a declaration. This is a big day for Theodore Dunne."

"I suppose," Theo said. "I know how I want things to turn out. The rest depends on you."

"Without thinking about it first? There is thinking to be done."

Theo laughed.

"Done thinking," Ester said. "I love you, too. So, what kind of dog should we get?"

Theo kissed her. "You don't want to savor this exchange for a moment?"

"I'm savoring. And I'm planning ahead," Ester said.

"Okay. A rescue dog. Whatever dog needs us the most, but probably not a really little dog or a super hairy dog. But what if we fall for a super hairy dog?"

"We'll pick up a vacuum on the way home," Ester said.

"Just like that?" Theo said.

"Just like that."

THANK YOU FOR READING

The story of the Crooked Rock Urban Indian Center will continue.

Book 3 is the story of Tommy meeting Elizabeth, the woman who will knock him off his feet.

Estimated release date: Summer 2018.

Join my mailing list to get the news when it's out. Your email will never be shared and you may unsubscribe at any time.

ENDNOTES

Indian Country is a diverse place. Tribal communities, individuals and organizations are different depending on their history, culture, traditions, geography and leaders—this is true of individual tribes, and is true of urban Indian communities. There is no typical organization that serves urban Indians.

I've created Crooked Rock as a place to serve my stories. My intentions are always respectful and based on my experience and observations as an Indian, and in the course of my work in Indian Country.

You might be wondering about the cover. Are those native people? Unfortunately, no. The cover is made from standard stock photos. The selection of stock photos of indigenous people is skimpy, and sadly, my numerous attempts to set up a photo session of my own failed. If you can provide pro-quality stock photos of cute Indian couples, please get in touch at pam@pamelasanderson.com. I would love to work with you.

ACKNOWLEDGMENTS

Thanks again to my early readers Kira Walsh, Marguerite Croft, Jennifer Malace and Hannah Parker. Your time and comments are always helpful and appreciated. More thanks to editor Lorelei Logsdon (www.loreleilogsdon.com) and cover artist Holly Heisey (www.hollyheiseydesign.com). And a big smooch to my ever-patient husband Bob Hughes who always empties the dishwasher.

ABOUT THE AUTHOR

Pamela Sanderson is a citizen of the Karuk Tribe and lives in the Pacific Northwest. She is employed as a legal assistant working on behalf of Indian tribes and tribal organizations. When she isn't working or writing, she enjoys baking, gardening and following Major League Soccer.

ALSO BY PAMELA SANDERSON

Crooked Rock Urban Indian Center

Book 1 Heartbeat Braves

Season of Us

CPSIA information can be obtained
at www.ICGtesting.com
Printed in the USA
LVHW091739120320
649865LV00004B/805